NICK ALLEN & THE LOST BOY

The further adventures of a young Nick Allen in
1960s St. Albans

ALLEN NICKLIN

"I feel that some people have a hard time with the truths around
us, not only the sexual abuse by priests, but all bad things. I call
it chosen ignorance. This modified form of ignorance is found
in people who, if confronted with certain truths realize that they
have to accept them and thereby acknowledge evil, and that scares
them. Opening up and letting the truth in might knock them off
their perceived centre. It is too hard, period."
Charles L. Bailey Jr., In the Shadow of the Cross

To the Men of Fields for their continuing support

Index

Prologue

Sunday 3 May 1959

Peter Waller was bored. He reckoned he was the most bored 8 year-old boy in the street, if not St Albans or even England or maybe the universe. It was a cold, miserable Sunday afternoon as he sat in a neighbour's kitchen watching his mother have her hair permed. It was bad enough having to put up with the awful smell of a *Toni* home perm, but to make matters worse they had to listen to *The Billy Cotton Band Show*[1] playing on the radio. He put his hands over his ears when he heard the cry 'Wakey! Wakey!' which was followed by that dreadful signature tune, *Somebody Stole My Gal*.

'Why don't you go out and play with Nick?' said Mrs Waller, who was seated at the kitchen table with a white towel wrapped round her shoulders while Mrs Allen rolled her hair around a variety of coloured plastic rollers.

'But they are playing football; you know I don't like football,' replied Peter, taking a big sigh.

Nick was the eldest son of Mrs Allen who along with Mrs Stewart was perming his mother's hair.

'Gordon and Paul are there as well, I'm sure they will let you play with them,' added Mrs Stewart, in a friendly tone.

'But I want to play Army games,' protested Peter.

Peter was a shy boy of medium build with short, neatly cut brown hair. His hobbies included reading, cub scouts, camping, but most of all – army games. Today he was dressed in the new Army outfit that his parents had bought him for his birthday. He hadn't worn anything else (apart from his school uniform) for the last two months. Along with the wooden rifle that his granddad had given him, he was the complete soldier. Ever since he could remember he had been interested in the Army and he couldn't wait until he was seventeen, when he would be called up for National Service. Both his dad and granddad had served in the army; his dad fought in the Second World War and his granddad survived the Great War. His dad didn't talk much about his time in the army; all he knew was that he was stationed in Burma, Malaysia and Singapore. But his granddad used to sit him on his knee and tell him lots of stories. His favourite story was when his granddad, who was with the British Expeditionary Force (BEF), engaged in battle with General von Kluck's First Army on the 23 August 1914. Early in the morning the German's attacked but were thwarted by the terrific rate of the rapid fire from the British professional troupes. Despite being totally outnumbered by a superior force the British had been spurred on by an avenging angel, clothed all in white, mounted on the classical white horse and brandishing a flaming sword. The Angel had rallied the troupes and enabled them to crush the enemy and halt their advance. Peter never tired of listening to the story of the 'Angel of Mons'.

'Okay, I'll go and play on green with them,' said Peter as he stood to attention, saluted, turned and marched out of the kitchen, down the passageway, then turned left towards the green.

The sky was leaden and he shivered as he went in search of his playmates. He could see the three boys playing football on the green. He guessed they were playing, three and in. One boy would be in goal, another a defender and the third boy would try and score. When the attacker scored three goals he would go in goal, the goalie became the defender and the defender the attacker and so on.

As he reached the field Nick shouted out, 'have you come to join us, Peter?'

'That's okay; I'll just keep guard, just in case the Germans attack,' replied Peter.

'Thanks Peter, we'll feel much safer now.'

With his rifle on his shoulder Peter started to march around the playing field. As he kept an eye on the boys playing football his mind wandered to another story his granddad had told him. It was Christmas Eve 1914 and his granddad was stationed in Northern France near the village of Laventie, when he heard the Germans singing *Silent Night*, so he and his mates started to sing *Good King Wenceslas*. Then the next day after some shouting between trenches and both sets of soldiers started to walk towards each other and then someone produced a football and before the officers could call them back a game had started. The game was about 50-a-side but unfortunately no one kept score, although his granddad always claimed he scored a hat-trick.

As he marched, Peter watched the boys change round. It was Nick's turn in goal and he would be Ron Baynham, Gordon, Syd Owen and young Paul would be Roy Dwight. Apparently there had been some sort of cup final yesterday between Luton Town and Nottingham Forest.

After about 30 minutes the three footballing boys decided to have a rest. They sat on the grass in between the jumpers that represented the goal. Gordon Stewart who was eight years old and in the same class as Peter looked out towards him and said 'he hasn't stop marching for the last half hour.'

Nick Allen, who was a year older replied, shaking his head, 'he'll make a great soldier one day.'

Paul Stewart, Gordon's younger brother just looked on, and then said 'I wonder what's for tea?'

As the boys watched Peter marching tirelessly along the edge of the field, a blue Hillman Husky pulled up alongside him. The window was wound down and a man started talking to Peter. After about a minute the man got out of the car pulled the front seat down and Peter climbed in. The man followed and before the three boys could move, the car drove off.

WEEK 1
Sunday 9 August -
Saturday 15 August 1964

Sunday 9 August

Nick Allen, a 14 year-old schoolboy with a mop of light brown hair, a nice smile and twinkling blue eyes lies contented on a bath towel in his back garden listening to Alan 'Fluff' Freeman announce that the Beatles were still number one in the pop charts with *A Hard Day's Night*. And the reason for his contentment – well, since returning from a week's holiday with his parents and little brother Richard, he had been dating a girl called Moira Harris and it was going extremely well. The only problem he had with having a girlfriend was that he hadn't seen his best friend Keith Nevin since he returned from his holiday, but that was to be solved as they had arranged to go on a foursome this evening. Another thing that pleased him was, instead of listening to *Pick of the Pops*, as he usually did, on the family radiogram in the living room, he had acquired a transistor radio. He smiled to himself as he recollected the events leading up to this recent acquisition.

During the previous year Nick had been involved in more than his fair share of scrapes and was lucky to still be alive after nearly freezing to death when he was trapped in a butcher's cold room. So his parents whisked him away for a nice week's holiday at the Dovercourt Bay Holiday Camp[2] in Harwich. For the majority of the week Nick immersed himself in all the activities available, swimming, football, sports day, donkey riding, knobbly knees, whatever was on offer, Nick volunteered. His parents had befriended a nice couple of similar age from Kilmarnock in Scotland, Mr and Mrs Muir. They had travelled down with Mr Muir's mother who had recently become a widow and their daughter, Suzanne. Not one to miss a chance, Nick had spent quite of bit of time with Suzanne, going for walks, treating her to the occasional ice-cream and being the perfect gentleman. Suzanne was reasonably attractive, pretty, with medium length wavy light brown hair and freckles. He had always had a thing for freckles. But what got him the most was her soft Scottish accent. He could listen to her speak for hours. Well, his patience paid off and by the end of the week they were regularly kissing and she had even allowed him to touch her breasts. That was the second pair, he noted, that he had caressed during his short love life.

Each night after dinner, but before the main evening's entertainment, a bingo session was held in the main ballroom. His parents and Mr and Mrs Muir along with Suzanne's grandmother grabbed themselves a table in a prime location and settled there for the evening. Sometimes Nick and Suzanne would join them; Nick's younger brother Richard, would be off with the other children at the Kiddies Club. Every night there would be a *Winner Takes All* raffle. Tickets were sold at a shilling each and the winner would pocket all the takings. On their last night, Nick was sitting next to old Mrs Muir when a Green Coat approached their table selling the *Winner Takes All* raffle tickets.

'Are you buying a ticket tonight, Mrs Muir?' asked Nick, as his sipped his glass of Coca Cola.

'I've told yer enough times laddie, call me Agnes, and no I'm not buying a wee ticket tonight. No one wins on a Friday,' replied Mrs Muir, in a strong Scottish brogue.

Nick looked puzzled, 'what do you mean no one wins on a Friday.'

'It's a fiddle, we were here last week and the prize was not claimed on Tuesday or Friday and it wasn't claimed this Tuesday either.'

'That could be just a coincidence.'

'That's as maybe, but I was speaking to a nice lady last week and she said that no one claimed the prize on Tuesday or Friday the previous week.'

This information was like a red rag to a bull and Nick, who described himself as a consulting detective, like his hero Sherlock Holmes, was taken in. Nick took a deep breath, grabbed Suzanne's hand, looked at her and said, 'give me a nudge when the interval comes.'

Suzanne gave him a strange look and said, 'okay' as she watched him rest his chin in his hands and drift off into a thoughtful trance.

As soon as the last game was played Suzanne duly gave Nick a nudge and with a quick shake of the head he said, 'how are you up for a little adventure?'

Even though she had no idea what he was talking about, she still replied, 'why not?'

'Okay, listen carefully. I think your gran's right, there is a scam going on and we are going to expose it.'

'How exciting,' replied Suzanne, softly clapping her hands.

'I'm not sure how many Green Coats are involved, but definitely Tommy, the main entertainer and I think that girl who's going round now selling the last minute tickets.'

'Oh,' said Suzanne, with a chuckle. 'Her name is Wendy, she's nice, but a wee bit thick.'

Wendy was a pretty platinum blonde with a very curvaceous figure. Nick had noticed many a husband on the receiving end of a sharp elbow from their wives when Wendy walked by. Tommy, on the other hand reminded Nick of a larger version of George Cole's character, Flash Harry in the *St Trinian's* films. Not the sort of bloke one would buy a second-hand car from.

'So, what's the plan?' enquired Suzanne enthusiastically.

'When she has finished selling her raffle tickets we'll follow her and see where she goes and what she does.'

'Is that it?' asked Suzanne, a touch unimpressed.

Slightly offended, Nick replied, 'what did you expect?'

'Something a bit more elaborate, I mean you were deep in thought for over thirty minutes.'

Nick giggled, 'no I just wanted a kip; I'm a bit tired today.'

Suzanne resisted the urge to hit him, looked up and said, 'look, I think she's finished, come on let's go.'

Nick and Suzanne quickly made some lame excuse to their parents and quietly followed Wendy out of the hall. Keeping a discrete distance they observed Wendy meeting Tommy in a corridor that led behind the stage. Before disappearing through a door they heard Tommy say to Wendy, 'Now you know what to do? Tear out all the tickets as usual and put them in the bucket; don't bother counting the money, I'll just make up some figure. No-one will suspect. Then just tear out one part of the next ticket in the book and leave it on the table, is that clear?'

'I'm not stupid,' replied Wendy, feeling rather belittled. 'I've done it before.'

'I know you're not; I just don't want any mistakes; that's all. Now in you go.'

Nick and Suzanne watched Wendy disappear through the door as Tommy gave her bottom a lecherous squeeze.

'What do we do now?' asked Suzanne.

'We wait; I need to get into that room,' replied Nick.

'She could be in there for ages.'

'I know.' Nick was thinking fast, he had to get into that room and see what was going on. 'Listen, this is what we'll do. She'll need time to tear out the raffle tickets, so we'll wait for about ten or fifteen minutes. If she hasn't come out by then we need to get her out.'

'And how do you propose we do that?' asked Suzanne.

'Not sure yet, but I'll think of something.'

Suzanne was thinking that standing around wasn't much of an adventure, especially on their last night. She was hoping for a romantic walk on the beach and kisses in the moonlight. Nick, for once wasn't thinking about getting inside Suzanne's knickers. After making small-talk for what seemed an age, Wendy re-appeared. As she approached the pair Suzanne said, 'Hello Wendy, I was just wondering…..'

'Sorry, love,' replied Wendy. 'Dying for a wee; catch you later.' With that she disappeared into the adjacent Ladies toilet.

'Now's your chance,' said Suzanne, practically pushing Nick towards the door.

As Nick suspected the door led to the Green Coats changing room. There were lots of cupboards, wardrobes and clothes racks full of costumes. In the middle of the room there was a table. Nick approached it and immediately spotted a small bucket full of folded raffle tickets. Next to the bucket, a pint beer mug full of money; lots of sixpences, shillings, florins and the occasional ten-bob note. Then Nick eyed what he was looking for – the raffle ticket book. On top of the book was a single raffle ticket – Green 326. He opened the book and noticed its counter-part was still attached. 'So that's how they do it,' whispered Nick, gently nodding his head. He quickly tore out the counter-part and put it in his pocket. Making sure that he hadn't disturbed anything, Nick made for the door, but just before his hand reached the door handle he heard Suzanne's raised voice.

'Hello Wendy, feeling better now?'

'Shit,' cursed Nick. He turned, looked round the room and quickly decided to hide behind a rack of costumes.

Nick smiled to himself as he experienced a small rush of adrenaline. He crouched behind the costumes and was just able to see Wendy as she entered the room. He watched as she stood in front of the mirror above a small sink. She was busy repairing her make-up when the door opened and in walked Tommy.

'Everything okay?' asked Tommy.

'Of course it is; why shouldn't it be?' replied Wendy.

'Just checking.'

'I'm not happy about this,' said Wendy, as she finished applying her lipstick. 'It's not right cheating the campers this way.'

'Listen, my girl,' replied Tommy, in an angry voice. 'You just do as you're told, or I'll let the boss know of your little sordid secret.'

'It's just not fair; I let you shag me once a week, ain't that enough for a girl without having to commit theft,' her Cockney accent getting broader by the second.

'Listen to me girl,' said Tommy, grabbing Wendy by the shoulders. 'Just you do as you're told or you'll be back in the gutter where you belong.'

Nick could feel his blood boiling and was tempted to run out and give Tommy a good thrashing. But he took a deep breath and remembered one of his mantras – revenge is a dish best served cold.

'Come on now girl, pull yourself together; we've a show to put on.' With that Wendy picked up the bucket and the Green 326 ticket, Tommy grabbed the mug full of money and they both left the room.

Nick waited for about thirty seconds before leaving his hiding place. Making sure everything was in order he carefully opened the door and stepped into the corridor. The split second his hand left the door handle Suzanne leapt on him, showering him with kisses.

'I was soo worried about yee,' said Suzanne, in her broadest Scottish accent.

'I'm fine,' said Nick. 'Come on let's get back to the ballroom before anyone suspects something.'

As they entered the ballroom the deathly silence was broken when a large northern lady shouted, 'HOUSE.'

The usual moaning ensued as Nick and Suzanne made their way back to where their families were gathered. Nick took his seat next to old Mrs Muir and took a sip of his Coca Cola, it was warm and flat.

'Hello laddie, where have yer been?' asked old Mrs Muir.

'Nowhere in particular, just out an' about,' replied Nick. 'Oh. By the way, as you have been so nice to me during the week I've bought you a *Winner Takes All* raffle ticket.' Nick fished around in his pocket until he found the green raffle ticket.

'Ah, that's very sweet of yer laddie, but yer shouldn't waste yer shilling on me, I told yer no-one wins on a Friday.'

'I think tonight might be different, trust me,' said Nick, as he gave Agnes his biggest smile.

Something made him look round at his father who was eyeing him suspiciously, 'alright dad; having a nice time?' His dad didn't answer. The numbers were checked on the northern lady's card and it was confirmed as a winner. The prize was given and it was eyes down for the next game.

At the end of the session Tommy took the microphone and announced it was time to make the *Winner Takes All* draw. The hush was immediate as Wendy approached Tommy with the bucket.

'I will now ask the lovely Wendy to make the draw,' announced Tommy. 'Tonight prize is a staggering fourteen pounds twelve shillings.'

Nick whispered to Suzanne, 'actually its sixteen pounds, five shillings.'

'How do you know that?' asked Suzanne inquisitively.

'Simple maths, 325 tickets at one shilling a piece.'

Wendy put her hand into the bucket to pull out the winning ticket. Nick noticed that her hand was closed. On removing it has she passed a ticket to Tommy who opened it and shouted out, 'it's a green ticket; anyone got a green ticket?'

Someone shouted out, 'we've all got green tickets. Get on with it, you tosser.'

'Charming,' said Tommy. 'It's a green ticket, number three hundred and twenty six.'

There was a sigh of disappointment until old Mrs Muir stood up, her thighs nudging the table, nearly knocking all the drinks over and shouted, 'it's me. I've won, I've won.'

'Are you sure?' asked the surprised Tommy. 'Green, three, two, six.'

'I'm not blind, yer tosser. I've won.'

The nearest Green Coat, an attractive brunette called Paula, took the ticket and shouted out. 'She's right Tommy, green, three, two, six.'

'Check the serial number, Paula. Make sure she's not cheating.'

Someone else shouted out, 'stop pissing around and pay the old girl.'

Tommy looked at Wendy; his anger was there for all to see. Wendy, opened mouth, was physical shaking.   Mrs Muir was up on her feet, bounding towards Tommy. She grabbed the mug full of money, raised it in the air to a chorus of cheers and returned to her seat before Tommy and Wendy could move. Nick sat there laughing his head off before old Mrs Muir started showering him with kisses. I could get used to this, thought Nick, before noticing his father looking very suspiciously at him.

For the rest of the evening everyone in the ballroom had a fantastic time, the Green Coats put on a show that was worthy of the West End. Every time Nick tried to dance with Suzanne, old Mrs Muir would grab him and dance to whatever the band were playing. If it wasn't a Waltz, it was the Twist or the Gay Gordon's. For an olden, Mrs Muir had plenty of stamina. As the evening wore on Nick wanted to be alone with Suzanne. Tomorrow they would say their goodbyes and it was a sure bet that they would never see each other again. Making the usual excuse of – just popping outside for a breath of air – Nick and Suzanne left the ballroom and slowly walked towards the swimming pool. The moon was in its last quarter, but there was enough ambient light for Nick to admire Suzanne's pretty face. Holding each other closely Suzanne smiled and said, 'Nick Allen, I want to thank you for an absolutely fab week. I think you are almost perfect.'

'What do you mean – almost?' replied Nick.

Suzanne removed her hand from Nick's waist and gently felt the bulge in the front of his trousers. 'Ah,' she said smiling, 'hundred per cent perfect.'

At fourteen years old, Nick had not yet managed to control his manhood. It seemed to have a will of its own and would become instantly erect whenever he came close to an attractive girl. He had heard at school that there was a substance called bromide and that the British Army used to put it in the tea of our solders to stop them getting aroused during the war. He had on many occasions nearly asked his local chemist for some, but being a cautious fellow he was worried about the long term side-effects.

Nick was thinking, this is it, when a booming voice from behind instantly extinguished his romantic intentions.

'I think we need a word, matey.'

Both Nick and Suzanne looked round to see the menacing figure of the Green Coat Tommy.

'Not a good time, Tommy. Maybe tomorrow, say after breakfast,' replied Nick, looking around, weighing up his options.

'I want my money, and I want it now.'

Nick chuckled, 'actually, I don't have it and unless you are totally thick I didn't win the money, old Mrs Muir did. Although I would have thought that mugging old ladies would be right up your street.'

'Don't get smart with me, sunshine. If you haven't got the money I'm gonna knock you into the middle of next week.'

Nick had moved slightly away from Suzanne and prepared himself for an attack by standing sideways on, to give his opponent a smaller target. Even though Tommy was at least three inches taller and almost twice as wide, Nick was not afraid. Then out of the shadows popped Wendy and she grabbed Suzanne from behind, pinning her arms to her side.

As Tommy advanced towards Nick, a voice from behind him shouted, 'don't you dare touch my son.'

Instinctively Tommy turned round and received a crashing right hook to the chin. Nick had often heard the term, his legs turned to jelly, but this was the first time he had actually witnessed it. Tommy's knees wobbled as he slowly sunk to the ground. This was the cue for Suzanne to join in the action. Wendy gave out a piercing scream as Suzanne's heel came crushing down on the top of her foot. With her arms now free she grabbed Wendy's head from behind her and executed the most perfect Judo throw over her shoulder.

All three viewed the two Green Coats sprawled out in front of them. Nick was the first to speak. 'I think our work here is done.'

'Come on you two, I'd better walk you home,' replied Mr Allen, quickly shuffling the two teenagers away.

After a few paces Nick said, 'that was one hell of a punch, Dad. I didn't know you could box.'

Mr Allen smiled and rubbed his knuckles, 'there are a lot of things you don't know about me son, but I used to box a bit in the Army. Actually I was regimental champion one year.'

'And as for you, Miss Muir; who taught you to fight?'

Suzanne laughed, 'I go to Judo classes twice a week; a girl has to protect her honour.'

Once they reached the chalet that Suzanne shared with her Grandmother, Nick kissed her goodnight and said he'll see her in the morning. When they reached the next row of chalets Mrs Allen was there waiting for her two men to return.

'Everything okay?' asked Mrs Allen, with a slightly worried look on her face.

'Everything is fine,' replied Mr Allen. 'Just need to have a few words with Nick before I turn in.'

Nick gently opened the door to his Chalet, his brother Richard was sound asleep. Nick and Mr Allen sat down on Nick's bed and Mr Allen asked, 'what was all that about.' For once Nick told his father everything; all about old Mrs Muir's suspicions and how he acquired the 'spare' raffle ticket and how Tommy was blackmailing Wendy.

'Okay, son, leave it all to me,' said Mr Allen, as he stood patting Nick on the head and made his way to the door.

''What's all the noise about?' came a voice from the other bed.

'Nothing for you to worry about,' replied Mr Allen. 'Now go back to sleep, Richard.'

'I've told you – call me Dick,' mumbled Nick's brother, before giving out a loud snore.

It didn't take long for Nick to get undressed, have a quick wash in the sink, brush his teeth and get comfortable in bed. It had been a long eventful day and he was very tired, and as he lay there thinking about recent events he realised that a certain part of his anatomy was fully awake. Not again, he thought as he lifted his blanket and whispered, 'be patient Little Nick, one day soon your time will come.'

With their bags all packed the Allen family relaxed over breakfast. As their coach didn't leave until eleven o'clock there was no need to rush. Unfortunately, the Muir family had a long drive back to Scotland, so they had breakfasted early. But, just as Mrs Allen was helping herself to a third cup of tea and waiting patiently for an extra rack of toast, the Muirs came to say their goodbyes. Old Mrs Muir gave Nick a big cuddle before he had chance to talk to Suzanne, but once she had released him, Nick and Suzanne exchanged addresses and promised to write to each other every week. Nick was a little sad, because he knew that he would never see Suzanne again but to compensate, a certain other girl called Moira Harris would be waiting at home for him.

The coach was on time and soon the Allen family were settled in their seats for the three hour journey back home. Nick was sitting window side to Mr Allen, who was surprisingly quiet for the first part of the journey. Bored with looking out of the window, Nick turned to his father and said, 'where did you disappear to after breakfast?'

There was a moment of silence before Mr Allen replied, 'just clearing up your mess.'

'Oh,' said Nick, casually, 'go alright?'

'Not bad.'

Nick sighed, 'just tell us what happened, you know you want to.'

Mr Allen smiled, 'okay, well I went along to see the Camp Manager, nice chap. He had heard that there had been a spot of bother, but didn't know the full details. So I thought, honestly is the best policy, and I told him all I knew. It turned out that he knew Tommy was on the fiddle but he couldn't prove it. '

'What happens now?'

'Tommy will get his marching orders today.'

'What about Wendy?'

'As it happens he was aware of Wendy's predicament, she's an unmarried mother. He was very sympathetic; apparently he has a sixteen year old daughter who is pregnant.'

'Will she get the sack?'

'No, he'll give her a final warning and he's going to adjust her working hours to suit her babysitting needs.'

Nick smiled, 'he seems like a reasonable chap.'

Mr Allen nodded, 'absolutely, top man.'

There was another pregnant pause before Mr Allen reached up to the luggage rack and took down a brown paper carrying bag. 'Oh, I nearly forgot, he gave me this to give to you, by way of thanks.'

Nick grabbed the bag and looked inside – a brand new Hitachi 2 band transistor 6 radio.

Moira Harris was not exactly in the best of moods as she applied the finishing touches to her hair with a squirt of hairspray. She had been 'officially' going out with Nick Allen for one week and she was really happy. He was good-looking, funny, attentive, maybe a little too randy, but most 14 year-old boys were. But to give him credit, if she said no, he didn't argue and he was very gentle. No boy of that age would be perfect, they were still learning about sex and love just as she was. She was quite fond of her last boyfriend, who just happened to be one of Nick's best friends; but he was two-timing her so she dumped him. She wasn't all that upset because she was secretly in love with Nick. Yesterday Nick had told her that they were going on a foursome with her ex-boyfriend and his new girlfriend. What was he thinking and why didn't he ask me first. She didn't fancy a row so she reluctantly agreed.

'So, where are we meeting them,' asked Moira, in a matter-of-fact tone.

Nick had finished his tea, had a wash, put on some clean clothes and was just finishing reading the *News of the World* when Moira appeared. In the background Sidney Carter was looking at love through songs old and new on an ITV programmes called *Hallelujah*.

'I've already told you, round at Keith's place,' gasped Nick. 'Look, if you don't want to go, just say. I can understand it. If I was you, I wouldn't fancy going out on a foursome with your ex-boyfriend and his new girlfriend.'

'No, I want to go; cos I'm very curious to meet the trollop that he was cheating with.'

Although Keith was one of Nick's two best friends, he had been very secretive about Brenda; so he was also intrigued to meet her. All he knew was that she was a year older than Keith (15) and she had large tits.

'Come on,' encouraged Nick, 'it will be interesting and we don't want to be late.'

Moira grabbed Nick's hand, gave him a peck on the cheek and said, 'as long as I'm with you, I'll have a nice time.'

Nick smiled, 'whatever she's like I can guarantee she will not be as pretty as you.'

After saying goodbye to Mrs Allen, they started to make their way towards Keith's house, which was a good ten minute walk. It was a beautiful Sunday evening and the few neighbours who were soaking up the last few rays of sun and busy attending their gardens smiled as they watched the young couple walk happily by. This bliss was suddenly shattered when Nick yelled out as he felt a sharp pain in the back of his head. Turning round he saw a withered women, completely dressed in black preparing to throw another stone.

'You bastard,' yelled the old women, as the next stone flew by Nick's head.

'Come on,' said Nick, pulling at Moira. 'Let's get away from here.'

The couple started to run. After about twenty yards Moira stopped and once she had caught her breath, she asked, 'what's that all about?'

'That's new, she's never thrown stones before,' replied Nick, looking pensive.

'What does she normally do?' enquired Moira. 'And why is she throwing stones at you?'

'She normally just swears and throws insults.'

'But why?' screamed Moira.

'You know who that is, don't you? That's Mrs Waller, and, you must remember, her boy Peter went missing five years ago, and she blames me.'

Moira gasped, 'of course, I'd completely forgotten about that. But why does she blame you?'

'She thinks that I was looking after him, but I was playing football with Gordon and Paul. To be honest, he was looking after us.'

'Doesn't it upset you?'

'I still have nightmares about it. I wish I had done something at the time, but it happened so quickly. One minute he was there, next minute he was gone.'

For the next two minutes they walked hand-in-hand in complete silence. This was broken when Moira said, 'I know, why don't we spend the rest of the holidays trying to find Peter?'

'What?'

'You're supposed to be a consulting detective. Why not? It could be fun and I'll be there to keep you out of trouble.'

Nick thought for a while before replying. 'Okay, we'll look into it. We'll mention it to Keith; I know how he likes a little adventure.'

'Actually, he doesn't,' replied Moira sheepishly. 'He only helps you out to keep you happy.'

'Are you sure?' said Nick, inquisitively.

Mrs Waller rushed inside and immediately filled the kettle and lit the gas hob. She then grabbed the teapot, removed the lid and hastily spooned two teaspoons of tea into it. Her breathing was rapid; she could feel her heart beating fast in her chest. She picked up a mug, and then threw it at the kitchen wall. As the shattered pieces hit the floor, she fell to her knees and burst out crying. It was only when the whistle on the kettle gave out its annoying shriek that she returned to her feet. Turning the gas off, she poured the boiling water into the teapot. Wiping her eyes with a nearby teacloth, she took a deep breath and then finding another mug she poured in the milk and waited for the tea to brew. When she was satisfied that the tea was to her liking she poured it into her mug and made her way to her favourite armchair in the living room. How long would this suffering last? It had been five years, three months and six days since her beloved boy, Peter, had disappeared. The Police were clueless and had all but given up on looking for him. And why did she always blame that poor boy, Nick Allen; he was only nine at the time, what could he have done? But she had to blame someone, anyone, and he was the easiest target. But why; why did it happen to her. Why was God punishing her, she was a good Catholic, never hurt anyone. She always went to confession even though there was very little to confess. But she had sinned once, a big sin and she had prayed repeatedly for forgiveness. Surely she shouldn't be punished that badly for just one indiscretion? They all said that time was a great healer, maybe, but not for her. Could he still be alive? She doubted it, but without his body to bury there could never be closure. How long could she live like this? Her husband had walked out on her three years ago, she didn't blame him, and she knew she had been hell to live with. He still paid the rent for her and sent her money every week. It wasn't a lot but somehow she survived. If only someone would find him; she put her mug down on the coffee table, fell to her knees again, kissed her rosary and prayed for a miracle.

Keith Nevin, who was one of Nick's closest friends, was a good two inches taller, had dark brown hair and a slight oriental look due to his mother being Vietnamese. He lived in a neat three-bedroom semi-detached house about a half a mile from Nick's house. When Nick and Moira arrived they were greeted by Mrs Nevin, a very pretty, petite, Vietnamese woman who escorted them to the lounge where Keith and Brenda huddled up on the sofa.

'Not disturbing anything, I hope,' asked Nick, with a smirk on his face, as both Keith and Brenda stood up when they saw the couple.

'Of course not,' snapped Keith, quickly pulling up the zipper on his trouser.

Nick and Moira just stood there with silly grins on their faces.

Composing himself Keith said, 'great to see you both, and let me introduce you to Brenda.'

Brenda took a step forward, offered her hand and said, 'pleased to meet you.'

Nick shook her hand and replied, 'pleased to meet you to.'

Moira just stood there. Nick looked at Brenda; she was of average height for her age, with a mass of long curly black hair, olive green eyes and a milky white complexion. She was pretty in a Victorian china doll way. Keith had told him that her mother was Irish and her father Italian. But her stand-out feature, as Keith had mentioned, was her amazing bosom.

'So,' said Brenda, 'you must be Moira, Keith's ex. He said you were pretty, but I can see now why he preferred me.'

Nick felt Moira squeeze his hand as she counted to ten before replying, 'well I can definitely see why he was attracted to you.'

'Ah, that's nice. I hope we'll become good friends. Haven't I seen you at church?'

'Yes, of course, I recognise you now,' replied Moira, forcing a smile.

'So,' said Keith interrupting. 'What have you been up to, Nick? Did you have a nice holiday?'

'Great, thanks. I'll tell you all about it later.'

'Nick wants you to help him with an investigation,' interjected Moira.

'Not again,' gasped Keith.

'Oh, how exciting, when do we start? Sit down and tell us all about it,' enthused Brenda.

'Have we got time? What time does the film start?' enquired Nick.

'We've got loads of time,' replied Brenda. 'This is more important.'

All four sat down, Keith and Brenda on the sofa, Nick and Moira each took an easy chair.

Nick was first to speak, 'five years ago, a boy who lived a few doors away from me, disappeared. His mother blames me and Moira here thinks we should try to find him.'

'Perhaps,' interrupted Brenda with a thoughtful expression on her face. 'He might have been taken and raised by monkeys, like Romulus and Remus. And that turned out alright, Romulus became the first pope.'

Shaking his head in disbelief, Nick replied, 'I think Romulus and Remus were actually raised by a she-wolf and Romulus was the founder of Rome, not the first pope. It was Tarzan who was raised by apes.'

'Are you sure?'

'Positive, anyway, I don't think there are many apes or wolves roaming around St. Albans.'

'Perhaps not,' replied a dejected Brenda.

'So, where do we start?' enquired Keith, without too much enthusiasm.

'I've been thinking, maybe I'll have a word with DI James,' responded Nick.

Brenda cut in, 'can we wait till I get back from holiday; I'm off to Italy tomorrow.'

Nick supressed a chuckle and said, 'we'll make a few enquires just to get going, then we'll ask your advice when you get back.'

Brenda clapped her hands and said, 'excellent, I'm sure it won't take us long to crack the case.'

'Good, that's settled. So, where are you going in Italy?' said Nick, quickly changing the subject.

'Rome, we're staying with my uncle. I'm very excited, Rome is full of history and artists and sculptures. Did you know that Michael Angelo painted sixteen chapels?'

'Incredible, is it your first holiday abroad?' asked Moira, trying to supress a giggle.

'Oh no. last year we went to Athens in Greece. We went to see the Acropolis, but it's not finished yet. You know, the Greeks are so lazy, they sleep all afternoon. It's amazing that any of their buildings are finished.'

'You're so lucky Brenda, I've never been abroad.' Moira looked at Keith, who had his head in his hands. 'I think we'd better go now, otherwise we'll miss the beginning of the film.

Brenda stood up and approached Moira, smiled and said, 'I know we are going to be the best of friends, let's walk together and let the boys talk about boring football.'

As Moira stood up, Brenda grabbed her hand and dragged her out of the room. Keith looked up at Nick and said, 'well, what do you think?'

Nick smiled, 'I think she's great, come on let's go.'

The film they had chosen to see was *Devil-Ship Pirates* starring Christopher Lee and was being shown at the *Gaumont* cinema in Stanhope Road. Nick had always liked the *Gaumont* cinema, especially the front that looked like a Greek portico with marble steps leading up to heavy oak swing doors. It was built in 1992 and was called *The Grand Palace*. It changed its name to the *Old Capitol* in 1945 after the *Odeon* group purchased the cinema in 1937 and was finally renamed *Gaumont* in 1950, to join hundreds of other *Gaumonts* in the country. The film was due to start at 8.30pm and the party arrived in plenty of time. After purchasing their tickets and some sweets from the kiosk they went back outside, thinking that it was a bit early to take their seats. As they chatted away, Nick couldn't help looking at all the other cinema goers, some he recognised and acknowledged. One person he did recognise was PC Adams, the elder brother of Dave Adams who was in his class at school.

'Excuse me a moment,' whispered Nick to his friends. 'There is someone I must speak to.'

Nick caught up with PC Adams, who was out of uniform, as he was buying his tickets. He was escorted by an extremely attractive girl.

'Sorry to disturb you officer; but could I have a quick word,' asked Nick politely.

PC Adams turned and recognised Nick immediately. 'Oh, it's

you. Look I'm off duty, can't it wait?'

'One quick question, then I'll be gone.'

'Go on, but make it quick.'

'Where can I find DI James tomorrow?'

PC Adams thought for a moment, and then replied, 'He'll be at *Jack's* café in Verulam Road, tomorrow morning at 8.00am. But you didn't hear it from me.'

Nick tapped his nose with his index finger and said 'thanks, I owe you one.'

Nick re-joined his friends and said, 'my friends, the game is afoot.'

Monday 10 August

Detective Inspector Philip James hated undercover work, although technically this wasn't really undercover work, but he was in disguise. He never felt comfortable wearing his casual clothes while on duty; he was a Detective Inspector for Christ sake and he should wear the clothes befitting his status – crisp white shirt, under a smart dark suit and a conservative tie. But today he was investigating the rising drug problem that was rearing its ugly head in St. Albans and this morning he had arranged to meet one of his informants at a local café. With a bit of luck he should be in and out in thirty minutes, then back home to change before reporting to the station. He would squeeze in a quick full English breakfast and a mug of tea, much more satisfying than the bowl of muesli and glass of freshly squeezed orange juice that his wife was insisting that he had for breakfast every day.

At 8.00am Nick finished his shift at *Headings and Watts* paper shop in Catherine Street and collected his bicycle from the builder's yard next door. Nick had recently been promoted from paperboy to marking the papers and generally helping around the shop. Mounting his bike he turned left into Etna Road, then right into Britton Avenue and left again into Verulam Road. *Jack's* Café was situated about one hundred yards up on the right. Feeling slightly nervous, he chained his bicycle to a drain pipe on the opposite side of the road. He would be able to keep an eye on it if he sat near the window. Even though he had never visited this establishment before, he knew it by reputation. A genuine greasy spoon café, frequented by local tradesmen and the down-and-outs of St. Albans; it was run by an ex-navy chef called John.

The café was about half full and as he entered he felt like he was in a Western film, walking into a saloon in Dodge City. For a few seconds the whole place went quiet as a dozen pairs of eyes stared at him. Seeing he was of no importance they turned away and continued with their meals and conversation. Nick quickly scanned the room but at first could not see DI James. Taking another look he noticed him sitting alone at the corner table. He realised why he missed him first time, DI James was not wearing his usual attire of a smart suit, tie and highly polished shoes. Today he was kitted out in jeans; a check shirt and what must be his gardening shoes. He was also unshaven. Nick thought he looked like a 1930s lumberjack; no, an undercover cop disguised as a 1930s lumberjack. Nick liked DI James; he estimated that he would be in his mid-forties, of medium height and broad shouldered. His thick brown hair and dark eyes must have made him quite desirable to some women. As Nick turned towards him, DI James, with a stern look on his face gave a delicate shake of the head. Nick understood, and turned towards the counter. John looked up and said, 'what can I do you for, boy?' John was a stout forty something year old with a round weathered face and a mop of dark brown hair. He was wearing a grubby white tee shirt under a blue with white striped apron.

'I'll have a mug of tea and a bacon roll, thank you.'

'Sugars?'

'Two, please.'

John poured the tea, gave it a good stir, passed it to Nick and then said, 'I'll call you when your roll is ready.'

'Thank you,' replied Nick as he picked up the mug, turned and made his way to a table next to the window, giving him a good view of his bicycle. Nick thought for a so called dive, the café was reasonably clean. Each table was covered by a plastic red and white checked table cloth, a glass salt and pepper pot, a bottle of HP sauce, a bottle of Heinz tomato ketchup and a plastic ashtray. As he made himself comfortable the cafe door opened and in walked the imposing figure of Ginger Mills. This local legend stood about five foot nine inches tall, sporting a ginger beard and a mop of ginger hair. With his trade-mark cowboy hat, leather waistcoat and large, very impressive belt; once seen never forgotten. A few diners looked up and nodded; Ginger smiled and acknowledged one or two of them. He walked towards DI James and sat down opposite him.

'Another tea here,' DI James called to John.

Nick sipped his tea, it was strong and sweet and he watched in awe as DI James and Ginger, heads close together, began their intense conversation. Straining to hear what they were talking about, Nick's concentration was broken by the sound of John shouting, 'one bacon roll.'

Nick thought for a moment before realising John was shouting at him.

'That's me,' he mumbled, before returning to the counter to collect his roll.

It was a good fifteen minutes before Ginger stood up, shook hands with DI James and left the café. Nick watched him through the window as he crossed the road and disappeared up Upper Dagnal Street to where the van that he lived in was parked. When he turned round, DI James was sitting opposite him. They looked at each other; DI James spoke first.

'Didn't know you came in here; no waitresses with short skirts for you to ogle at.'

'Didn't know the C.I.D. made their inspectors dress like scruffy lumberjacks,' retorted Nick.

'Touché.'

'So, is Ginger Mills one of your snouts?' said Nick eagerly.

'He may be helping us with one or two of our enquiries.'

'Anything I can help you with?'

'I don't think so... ... anyway, why are you here, and how did you know where I'd be?

Nick laughed. 'I have my informants as well, and I'm not here out of choice that's for sure,' he replied, looking round. 'Actually, I was hoping you could help me with one of my investigations.'

DI James took a deep intake of breath, remembering how only a few weeks ago Nick nearly froze to death on one of his "investigations".

'Do you remember, about five years ago a boy called Peter Waller disappeared? Well his mum blames me for his disappearance. She shouts and swears at me every time I walk past her house. Now she's taken to throwing stones. So Moira suggested that I should use my summer holiday to find him. So I thought you could have a look in your files.'

Nick noticed that DI James looked very thoughtful and it was a whole minute before he answered. 'The first case I was assigned to after my transfer from Tottenham was the Peter Waller disappearance. After five years it's the only case I've been involved with, that remains unsolved.'

'I didn't know that,' it was all Nick could think of to say.

'The only witnesses were three young boys, all under ten years old. I guess you were one of them.'

'That's right.'

'Interesting; did I interview you?'

'No, we gave our statements to a wooden top. Not much to say really. We couldn't see the faces of those in the car, but there were definitely three of them.'

'But you did give a good description of the car and that was all we had to go on.'

'Did you have any suspects?'

'We traced all the owners of blue Hillman Huskeys in the area, checked their whereabouts for that afternoon. All except one had a cast iron alibi. He was known to us. Bit of a juvenile delinquent, always in trouble. Apart from a few fines we never nabbed him for anything major. His mum always gave him an alibi. He seemed to settle down after his National Service and that was the only time he came onto our radar.'

'What was his alibi?'

'Listening to the wireless with his mum, and she confirmed it.'

'And did you believe her?'

'We couldn't prove otherwise.'

'What else can you tell me about… …err?'

'His name is Billy Watkins, must be about 26 years old now, average height, skinny, bit of a Teddy Boy and not the full shilling. His mum doted on him, very protective. I think that's why she always gave him an alibi.'

Nick took a sharp intake of breath then exhaled. 'I think we should start with him. Do you know his address?'

'Can't remember off hand, but I'll check it out and give you a bell later. But, be careful, Billy has a nasty temper.'

'I will.'

'Listen, I would love to close this case, so please keep me informed and I'll try to help you as much as I can.'

'Thanks.'

'Look, I've got to go now, but I'll be in here same time next Monday if you have anything to report.' With that he got up and left.

Nick sat there for a while thinking over what DI James had said and trying to formulate his next course of action.

Keith Nevin was in a reflective mood as he cycled the half mile to Nick's house. Brenda had caught her plane and was now holidaying in Italy. He'll miss her a bit, especially when they were alone. What she lacked in intelligent conversation was definitely made up for in the passion stakes, she was an animal. It was a shame that Moira found out, it would have been the perfect situation – Moira for the intellect and Brenda for the passion, still can't have everything. But having two girls on the go meant that he didn't have much time to see Nick and he felt guilty that he wasn't there when he nearly died last month. He remembered that whilst Nick was freezing to death in that butchers cold store he was bathing in the delights of Brenda's magnificent bosom. Keith had been friends with Nick since they first met at Grammar school. It was after the first half-term in the first year. He had started there late because they had only just moved from the East End to St. Albans. At the morning break on his first day he didn't know where to go, or what do. Then Nick appeared and said 'come with me' and they have been friends ever since.

'Did she get off alright?' asked Nick, as Keith approached him. Nick was sitting in his back garden enjoying the afternoon sun and listening to Radio Caroline on his new transistor radio. The delicate tones of Marianne Faithful singing *As Tears Go By* filled the air.

Sitting himself down on the grass Keith replied, 'no problem.'

'Are you going to miss her?'

Keith thought for a while before answering, 'maybe, a little. It's great to have a girlfriend, but I miss when it was just the three of us, putting the world to rights.'

'A little bird told me you only came along just to please me.'

'Who told you that?' gasped Keith. 'Oh, I bet it was Moira. I only said that to make her think I preferred seeing her to you.'

Nick smiled, 'of course you did.'

'How did you get on with DI James, this morning?' said Keith, quickly changing the subject.

Nick gave Keith a quick summary of this morning's meeting at Jack's Café.

'Well that's something; has he phoned with the address?'

'Yes, DI James was as good as his word; our suspect lives with his mum, in Leyland Avenue.'

'I take it that will be our first port of call?'

'Absolutely; got your bike?'

'Of course.'

'Then let's take a little ride to Cottonmill.'

Billy Watkins was in a happy mood, it was the first day of his annual holiday and he was planning to spend a few days in Margate. He would drive there tomorrow, find a cheap bed and breakfast and spend the majority of his time in Dreamland. Opened in 1920 and inspired by Coney Island, Dreamland was described time and time again as the heartbeat of Margate and is one of the oldest and best-loved amusements parks in the UK. But first he needed to give his car a good clean, he'd been neglecting it lately and his mum had been nagging him. 'It reflects badly on me,' she would say. He kept promising himself that he would move out soon and find a place of his own. But he loved his mum and felt responsible for her ever since his dad died.

Leyland Avenue is a cul-de-sac off Cottonmill Lane on the Cottonmill estate. It took the boys about fifteen minutes to cycle there. Their luck was in; as they casually cycled down the cul-de-sac, they spotted the recognisable figure of Billy Watkins busily washing an Alpine Green Vauxhall Victor Super. Turning round at the end of the cul-de-sac, Keith turned to Nick and said, 'that's lucky, he must be on holiday or out of work. So how are we going to approach this?'

'Just follow my lead, but remember he's got a bit of a temper, so don't antagonise him.'

The boys nonchalantly cycled towards Billy and stopped next to him.

'Excuse me, Sir,' said Nick. 'We are lost; can you direct us to Priory Walk?'

Billy turned and looked curiously at Nick. Seeing he was just a young boy, who was no threat to him, he smiled and replied, 'turn right at the end of the road, over the bridge and it's on the right.'

'Thank you very much, Sir,' replied Nick. 'And I must say that's a fab car; is it yours?'

'You like it?' replied Billy enthusiastically. 'I've only had it a few months, it goes like a bomb.'

'I can't wait to learn to drive,' added Nick.

They stood there for a few minutes admiring Billy's car, before

Keith said, 'When I pass my test, I think I'll buy a Hillman Huskey. Get used to driving on the roads before I buy a more powerful car. What do you think?'

Without thinking, Billy replied, 'I used to have one of them a few years ago; nice little car.'

'Yes they are,' continued Keith. 'A nice blue one, I think; what colour was yours?'

A little wary, Billy answered, 'blue.'

'What a coincidence; so why did you sell it?'

'Why do you want to know?' replied Billy nervously.

Keith shrugged his shoulders and replied, 'just making conversation.'

Nick could see that Billy was getting a little agitated, 'and you sold it about five years ago?'

Billy snapped, 'I never said that. Go away and leave me alone.'

Nick thought it was time for the kill and said, 'just after you kidnapped Peter Waller?'

Before Nick could move Billy had picked up his bucket and threw the contents over him.

'Let's get out of here, he's fucking mad,' screamed Keith, and the two boys pedalled quickly away. 'We'll get you; we know you did it, you fucking nutter'

'You okay?' asked Keith, once they had cycled out of sight of Billy.'

Nick chuckled, 'I must look like a drowned rat.'

'A bit,' laughed Keith. 'But seriously, what have we achieved?'

'I think we can one hundred per cent say that our mad friend Billy was definitely involved.'

'So, one suspect down, two to find.'

'Correct; but the problem now is, how are we going to find them. We daren't go near Billy again, so we're no better off than the police, except we know definitely that he was involved.'

'Unfortunately we can't prove it and just because he threw a bucket of dirty water over you, doesn't make him a kidnapper.'

'We need to find another way of getting to him, and I've no idea how we are going to it.'

The boys cycled home, Nick needed to change his clothes and it was almost tea-time. He said goodbye to Keith and said he would ring him tomorrow.

Mrs Allen, a pretty petite woman in her late thirties, stood over the sink peeling potatoes for the evening meal. She felt contented with her life and was happy living in their two-bedroomed council house. A far cry from the cramped flat she lived in with her brother and sister in Shoreditch before she was married. She met her husband Stan after the war. They had corresponded during the war after Stan had picked her out of a group photo of girls with their shirts hitched up standing in the sea. After they had married they lived with his parents in Shirley Road. Two years after Nick was born they moved to this newly built house on the Batchwood estate. Since then Nick's little brother Richard had arrived. Her only worry was Nick, who seemed to get into a lot of trouble. It's not as though he was a bad boy, just the opposite. He cared for people, hated injustice and felt that he had to solve everyone's problems, which often put him in danger. She just hoped he would grow out of it soon. Understandably she was not impressed with her son as he walked into the kitchen. Although his t-shirt had dried a bit, it was covered in dirty stains and his hair was more of a mess than usual.

'Look at the state of you, what have you been up to? ... ... No I don't want to know.' gasped Mrs Allen.

'We need to talk, Mum. What's for tea?' said Nick, as he slumped into a kitchen chair.

'Leftovers, now tell me what's bothering you?'

'I'm trying to find out what happened to Peter Waller.'

'And how long has this been going on?'

'I only started today.'

'Today; and you're in this mess already,' said Mrs Allen, sitting down opposite Nick and giving him a cup of tea.

'We had an early breakthrough,' said Nick, before taking a sip of his tea. 'Got any biscuits?'

'No, you'll spoil you tea. Now finish your drink, go and get cleaned up, then we'll discuss this with your father at the dinner table, when he gets home.

Monday's tea was always leftovers. Whatever roast they had on Sunday they would have cold on Monday; this week it was roast beef. Mrs Allen sliced the remaining joint and served it cold with roast potatoes, gravy and peas, fresh from the garden.

'I thought you were going to take it easy with your investigations,' said Mr Allen, as he moped up the remaining gravy with a slice of dry bread.

'I was, but this is different. Mrs Waller blames me for Peter's disappearance and she's always swearing at me and now she's started throwing stones; I do feel sorry for her. I mean its five years, he must be somewhere,' said Nick, as he finished the last roast potato on his plate and giving out a large burp. 'Pardon me, but that was lovely, Mum.'

'If I'd 'ave had done that you would have clipped me round the ear,' said Nick's little brother, Richard.

'In some countries it's a sign of appreciation,' replied Nick.

'Funny how you always have an answer for everything.'

'Well if you spent more time reading books instead of comics, you might learn something.'

'That's not fair,' screamed Richard. 'You buy me the bloody things.'

'Now, stop it,' intervened Mrs Allen. 'Mind you language Richard and stop winding your little brother up, Nick.'

'May I leave the table, Mum? asked Richard, deciding not to carry on with the argument.

'Of course you can, Richard,' replied Mrs Allen.

'And I keep telling you, call me Dick.'

Once Richard had left, Mr Allen continued his questioning, 'so how do you propose to find him?

'I'm not sure, the police are clueless as usual, but DI James gave us one lead which we followed up.'

'I take it, it didn't go well,' said Mr Allen suppressing the urge to laugh.

'If you're referring to the fact that our suspect poured a bucket of dirty water over me, you may be right. But it's 99.9% certain that he was involved, so we've learnt something. Unfortunately we might have difficulty talking to him again.'

'What's your next move?'

'I'm not sure, but I'll sleep on it.'

'Are you out tonight? asked Mrs Allen.

'No, I think I'll have a night in. Moira's washing her hair; and *No Hiding Place* is on the telly.'

Tuesday 11 August

Nick had a restless night's sleep, tossing and turning and having weird dreams. One minute he was talking to Suzanne and then Moira threw a bucket of water over him. Next he was being chased by Billy Watkins and Tommy, the Green Coat. There were other dreams which he couldn't recall, but what he did remember was that at the end of each dream his mother was there to comfort him. When his alarm clock told him it was time for work he knew he had the solution. If he couldn't get to Billy he would try to extract the information he needed from Billy's mother. He wasn't sure how this was to be achieved but he knew where to start.

Winifred Watkins was in two minds, one, she was glad that her son Billy had gone away for a few days. It would give her chance to give the house a good clean and put her feet up and not worry about making sure that she had his dinner and tea on the table for when he came home. Why he had to come home every dinner time God only knows. Why couldn't he take sandwiches or go to a café with his workmates. But she would miss him and worry about what he got up to. It had been a struggle bringing him up on her own since her husband died, but luckily he hadn't been in trouble for a few years, so hopefully he would be okay. She had just finishing a pile of ironing and was looking forward to a nice cup of tea and a cigarette. Picking up her copy of the *Daily Sketch* she took her cup of tea into the front room and sat herself down in her favourite chair. It was then she realised that she had run out of cigarettes.

Nick phoned Keith during the morning and explained what he intended to do. He didn't know how long it would take so he would go it alone. He thought that if he hung around outside Billy's house around lunchtime, Billy Watkins' mum might appear; just hoping that Billy wasn't at home. He sat on a garden wall opposite Billy's house, happy to the fact that there was no sign of Billy's car. He pulled out a *Toffee Crisp*, tore of the wrapper and took a mouthful. Whilst waiting, his mind started wandering; after a while he started to think about sex. He had been going out with Moira for eight whole days and he had never been happier. She was perfect, good looking, funny, and intelligent; all that he could ask for. Although they hadn't had the opportunity to be alone, she had allowed him to touch her breasts a few times whist snogging, but only through her jumper. Once he put his hand under her blouse to rub her back, he couldn't believe how soft her skin was, it was like running your hand over the finest silk. He wondered how far she would let him go; when would he reach second base? He felt confident that he knew what to do when the time came. This confidence was gained from the advice he had received from a class mate called Richard Martin, who seemed to know a lot about girls and sex for a fourteen year old. The first problem about shagging a girl he said was not to make her pregnant. The best way to achieve that he said, was to wear a Rubber Johnny. Although, he added, it was like having a wank whilst wearing a pair of *Marigolds*. Another method, which most of his mates used, was the 'whip it out and wipe it' method. He explained that you would pull your dick out just before you come. The problem with this he explained was that if you did it regularly, the girl would get frustrated and start growing whiskers on her chin. The safest and best method he recommended was the rhythm method. This he added was favoured by the Catholic Church. Unfortunately, he chuckled, most Catholics thought it meant making love whilst listening to the Glen Miller Band, hence why so many Catholics have large families. Continuing, he explained that, scientifically (how does he know this stuff) if you shag a girl, either two days before or two days after her period, you could leave it in without the fear of her becoming pregnant. Nick thought about the whiskers on the chin and an old lady who lived alone at the end of his road. Old Mrs Foster, she had loads of whiskers on her chin and all the kids used to sing –

There once was a man named Michael Finnegan,
He grew whiskers on his chinnegan,
The wind came up and blew them in ag'in,
Poor old Michael Finnegan (begin ag'in)
There once was a man named Michael Finnegan,
He grew whiskers on his chinnegan,
Shaved them off and they grew in ag'in,
Poor old Michael Finnegan (ag'in ag'in ag'in)

Nick was quickly brought back to reality by the sound of a front door slamming; he looked up and observed an elderly lady who he assumed was Mrs Watkins.

Following at a safe distance, Nick watched as Mrs Watkins walked to the end of Leyland Avenue, cross over Cottonmill Lane towards the small parade of shops. Parking his bike on the kerb he followed Mrs Watkins into *Archers* the Newsagent. Mrs Watkins went straight to the counter and asked for ten *Kensitas* tipped; Nick discretely browsed through the comics on the shelf.

'How's your friend Mrs Buckingham, is she feeling better?' asked the lady behind the counter.

'She's on the mend, but it looks like I'll be going to Bingo on my own tomorrow,' replied Mrs Watkins.

'You don't mind that?'

'Oh no; I'll find someone to sit with, they are a very friendly crowd.'

It was one of those light-bulb moments – Nick had a great idea. He quickly grabbed a copy of *Hurricane* and walked to the counter. Putting on his best Irish accent he said, 'excuse me missus, but I couldn't help overhearing you mention that you were going to the bingo tomorrow.'

'That's correct, young man,' said Mrs Watkins, smiling at the young lad.

'Well, me and me maam have just moved here from Ireland, so we have, and we don't know St. Albans very well. And she loves her Bingo, so she does. So can you tell me where it's being held?'

'Certainly, it's at the Market Hall in St. Peters Street. It's start at 7.30 pm.'

'Thanks very much, me maam will be very grateful, so she will.' Nick gave the shopkeeper 6d and left the shop.

'So, what's the plan?' asked Keith, as the boys walked towards Verulamium Park for a spot of illegal fishing. Verulamium Park is set in 100 acres of parkland which was purchased from the Earl of Verulam in 1929.

'Well, I'm going to try and talk my mum into going to bingo tomorrow night. I'll get her to make friends with Billy's mum and try and extract the information we need,' replied Nick, confidently.

'Do you think she will?'

'She'll play hard to get, but I'm sure she'll be up for it.'

Although fishing is prohibited in the lakes of Verulamium, Nick and Keith were confident that they could get at least an hour's worth before the Park Ranger appeared. They set themselves up on the bridge that separated the main lake from the smaller boating lake. This gave them an excellent vantage point to look out for the dreaded Ranger. Although neither boy had a proper fishing rod they made do with a couple of eight foot bamboo canes borrowed from Nick's dad. A cheap reel, line, hooks, split shot and floats where purchased from the local fishing tackle shop. Thirty minutes were spent with a pair of pliers, some stiff wire and a roll of Sellotape; now the boys were ready to go. Using stale bread as bait, they cast out and waited for their first bite. It was a glorious afternoon and the park was alive with parents and children making the most of their school holidays. There were a few other lads daring to spend the afternoon illegally fishing; Nick noticed an old friend, his name Ernie Tomkins. Ernie was a year older than Nick and they had met when Nick joined the scouts and they became good friends. Nick gave him a wave and noticed that Ernie had a new split cane fishing rod and was having a good day as he seemed to catch a fish nearly every ten minutes. Ernie had left school at Easter and was now working for a local building firm.

'He's doing well,' commented Keith. 'What's he catching?'

'Mainly Roach I think; the lake's full of them; although those smaller ones are Gudgeon. They say there are some Pike in there, but I've never seen one,' replied Nick.

'What about King Kong, the giant Pike; wouldn't it be great to catch that.'

'I think that's a myth, have you ever seen it?'

Keith shook his head, wound in his line and re-baited the hook. The time seemed to fly by as the boys chatted away; Ernie had packed up and waved goodbye and the park was gently emptying as tea-time approached.

'I suppose we'd better start making a move,' said Keith, in a non-committal tone.

'Give it a few more minutes,' replied Nick. 'We've been here two hours and haven't had a single bite between us.'

It was that point when Nick noticed some movement on his float. Keith had also noticed it. Unfortunately he had also noticed something else. In the distance a figure wearing a peaked cap and riding a scooter was heading their way. Nick hadn't noticed, he was about to strike. With a sudden jerk to the left, the fish was hooked.

'Yeah, baby, look at that; it's a beauty,' shrieked Nick, as he started to reel in a decent sized roach.

'Ranger on the horizon,' screamed Keith.

Nick looked up and in blind panic shouted, 'what shall I do?'

'Leg it.'

Nick's wrist was going ninety to the dozen as he desperately reeled in the prized fish. Keith had bundled all his tackle and bits and pieces into his brown paper carrier bag. The ranger was closing in. It was no good, Nick had to run.

'Make for the woods,' yelled Nick, as he quickly grabbed his things.

Hoping to lose the ranger amongst the trees, the boys hot-footed themselves from the bridge towards the small wooded area, that separated the park from St Michaels Street. It was a sight to remember as the two boys, with brown carrier bags in one hand, fishing rods in the other; one with a distressed roach dangling from it, were pursued by a man in uniform on a black scooter. The front wheel of the scooter was barely a yard from Nick's heel when the boys reached the trees and disappeared from sight of the small cheering crowd. The Ranger tried to follow, but there was no way he could keep up with the nimble feet of the two youthful boys. Once they realized they were safe, they stopped to catch their breath.

'That was close,' gasped Nick. Then remembering his catch, he looked at the end of his rod, but the fish had gone, 'bloody hell - where me tea?'

Keith just laughed.

'That was fun,' said Nick

'Mum,' said Nick, as he tucked into his evening meal of sausage, beans and mashed potato. 'How would you fancy going to Bingo tomorrow night; my treat?'

'What's the catch?' replied Mrs Allen, without looking up.

'I don't know what you mean,' replied Nick, sounding hurt.

'Is this part of your "investigation"?'

'Might be; ….okay it is.'

'Explain.'

'What I thought was - that you could go to the Bingo at the Market Hall tomorrow night. Auntie Marge could go with you, if she wants. Then, while you are there, you could make friends with a lady called Mrs Watkins. I'll come with you and point her out. Then you get her talking about her son Billy and find out all you can about him, especially who his friends are and specifically who he was hanging out with five years ago.'

'That all?' said Mrs Allen, looking inquisitively at Nick.

'That's all; you have a nice night out, I get the information I need and you never know – you might win.'

Mrs Allen sighed, then said, 'okay, just this once.' Secretly inside she was very excited to help Nick with one of his investigations.

Wednesday 12 August

Nick was just finishing off his lunch, spam fritters and baked-beans, when the phone rang. He answered it.

'Hello, Nick Allen speaking.'

'It's me,' replied Keith. 'Fancy going swimming this afternoon?'

'Sounds good, come round when you're ready.'

The Cottonmill Swimming Pool was built in 1905 by George Ford with Mr Bushel, a builder, at a cost of just £1275. It was not one of Nick's favourite places, the water was always cold, but it was a good place to socialise. He always remembered the first time he was taken there; he was about eight years old and could not swim. His parents had often taken him to paddling pools but this was the first time he'd been to a real swimming pool. He was a bit nervous of deep water but someone had told him that if you jump in you would automatically float to the top. So after changing, he jumped straight into the pool and sat on the bottom waiting to float to the top. Luckily Mrs Stewart was watching and jumped in and hauled him to the surface. It was a few years before Nick returned there.

After spending about twenty minutes in the pool, they grabbed their towels and made their way to the viewing balcony, situated over the men's changing cubicles. Sitting in the front row they had a good view of the whole pool, to the right was the shallow end and a small slide. To the left, the deep end and the diving boards. But in front, on the other side were the girls changing rooms and between the cubicles and the pool there was enough paved area for sunbathing.

'Seen anything you fancy?' asked Keith, who was eyeing up a couple of mature ladies sitting on the edge of the pool with their feet splashing in the water.

'I'm not looking,' lied Nick. 'I'm thinking about the case.'

'Are you sure? Look over there, there's the Cottonmill crowd and if I'm not mistaken I can see Margaret Russell. I know you fancy her and I can also see Heather Turnbull; you had a crush on her a few years back.'

Nick smiled, 'she is nice, isn't she?'

'She's okay, but we'll stop ogling for a moment and discuss our next move. Have you had any ideas? Nick, are you listening.'

'Sorry, miles away. What did you say?'

'I thought you wanted to discuss the case,' said Keith, looking towards the heavens.

'Of course I do, but doesn't she look good in a swimsuit, just look at her lovely bottom.'

Keith punched Nick on the arm.

'Ouch, no need for that,' said Nick, frantically rubbing his arm.

'What have you got planned?'

'Well as I said yesterday I talked to my mum about helping out and she's up for it. She's agreed to go to the Bingo tonight. So you and I will escort her and Mrs Stuart to the Market Hall and point her in the direction of Mrs Watkins.'

'Sounds good.'

'Let's just hope she's a good talker.'

The Market Hall was situated behind *British Homes Stores*, down an alley that led towards the cattle market. At 7.10pm, Nick, Keith, Mrs Allen and Mrs Stuart stood outside *British Home Stores* in St. Peters Street waiting for Mrs Watkins. Nick had checked on the bus timetables and had estimated that Mrs Watkins's bus should arrive at 7.15pm. The ladies were busy looking at the window display when Nick spotted Mrs Watkins alight her bus.

Giving Keith a slight nudge, he said 'look there she is; the old girl in the blue hat.'

Nick turned away, so that she wouldn't recognise him. As she walked past, Nick alerted his mum.

'Okay mum, this is it. The lady in the blue hat is our target. You have your instructions; remember - failure is not an option.'

Mrs Allen smiled and shook her head. 'Come on Marge, let's go and do our duty.'

Nick and Keith watched as his mum and Mrs Stuart, quickly walked to catch up Mrs Watkins. They caught up with her as she reached the queue at the door of the Market Hall. By the time they disappeared into the hall the three ladies were deep in conversation.

'What shall we do now?' asked Keith. 'We could go to the Pioneer Club; do you fancy it.'

'Yeah, why not,' replied Nick. 'We could check out the talent.'

Keith was confused, 'aren't you happy with Moira?'

'Mate, I'm ecstatic. She's the best thing that's happened to me. But it doesn't mean you can't look at other birds.'

'I suppose not.'

'Look at it this way,' Nick explained. 'Say you bought a brand new *Rolls Royce* car. You would love it, cherish it for ever. Never want to change it; it becomes part of your life. But that doesn't stop you looking at cheaper models; understand?'

'And occasionally giving them a test drive.'

'You said it.'

They walked up St. Peters Street, turned right at the *Blacksmiths Arms* and made their way down Hatfield Road to the Pioneer Youth Cub that was situated in the old Fire Station. It was a quiet evening with only a handful of teenagers in the club. Nick and

Keith decide to have a game of table tennis as the table was free. After two games and with each winning one game, they decided to play a decider before heading off. With the score at 15-15, Nick noticed a familiar figure approaching them. Dressed in his usual attire of black tee-shirt, blue jeans, studded leather jacket and green hob-nailed boots, was Digger Barnes.

'Hello Nick, how are you? Haven't seen you since our little fracas,' said Digger with a wry smile. Digger had rescued Nick from his mad Geography teacher a few months back.

Nick smiled and shook Digger's hand. 'It's nice to see you as well.'

Keith acknowledged Digger with a smile and a small wave.

'Staying out of trouble are we? Or have you got something going on?' asked Digger.

'Nothing too exciting, just a missing person.'

'Well if you need any help, you know where to find me.'

'You can rely on that,' laughed Nick. 'You're top of my list of important and useful contacts.'

'Glad to hear it.' And with that Digger disappeared out of the door.

'I've had enough,' said Nick. 'Let's call it a day. I can't concentrate; keep wondering how mum is getting on.'

So the boys left the club and made their way home, but not before popping in the *Painters Arms* public house to buy a bottle of Grapefruit Juice.

'Why don't you go to bed?' asked Mr Allen, as he watched his son pace up and down the living room.

It was just after 10.00pm and Nick was anxious to de-brief his mother.

'How can I sleep? I need to know what she's found out. What's keeping her; she should be home by now.'

'Patience was never your strong point.'

'What?' Nick exclaimed. 'Me; I've got the patience of a saint. I'm known throughout St. Albans as – Nick the Patient.'

'I think that's because you spend so much time in hospital,' laughed Mr Allen.

At that point they heard a noise in the kitchen.

'Mum's back,' said Nick, rushing to see her.

Mrs Allen was in the kitchen taking off her coat.

'How did you get on, what did she say? enquired Nick, excitedly.

'For God's sake boy, let me get in. It's been a long night, now put the kettle on and let me take my shoes off.

'Sorry, Mum,' replied Nick, as he filled the kettle.

Mrs Allen hung her coat up in the hall, kicked her shoes off, and then went to see her husband in the living room. Nick made a pot of tea, filled three cups, put them on a tray and then re-joined his parents. Placing the tray on the glass coffee table he sat in his favourite chair and said, 'well?'

'I won ten shillings,' beamed Mrs Allen.

'What about Mrs Watkins?' gasped Nick.

'Can we do this in the morning, I'm very tired?'

Nick just gave her one of his looks.

'Okay then, I'll get no peace until I do. Well, your friend Mrs Watkins or Winnie, as she likes to be called, is a very nice lady, but she can't 'arf talk. Never stopped; likes talking about herself, not really interested in what you had to say, not that I got much of a word in. She lost her husband when her son Billy was quite young, industrial accident or something. She dotes on him, she admits that he's not quite the ticket, but he seems to be okay at the moment. He was a bit of a tear-way when he was a lad, got into a lot of trouble. She blamed it on the company he kept, said they led him astray. Many a time she had to lie to the police to save him. Then, after he did his national service he seemed to settle down. He secured a job as a mechanic at *Marlborough Motors*, made friends with a nice chap called Eddie Reynolds, who took him under his wing and everything was hunky-dory for a while. Then, about five years ago, there was some problem, which she never quite worked out and she had to give Billy an alibi. As I said, she never understood what it was and it's never been mentioned since. But, the strange thing was that his friend Eddie committed suicide a few days later. Set Billy back; he had a sort of a break-down. He was off work for a long time, never left the house. He seems okay now and his work was very understanding.'

Nick was excited, 'Mum, you have done brilliantly. Carry on like that and I'll have to put you on the payroll.'

'So' intervened Mr Allen. 'What have you learnt from that?

'Well,' replied Nick, 'that confirms what we had already suspected, Billy was involved and this Eddie bloke could be one of the other two who we saw in the car. I also think that Billy was just the driver, he's too thick to plan something like this.'

'Mind you, it doesn't help that this bloke Eddie topped himself.'

'Yes, that's a bit of a nuisance,' chuckled Nick

'So what's your next move?'

'I need to find out a bit more about this Eddie Reynolds bloke. I think I'll have a word with DI James; they must have a record of the suicide. Also I have a feeling that there is some connection between the kidnappers and the Waller family.'

'What makes you think that, son?' asked Mr Allen.

'I just don't think that Peter would get into a car without knowing someone there. Who would be the best person to talk to about Mrs Waller?'

'That would be Moira's mum,' stated Mrs Allen. 'They were the best of friends before, you know what happened.'

Thursday 13 August

It was a miserable morning, overcast and the weatherman had forecast rain. Keith had called on Nick and with nothing better to do they decided to play a game of *Subbuteo* in Nick's bedroom. Nick brushed down the green baize pitch and set out the playing figures. Nick took the blue players whilst Keith had to settle for the reds. At the moment Nick was about to kick-off they heard a knock on the front door.

'I wonder who that is?' asked Keith.

'Nobody for me,' replied Nick. 'All my friends come round the back.'

From the bottom of the stairs came the booming voice of Mrs Allen, 'Nick, it's for you,'

'Who is it?'

'A prospective client,' was the reply.

Nick looked at Keith and raised his eyebrows, 'our fame is spreading.'

The two boys quickly jumped to their feet and rushed down the stairs. Mrs Allen was waiting at the bottom. 'I've shown him to the living room.'

'Thank you Mrs Hudson, we'll take it from here.'

After composing themselves and adopting a professional manner the two boys entered the living room. Standing there was a plain looking boy of similar age, dressed smartly in a blazer, trousers, shirt and tie; he introduced himself as Christopher Wright. Nick gestured for him to sit down.

Nick asked, 'well Christopher what can we do for you?' From nowhere Keith produced a pad and pencil.

'I've been informed that you are a private investigator and I'm in need of your services,' replied Christopher, confidently.

'Consulting detective, but no mind; who recommended us?'

'A friend of mine, Tom Clarke; apparently you helped him find his rabbits when they disappeared a few months ago.'

Nick looked at Keith and gave a little smile,' ah yes, I remember that case.' What Tom had failed to tell Christopher, that it was Nick and his friends who had kidnapped his rabbits and held them hostages until he had given them the information they needed to help their Sports Master who had been suspended from school. The outcome resulted in Tom having to change schools. Nick thought it was nice that he didn't hold a grudge. 'So how can we help you?'

Christopher took a deep breath and said,' it's a bit delicate, but I think my girlfriend is cheating on me.'

'Interesting, I think you had better start from the beginning.'

'Her name is Jennifer Hewitt and I love her dearly. We've been going out for at least five weeks, but a friend of mine informed me that he had seen her out with other boys.'

'Have you asked her?'

'Of course and she fervently denies it. She says she hasn't looked at another boy since we met.'

'How often do you see her?'

'It varies, every other night during term time and whenever we can during the holidays.'

'I see and when are you seeing her next?'

'This afternoon; she has a piano lesson at 2.00pm, then we'll meet in *Christopher's* coffee bar.'

'Where does she go for her lessons?'

'Don't know.'

Keith, who was busy taking notes, butted in and asked, 'what does she look like.'

'Oh,' said Christopher, 'I thought you might ask that, so I brought a photo.' He put his hand inside his blazer and pulled out a black and white school photograph of his beloved Jennifer and handed it to Nick. 'Isn't she lovely?'

Keith lent over to have a look; Jennifer was a very plain, stern looking girl with non-descript, shoulder-length dark hair. 'Yeah, she's lovely.'

'Can you tell us about her family,' continued Nick.

'She lives with her parents and one sister.'

'Older or younger?'

'Who?....Sorry I'm not sure; I don't think she gets on well with her sister.'

'One last question; where does she live?'

'New Greens, I'll write the address down.'

Nick thought for a minute before saying, 'I think that's all we need, if you come back next Thursday we'll give you a full report.'

Christopher stood up and said, 'thank you very much. Oh, just one thing, what are your fees?'

'Don't worry about that,' replied Nick, who had no idea what to charge. 'We'll sort that out next week. I'll see you out.'

When Nick returned, Keith was looking at Jennifer's photo, 'I wouldn't say she was pretty, would you?'

'Well she's definitely not my type,' replied Nick.

'I don't think she's cheating, I mean, she must be grateful to have one boyfriend.'

'Maybe, but it's not for us to speculate, we need to investigate. See what I did there?'

'Very good; so where do we start.'

'A little walk to New Greens, I think.'

Jennifer Hewitt lived in Maple Avenue, which was not that far away, so they decided to walk. As they turned into Toulmin Drive, Nick suddenly stopped and said, 'isn't that her at the bus stop?'

Keith looked and replied, 'I think your right. What shall we do?'

'Fancy a bus ride?'

The boys nonchalantly walked up to the bus stop and stood in the small queue behind Jennifer. Nick discretely took out Jennifer's photo to double check. Keith nodded in agreement. It was only a few minutes before the 325 bus arrived. Sticking as close as they could so that they could hear her destination, they followed her onto the bus. She alighted from the bus in St. Peters Street and made her way towards the bus station, the boys followed at a discrete distance. At St. Peters Close, a small cul-de-sac, she turned left; the boys then sprinted to avoid losing her. They just managed to spot her before she disappeared into a large Edwardian house.

'What do you think she's doing here?' asked Keith.

'I'm not sure, but if I didn't know better I would say she was going to her piano lesson,' replied Nick.

'It certainly looks like the type of house to have a piano, but didn't Christopher say she was having it this afternoon.'

'But he's so obsessed with the girl I doubt he even knows what day it is. Still, we must be professional so we need to be sure.'

'Agreed; so I'll keep watch while you have a look,' said Keith, taking a step back.

Nick shook his head and said, 'thanks.'

Weighing up his options Nick thought he could sneak up to the large bay window at the front of the house unseen first, before taking any drastic action. He was in luck; sitting with her back to the window, Jennifer was adjusting her sheet music on the piano. A tall elderly gentleman was standing next to her. Nick turned to Keith and gave him the thumbs up before re-joining him by the front gate.

'So what do we do now? asked Keith.

'Well, we need to follow her after the lesson; how long are piano lessons?' replied Nick.

'I would think an hour or 45 minutes,' said Keith, shrugging his shoulders.

'Sounds about right; let's get a milkshake at *Sally's*, then we'll follow her.'

'This is getting expensive, bus fares and drinks,' moaned Keith.

'No problem, laughed Nick. 'We'll claim it all back from Christopher in expenses.'

Anna Yarker enjoyed her job as a waitress at the *Sally's Inn* café. She enjoyed meeting people and her friends regularly popped in to see her. Unfortunately life was not easy for her; she lived with her mother, who was not in the best of health. Since her father walked out on them five years ago it has been a bit of a struggle to make ends meet. Despite her illness, she suffered from Rheumatoid Arthritis, her mother managed to hold down a part-time job at the local stocking factory. To help out, Anna worked as many shifts as she possibly could at the café. Her mother had begged her to leave school this summer and get a full time job, but she was determined to stay on for the fifth year and take her 'O' level GCEs. Her greatest disappointment, so far in life, was failing her eleven plus. She had always been the brightest girl in her class and it came as a great shock to everyone including her teachers when she failed. Anna put this failure down to stress, as the exams were only a week after her father left home. Her ambition was to become a fashion designer and her plan was to complete her 'O' levels, then go on to college to study fashion. One of the things she did enjoy about working in the café was teasing the young boys that came in to ogle her. Even though she was only fifteen, she was fully aware of her sexuality and the effect she had on the young lads. Although she regularly dated she had decided not to have a steady boyfriend yet. There were three specific boys, who were about a year younger, that she particularly liked teasing. They were always trying to chat her up, but she had to admit to herself that she quite liked one of them. His name was Nick, and he had the most beautiful blue eyes and a gorgeous smile. One day, she thought, when he's a bit older, she let him take her out. But for now he would have to make do with her teasing and trying to look up her skirt.

Sally's Inn café was Nick's favourite coffee bar and was situated at the top of St Peter's Street opposite the War Memorial. It was run by a former actress, Sally Barnes, who was best known for appearing in such films as *Holidays With Pay* (1948), *Somewhere in Politics* (1949) and *Make Mine a Million* (1959). As they entered they were greeted by their favourite waitress Anna Yarker. Everyone fancied Anna; she had a short hair style, similar to Mary Quant, it was dead straight, with a fringe and came under her chin in a bob. She also had lovely long legs that seemed to go all the way to her armpits and she was very pretty.

'Not you two again; got nothing better to do?' asked Anna sarcastically.

'Is that anyway to talk to your favourite customers? We'll have two strawberry milkshakes and one of your very special smiles,' replied Nick.

'Sorry, out of smiles today.'

The boys found an empty booth and sat down to enjoy their milkshakes.

'Why is she always so rude to us,' asked Keith.

'She's just playing hard to get, pretending she doesn't fancy me,' said Nick.

'Just listen to yourself, now forget her for just a minute and concentrate on the case.'

'Okay, well I suggest we stay here for a while, discuss the problems of the world whilst trying to seeing what colour knickers Anna is wearing today when she bends down, Then we'll wait outside for Jennifer and see where she goes.'

'My mum bought me a new pair of 501's, the other day,' said Keith, with a funny look on his face.

Nick noticed, 'and?'

'She wasn't very pleased when I tried to shrink to fit them.'

'What does that mean?'

'You mean there's something you don't know.'

Nick ignored the remark.

'It's what you have to do to *Levis* to make them fit your body. First you fill a bath with hot water and submerge them. Then you weigh them down, I found a couple of house bricks, and leave them for about twenty minutes. Then hang them somewhere to dry; when they are nearly dry, still moist, you put them on so that they shrink to your exact body shape. The trouble is that you can't sit down until they are totally dry. I'd manage to get most of it done before mum came home, but she wasn't very pleased when she caught me walking up and down the garden path in wet jeans.'

After 45 minutes they were no nearer to discovering the colour of Anna's underwear although they were close on a couple of occasions, so they decided to leave. Crossing the road they sat on the wall surrounding St. Peters Church, it gave them an excellent vantage point to observe the movements of Jennifer Hewitt. They didn't have to wait long, at exactly 12.00 hours Jennifer appeared, walking out of St. Peters Close she turned right and made her way down St. Peters Street towards the town centre. Following at a discreet distance they tailed Jennifer through the town into French Row. Waiting outside *Christopher's* coffee bar was a smart looking boy about sixteen years old, who was extremely pleased to see Jennifer. They greeted with a passionate kiss, which Nick thought was a bit too heavy for public viewing, before entering the café.

'Did you see that,' said Keith. 'That's definitely not Christopher;

what do we do now?'

'Okay, so we know she's cheating, but we need evidence. I've got my camera; all we need is a photograph,' replied Nick.

'And how do you propose to do that?'

'We go in, order a drink then I'll discretely take a picture.'

'I'm running out of money.'

'So am I,' replied Nick, checking the change in his pocket.

They were now standing outside the café and could see Jennifer and her beau, being seated by the waiter.

'Don't worry,' said Nick. 'I think I've got enough for two cups of tea, but I've a feeling we won't need it, just follow my lead.'

The boys entered the café and were shown to the table next to their prey. After a few minutes the waiter approached them, took out his notebook and asked if they were ready to order.

'Tea for two,' answered Nick.

'It's after twelve so you must order food or I'll have to ask you to leave,' replied the waiter.

'Okay, your loss, we'll leave, but I must just have a word with the couple at the next table.'

Nick stood up; Keith looked on as he approached Jennifer.'

'Sorry to bother you,' said Nick, holding his camera. 'I'm doing research for a school project. It's entitled "what school kids do in their summer holidays." Obviously, like you, we hang out with our friends in coffee bars and you're such a happy looking couple I was wondering if I could take a photo of you two to illustrate my project?'

'Of course, it would be our pleasure,' replied a beaming Jennifer.

Nick took a couple of snaps, said his thanks and left the café with Keith in tow. Outside Keith said, 'quick thinking Nick, I think our work is done.'

'Maybe, but I think we need to see what she does this afternoon. Will she go for another piano lesson?'

'You think Christopher made a mistake with the time?'

'I'm not sure,' said Nick, scratching his head. 'I don't really want to wait here until she finishes her meal. I don't think she'll have time to go home first before her next lesson, so this is what we'll do. We'll go back to my house get a bite to eat, and then make our way back to St. Peters Close. We'll see if she goes for another lesson. If she does they'll be no need to hang around as we know she's meeting Christopher afterwards. If she doesn't turn up, either he's mistaken or she's a lying, two-timing scumbag.'

At 1.55pm and suitably refreshed the two boys were positioned back on the church wall waiting for the deceitful Jennifer Hewitt. They didn't have to wait long; at 1.58pm Jennifer appeared and proceeded to her piano lesson.

Keith was the first to speak, 'interesting, what do you make of that.'

Nick thought for a while before answering, 'definitely interesting; she's changed.'

'What do you mean?'

'Well, this morning she was wearing slacks; now she's got a skirt on, and a different top.'

'Would she have had time to go home and change?'

'If she caught a bus, it's possible.'

'So, what shall we do now?' asked Keith as he jumped off the wall.

'Let's pop down to the Record Room and see what records we can't afford to buy.'

Friday 14 August

Mr Allen lit a *Manikin* cigar before picking up the *Herts Advertiser*. After a few minutes he moaned, 'have you seen this?'

'What's that dad?' replied Nick, as he tried to concentrate on his favourite TV show, *Ready, Steady. Go*. Tonight's episode featured the Swinging Blue Jeans and Georgie Fame.

'That bloody Ernest Marples has refused to ban heavy traffic through St. Albans. Did you know that over 3000 Lorries a day travel along London Road and Verulam Road? What was the point of building the bloody M1; the man's a complete idiot. He's stopped it in other towns, but no, not here. That's the trouble with politicians, especially the bloody Tories, got their brains in their underpants. Do you know what they are saying? Eh; that Ernest bloody Marples in the 'Man in the Mask'.'

'What's that, Dad?' asked Nick, only half listening to his father.

'One of those sex parties that your friend Christine Keeler used to attend. Apparently, a waiter walked around naked apart from a Masonic apron and a mask and a sign bearing the legend: "if my services don't please – whip me." Well rumour has it – it was Ernest Marples. You know I can't wait for the General Election when we get rid of this lot.'

When the programme had finished, Nick said goodbye to his parents and made his way to Moira's house. Tonight they were off to the Market Hall to see a group called The Sneakers. It would be a good night, 4/- each entrance fee, money well spent. During the interval Nick took Moira round the back of the hall to the cattle market. Finding a quiet spot by the chicken coops Nick could spend some time snogging Moira uninterrupted. She allowed him to put his hand inside her blouse and squeeze her breasts, they felt great and he hoped that one day soon he would see them in daylight. After a few minutes he thought he might risk trying for second base. He slowly removed his hand from her blouse; let it run down her body then up under her skirt. He didn't get very far before she pushed it away and said, 'what are you doing?'

Nick felt foolish, 'sorry, I just thought....'

Moira smiled and pulled him back and continued snogging him. He placed his hands on her behind and pulled her closer to him. He was so aroused; he didn't know what to do. Needing some air, he gently pulled his head away and looked into her eyes. Even in the dark she looked so beautiful, he would marry her tomorrow, if he was old enough.

He said, 'sorry about that, but you get me so worked up, I'm totally confused.'

She smiled and replied, 'I know you are, it's there for all to see and I feel randy too, but we're only fourteen. If I let you touch me there, we will both want to go all the way and we could easily make a mistake and I'll get pregnant. Anyway when I do let you touch me there, I want it to be somewhere special and a lot cleaner. So come back here, pucker up, grab my tits and kiss me.'

A loud crash on the drums indicated that the band was ready to start their second set. As Moira adjusted her bra and top another couple appeared from nowhere, giggling and laughing.

'I know her,' said Nick. 'That's Jennifer Hewitt, you know the girl I told you about and she's with yet, another fella.'

'Are you sure,' replied Moira. 'It's a bit dark.'

'That's definitely her and that's definitely not my client or bloke she was with yesterday.'

'Well I think that case is closed then.'

They returned to the hall and enjoyed the second half of the gig. It was when the band started to play *Good Golly Miss Molly* that the real fun started. After a few bars, a lad, older than Nick, with long curly hair and glasses, jumped on the stage. He stood next to the singer and started singing. It was Cuddles, (real name Roy Osbourne) who fancied himself as a singer. He managed to sing a couple of songs before being escorted from the stage to ecstatic cheering from the crowd.

The priest stood alone in his room and thought about tomorrow. He would be there, his new 'special one'; young, fit, and handsome. He looks into the mirror and examines his conscious; he admires his body and hungers for it to be touched by a young boy's hand. He is reminded of his vow of celibacy but knows it does not work for him or for most of his peers.

Saturday 15 August

Mary Harris smiled to herself as she thought about what her daughter had just told her. Apparently her new boyfriend, Nick

Allen, wanted to interview her regarding his latest investigation. She had heard a few rumours about some of the antics her new boyfriend had got up to and most of them sounded a bit far-fetched. But she was fully aware that Moira had saved his life a few weeks ago. She was pleased that her daughter had a boyfriend but on the other hand having two very pretty teenage daughters was a worry. As soon as they had started their periods she had told them the facts of life. She could only hope that they would be sensible and heed her warnings. As for this new boyfriend, she was a bit worried. She liked him; actually she liked him a lot, perhaps a bit too much, even though he was only fourteen. A couple of times she thought that she had been a little over friendly, but hopefully no one noticed.

It was another glorious day, the sun was high in the sky and temperature was in the top 70s. Nick was in a good mood today, his favourite singer, Cilla Black had performed her latest single *It's For You* on the *Saturday Club*[3] this morning. He also enjoyed songs from The Four Pennies and The Fortunes. To keep himself comfortable Nick was just wearing his navy blue football shorts and a white football shirt. He wasn't looking forward to interviewing Moira's mum, she made him feel uncomfortable. Don't get it wrong, Nick thought the world of her, but she always seemed a little too familiar with him. But it had to done for the sake of the investigation. Mr Harris was working on his allotment and Moira's sister Elizabeth was out with her friends.

'So, Moira tells me you want to ask me a few questions about Mrs Waller,' said Mrs Harris, in her soft Irish accent, as he walked into the living room.

'That's correct,' replied Nick nervously. 'It shouldn't take up too much of your time.'

'Take as much time as you like, I've no plans for this afternoon. But first I'll make a pot of tea, please make yourself comfortable.'

Mrs Harris disappeared into the kitchen; Nick sat himself down on the sofa.

'Moira love,' shouted out Mrs Harris. 'Will you pop to the shop and get a packet of *Custard Creams*; you know how your dad likes one with his cup of tea when he gets home.'

Moira was just coming down the stairs, smiled and replied, 'no problem, Mum.' She popped into the lounge, walked over to Nick, kissed him on the cheek and said, 'won't be a minute.'

Moira disappeared, as Mrs Harris walked in carrying the tea tray. After pouring out two cups and passing one to Nick, she said, 'would you like a *Custard Cream*?'

Nick took one then replied, 'I thought you were out of them.'

Mrs Harris just smiled and said, 'silly me.'

She then took a couple of sips from her cup before placing it back on the glass coffee table. 'So Nick, what do you want to know?'

Nick cleared his throat then began, 'We need to know all about Mrs Waller, is there anything in her past that may have some bearing on our investigation?'

Mrs Harris thought for a while then said, 'Okay, I met Alice Carter; Carter was her name before she married Cyril Waller, just after I came over from Ireland. We shared a room in a house in Ramsbury Road. She was very beautiful and had lots of male admirers … ….'

Whilst she was speaking, Nick had noticed that she had placed her hand on his thigh and voluntary or involuntary, moving it up and down as she talked. Nick could feel the warmth of her hand and the smell of her perfume, which he would swear she didn't have on before she went into the kitchen. This combination was having a strange effect on him. He hadn't taken in a word she had spoken for the past two minutes. He was frantically, mentally, trying to stop what was happening inside his football shorts. It was no good; wearing loose football shorts was a mistake as he looked down at the bulge that was prominently on display. Mrs Harris seemed not to notice and carried on with her narrative. Suddenly Nick looked up when he heard the front gate open, indicating that Moira had returned. Mrs Harris also heard the noise; she stopped talking, turned, looked at Nick and at the same time grabbed his erection.

She looked him in the eye and said, 'I hope you're keeping this big boy under control, we don't want my Moira getting into trouble now, do we?'

Nick was visibly shaking, 'Of course not, wouldn't think of it. I've never touched her.'

'That's good, and we'll keep it that way, understood.'

'Absolutely.'

The front door opened and Moira shouted, 'I'm back.'

Mrs Harris smiled, gave Nick's penis a gentle squeeze, and said, 'not bad,' before releasing it.

Nick quickly looked around, grabbed a cushion from an adjacent chair and put it on his lap to cover up his embarrassment.

Moira waltzed in the living room and asked, 'have I missed anything?'

'Not much,' spluttered Nick. 'Your mum has just started.'

Moira sat in the chair opposite.

Mrs Harris continued, 'as I was saying, Alice Waller nee Carter, and I shared a room in Ramsbury Road. We became very close and I was a bridesmaid at her wedding. She had many admirers but there were two main suitors. They were Cyril, who she eventually married and his best friend Eddie. It was a toss-up which one she would eventually marry, but I think she made the right choice. Eddie was nice, but a little strange. We often joked about him, saying we wasn't sure who he loved the most – Alice or Cyril. But Eddie was a good friend to both of them, never held a grudge when Alice chose to marry Cyril. I remember the wedding very well, it was a perfect day. Eddie was the Best Man, and he gave a very heart-warming speech. They stayed friends, very close friends, for a few years after the wedding, and then he just disappeared off the scene. Cyril was working for Southern Express Transport Ltd in Harpenden, as a long distance lorry driver. He was often away overnight, so Eddie used to keep her company. I asked her a few times what happened to him, but she just shrugged her shoulders and said he just stopped coming round.'

Nick listened intensely, and then said, 'what was Eddie's surname?

Mrs Harris thought for a moment, then said, 'Reynolds, that was it, Eddie Reynolds.'

'Eureka' exclaimed Nick. 'You've found the connection. Mrs Harris, I could kiss you.'

'I know you could,' replied Mrs Harris, with a mischievous grin on her face.

Nick blushed, and then continued, 'we now know that Eddie Reynolds was the second man in the car. Now we just need to find the third man,'

'Are you going to talk to Eddie?' asked Mrs Harris.

Nick chuckled, 'that would be a little difficult. Didn't you know, he committed suicide about the time of Peter's disappearance? We think that he was so full of remorse at what had happened to Peter that he topped himself.'

'Oh dear, I never knew,' replied Mrs Harris as she quickly crossed herself.

Nick could see that Mrs Harris was clearly upset about the news. Moira grabbed his hand and gave him a comforting smile.

Mrs Harris composed herself, and then said, 'I can't believe he was involved. He was a good Catholic and thinking about it, he never met Peter. I'm not even sure he knew he existed.'

'Did Eddie have any relatives, parents, brothers or sisters?' asked Nick.

Mrs Harris thought for a moment, before saying, 'no, he was an only child and his parents were killed in the Blitz. What are you going to do now?'

'On Monday I'll have a chat with my contact in the police and see if he can throw any light on our mysterious dead friend.'

The three of them chatted a while before Moira said, 'sorry Nick, I have to go out now. I promised to meet Dympna at three. You don't mind, do you?'

Trying hard to hide his disappointment Nick replied, 'of course not, you go and enjoy yourself. Don't worry about me; I've got lots to do.'

Mrs Harris gazed out of the window as Nick and Moira walked hand in hand down the garden path. What had she done, what the hell had possessed her to do that? It was his fault wearing those shorts. She did like muscular legs and for a fourteen year old he did have lovely muscular legs. Perhaps putting the perfume on was a mistake, it always turned her husband on. But it was funny, seeing him sitting there, all embarrassed with a hard on. She would definitely have to go to confession tomorrow.

Algernon Teggegh looked into his bedroom mirror and adjusted the woggle on his scout scarf. Not bad, he thought as he gave his thick ginger hair another brush; that should do the trick. This afternoon his scout group, the 15th St. Albans, were having a practice football match at the Cunningham Hill playing fields and he was 100% sure that lots of lovely girls would be watching. As he wasn't playing, football wasn't his game; he could mingle with the crowd. They would say how smart he looked in his uniform and then by the end of the game he would have bagged himself a girlfriend. He needed a girlfriend, someone to talk too, someone to take to the pictures, someone to love him. If he was really honest with himself he just needed a friend. There was a new boy called Donald who had recently joined the scouts, he seemed nice. He had invited him back to his house after the game; a back-up, just in case he didn't get a girlfriend.

Algernon didn't have many friends and his home life wasn't exactly a laugh a minute. He lived with his parents and his little sister in a big house in a posh part of St. Albans. His father, who worked as a civil servant, was a strict disciplinarian who showed little or no affection to his children and even less to his wife. His mother, who always boasted that she gave up a promising career as a concert pianist to bring up her children, was never around. She was always going to some committee meeting, Women's institute, PTA, Rotary Club and other good causes. As for his ten going on twenty year old little sister, she was just a pain in the arse. But today he thought things were going to be different.

It was about 3.00pm when Nick entered the kitchen through the back door and was surprised to see Mrs Patrick sitting at the kitchen table sipping a cup of tea. Mrs Patrick was Nick's other best friend, Don Patrick's, mother. She had stopped Don playing with Nick after her son was badly shaken up after an incident during his last investigation. He was in the process of turning round and walking back out when his mother said, 'Don's mum would like a little word with you.'

Nick eyed Mrs Patrick suspiciously as he sat himself down at the kitchen table opposite her. Even though it was quite a warm day, Mrs Patrick was wearing a light coloured raincoat and a headscarf. 'I'm worried about Donald,' she said nervously. 'He hasn't been the same since I stopped him playing with you.'

'And that's my fault because?' replied Nick, instantly regretting his tone.

'Don't be cheeky to Mrs Patrick, Nick. Now apologise at once,' shouted Mrs Allen.

Suitably chastised, Nick dropped his head and said, 'sorry, I didn't mean it like that. If there is anything I can do, you only have to ask.'

'Well, if I let him play with you again, perhaps you might be able to cheer him up.'

'That would be great, I really miss him. So tell me, what is exactly wrong with him?'

'He just seems to be quiet and moody. He never talks to me; before he was full of stories and ….well, you know.'

'So how does he spend his time?'

'He's joined the scouts and he's spending more time at the church. He's hoping to become an Altar Boy very soon. We're very proud.'

A smile appeared on her face for the first time this afternoon. Nick reckoned that Mrs Patrick would be a couple of years older than his mum; she had a pretty face but little trace of make-up. Her hair, what he could see was greying and maybe she was a few pounds heavier than she ought to be.

'So where is Don this afternoon?' asked Nick.

'He's having a trial for the scout football team; I think he said it was at Cunningham Hill.'

Nick stood to attention, 'then that is where I shall go.' He turned, waved goodbye, grabbed his bike and was on his way.'

Father John Flanagan blew his whistle to end the practice match and Don Patrick walked slowly back to the changing room. He was pleased with his performance, right half was definitely his best position. It was the first time he had enjoyed himself for a long time. Since his mum had stopped him playing with Nick he'd been at a loose end. He'd joined the scouts, at his mum's suggestion, spent more time at church, again his mum's suggestion. He also missed his other friend Keith, who hadn't called him for a while.

It was a two mile ride to the playing fields and whichever route he took involved a steep hill. Nick had to admit to himself, he missed Don's company. It was almost six weeks since they last saw each other and although he was extremely happy he felt there was a small void in his life. He had known Don now for about eight years. They first met at the medical clinic in 1956; they were both there for their first Polio injection. Nick remembered how much it hurt, but not as much as the triple vaccination he received in 1961. He had a nasty reaction to the injection which would protect him against Diphtheria, Tetanus, and Whooping Cough. His left arm went completely stiff and painful to touch. To make matters worse, his mother kept him of school for a day and not only did he miss playing for the school football team he also missed the team photograph.

In no time Nick had reached the Cunningham Hill playing fields; the entrance was via Dellfield, a notorious council estate. As Nick climbed the steep concrete steps carrying his bike, his journey was made difficult by a rush of boys carrying their sports bags coming down the steps. When he had finished his ascent, he looked around at the empty playing field. The field was large enough to easily house two full size football pitches. Nick had played here on a few occasions. The changing facilities consisted of one brick built shed which could accommodate four teams, at a pinch. There were no showers, just an old sink with one cold water tap in the corner. Nick was worried that he had missed Don, as the playing field seemed deserted. Then he noticed a solitary boy, kitted out in his scout's uniform hovering around outside the changing room. He approached the boy.

'Excuse me,' said Nick to the boy, trying to catch his attention. 'I'm looking for Don Patrick, has he gone?'

The boy sniggered, 'No, he's still in the changing room.'

Nick looked at the boy and thought how much he reminded him of Alfred E Neuman, the boy who appeared on the front of the *Mad* magazine. He had a mop of ginger hair, freckles, stick out ears and a gap between his two front teeth. But Nick had to admit that he was immaculately turned out in his scout uniform.

'Why are you wearing your uniform?' asked Nick. 'I didn't see any of the other boys wearing theirs.'

'I thought it might attract a girlfriend. They say that girls like a man in uniform,' replied the boy.

'Did many girls turn up? I didn't see any around.'

'None at all; I was hoping that some would come and watch the practice.'

'So you weren't playing then.'

'No, I'm useless at football. In fact I'm useless at most things, especially at trying to get a girlfriend. The main problem is that I'm ugly and there is nothing I can do about that is there?'

Nick didn't reply.

'Do you think I'm ugly?'

No, of course you're not ugly,' replied Nick trying to be diplomatic. 'You're not the best looking bloke I've seen, but I wouldn't go as far as to call you ugly.'

'So why haven't I got a girlfriend?'

'I don't know….perhaps your approach is wrong.'

'You're just trying to be nice. Let's face it, I'm ugly and ugly blokes don't get girlfriends.'

The boy started snivelling and Nick started to feel sorry for him.

'Come on,' said Nick. 'Don't cry; there is a girl out there for you. You just haven't found her yet.'

'Do you think so?' replied the boy, before pulling out a handkerchief and giving a big blow.

'Of course there is,' said Nick, putting his arm around the boy's shoulder and giving him a hug. 'What's your name?'

'Algernon Teggegh.'

'Jesus, that's enough to put off any girl, what do your friends call you?'

Algernon looked surprised. 'Why, Algernon of course.'

'Okay; I think you should shorten it to Al or Algy.'

'Do you think so?'

'Absolutely, and you need to do away with the scout uniform. Girls do like men in uniforms, but they have to be Army Officers or RAF.'

'I understand, but that's not going to alter the fact that I'm ugly.'

Nick was feeling himself getting a bit annoyed, but he persevered. 'Lots of ugly blokes get girlfriends.'

'Such us?'

Nick thought for a second, 'Mick Jagger is dead ugly and he's shagging everything in sight, and Sid James, who has more lines on his face than a London Underground map, he's a top shagger.'

'Yeah, but they are famous. Famous people get all the birds.'

'That's true, but girls do go for boys that are good at things. What are you good at?

'Nothing.'

'Right; maybe you could improve your appearance.'

'How?'

Nick sighed, then answered, 'if you grow you hair that would cover up your ears, and … … ….are your parents rich?'

'Of course,' replied Algernon, giving Nick an, aren't all parents rich, look.

'Well, ask them to send you to a dentist to get your teeth fixed.'

'That's a good idea, do you have a girlfriend?'

Nick smiled, 'as a matter of fact, I do.'

'So what are you good at?'

Nick shrugged his shoulders, 'I don't know, suppose I'm just lucky.' Nick then looked at his watch and thought, what's keeping Don?

'There is another problem,' groaned Algernon, 'I have a very small willy.'

Nick looked to the heavens, 'what?'

'I have a very small willy. I'm never going to get a girlfriend with a small willy.'

'Who said it was small,' asked Nick, thinking how much more he can take before he loses it.

'I did,' said Algernon, as he started to undo his belt. 'Do you want to see it?'

'No I bloody don't,' screamed Nick. 'What's wrong with you?'

Algernon looked offended, before asking, 'what can I do about it?'

'I don't know… …..tie a brick to it.'

'Will that work?'

Nick turned to Algernon and asked, 'why is it taking so long for Don to get changed?'

Algernon smiled and said, 'I'm sure I don't know.'

Nick grabbed Algernon by the scarf and said menacingly, 'I've just remembered what I'm good at.'

Algernon looked scared and muttered, 'what's that.'

'Making ugly boys tell me what I want to know.'

'Okay, okay, just don't hurt me.'

Nick released his grip on the boy. 'Go on.'

'He'll be in there with Father John. He's the special one this week.'

'Special one; what does that mean?'

'Well, he likes to have a special boy to assist him. He will help out before Mass and other things and in return he will receive special treats.'

'Have you ever been a special boy?'

Algernon sunk his chin onto his chest and said, 'of course not, he wouldn't pick me, I'm ugly.'

Nick looked him and said, 'if you mention being ugly again I'll give you a slap, understand?

'Sorry.'

'Just a minute, why are you here? All the other boys have gone home.'

'Oh, I'm waiting for Donald; he's my new best friend. We are going to practice tying knots round at my house.'

'Well Algernon, not today. His mum has sent me to bring him straight home, so if I was you I'd bugger off now. Go home, tie a brick to your willy and learn to sing.'

Algernon, clearly upset, turned and walked away.

Fed up with waiting Nick walked over to the changing hut, pushed the door open and walked in. The sight that faced him was not what he expected. Standing on the bench, wearing just his underpants and looking totally embarrassed stood Don. In front of him, holding a tape measure was Father John. 'What do you want?' screamed the angry priest.

Composing himself, Nick ignored the question and spoke directly to Don, 'come on, get your clothes on, your mum needs you urgently.'

Don didn't need telling twice, he jumped off the bench, grabbed his trousers and quickly pulled them on. As he pulled his tee-shirt over his head his feet were fishing for his shoes. Neither Nick nor the priest had moved, both staring intensely at each other. Nick was good at this, spending hours practicing on his next door neighbour's dog.

'I'm ready,' gasped Don, as he stuffed his football boots in to his kit bag.

'Let's go,' Nick replied as he turned and ushered Don out of the building.

Once outside Nick grabbed Don by the arm and screamed, 'what the hell's going on?'

'Nothing,' replied Don, pushing Nick away. He turned and headed for the steps. Nick quickly retrieved his bicycle and followed Don down.

'Where's your bike?' asked Nick.

'Haven't got it, Father John gave me a lift in his car.'

Nick was struggling to keep up with Don. Carrying his bicycle down those steep steps was an art in itself.

When Don reached the bottom, he turned and looked at Nick and said, 'what are you doing here, anyway? You know that I'm not allowed to hang out with you.'

When Nick finally managed to reach the bottom of the steps, he replied, 'well, your mum has had a change of heart. She came to my house, had a word with my mum and as long as I don't get you into trouble, we can be friends again.'

'Oh, that's nice,' replied Don, with not much enthusiasm.

'Well, if you would rather tie knots with your new freaky friend and have your dIck measured by that pervert priest, I'll leave you to it.' Nick mounted his bike and started to slowly pedal away.

'No,' shouted Don. 'I'm sorry, look I'm glad you are here. It's just a bit complicated.'

Nick stopped and waited for Don to catch up.

'Algernon's alright,' said Don.

Nick gave Don his, are you sure, look.

Don smiled, 'actually, he's a pratt. I felt sorry for him, he hasn't got many friends.'

'Apparently he hasn't got a girlfriend either.'

'Did he tell you that?' replied Don, with a hint of a smile.

'In great detail,' laughed Nick. 'So what was that priest doing in there?'

'He was checking my development,' Don was struggling to explain. 'He was measuring my muscles to see if they are developing properly. He has a chart and he records the measurements.'

'So he didn't measure your dick?'

'Of course not, you're disgusting. He's a priest; they don't do that sort of thing.' Nick noticed that Don was blushing profusely.

Nick decided not to push it any further and changed the subject, but he would be keeping a close eye on Don and that priest.

'So, how did the practice go?'

Don cheered up slightly and replied, 'very well, with a bit of luck I should get into the team. Did you know that the 15th St. Albans scout group are unbeaten in two years?'

'Point of order,' Nick smirked, 'I believe they were beaten 2-1 by a team made up of the rest of the league at Clarence Park, back in May.'

'Okay, I'll give you that one, but I don't think that counts.'

Nick's mind started to wander, 'just think, if I hadn't been kicked out of the scouts I might have played in that game. Did you know that Barry Dudley scored both their goals?'

'Then let that be a lesson to you, that sort of thing only happens to good, normal, church going people.'

Nick was offended, 'are you saying I'm not normal. I occasionally go to church and I'm very good.'

'Huh, good at getting yourself and other people into trouble.'

Nick was now getting very upset, 'what's got into you; you were always up for a bit of adventure.'

'Father John says … … … ….'

'I don't want to hear what bloody Father John has to say, what I say is that you should keep away from him. What do you think your mum will say when I tell her what I saw?'

Nick could see the look of fear on his face and pleaded with Nick, 'please don't tell her, I'll do anything.'

'Just forget about the church for a minute, I've got a big investigation going on and I need your help.'

Don thought for a minute, 'okay I'll help you as long as you don't tell my mum. But you can't stop me going to church.'

'It's a deal, as long as you don't get into a situation where you are alone with that Father John bloke; agreed'

'Agreed!'

'Don't you miss being in the scouts?' asked Don, as they walked up Camp Road towards the *Crown* public house.'

'Not really; I did at first, but then I wouldn't be able to fit it in now, what with all these cases I keep getting,' replied Nick.

'Suppose not, but when you were, what badges did you get?'

'Let me think – ah yes. I achieved three, First-aider, Cyclist, and Jobs man.'

'Were they easy to get?' asked Don enthusiastically.

'Well, the First-aider wasn't, we had to have lessons. They were held at the 9th scout hut, on the corner of Lemsford Road and Sandpit Lane. Then we had a test afterwards. That was the hardest of the three. For the Cyclist badge I had to cycle from one place to another, answer some questions on cycling, you know Highway Code and all that. Then you had to pretend to have a puncture on your bike. Take off the wheel; remove the inner-tube and stick a patch on it. Then put it all back together again.' Nick gave a little laugh. 'My problem was when I put it all back together, I pinched the inner-tube, so then I actually had a puncture. I had to go back another day to do it again; got there in the end. As for the Jobs Man badge we just had to do various odd jobs for some bloke. I had to clean out some gutters. That's right and I had to show him a sock that I had darned.'

'You darned a sock?' asked Don, well impressed,

'Of course not, mum did it; I just said I did it. I would have got the sportsman's badge, all you had to do was get a letter of confirmation from school to say that I had represented the school at a sport on at least two occasions and answer some questions on cricket and football; doddle really.'

'What sort of questions?' asked Don.

'Let me think now, my mate Dave got it and he was asked how far apart the stumps were on a cricket pitch; easy, twenty two yards and who played in goal for Fulham, that sort of thing.'

After seeing Don safely home, Nick pedalled furiously back to his house and immediately phoned Keith. Although Don wasn't forbidden to hang around with Keith they had hardly seen each other for the last month. News of their re-kindled friendship was music to Keith's ears. After telling Keith all about his encounter with Father John, they arranged to meet tomorrow morning outside Nick's paper shop.

With all this excitement Nick nearly forgot that he had planned to watch *Dr Who*. His little brother Richard was already seated, waiting expectantly. Together the enjoyed the episode entitled *Guests of Madame Guillotine* in which the Doctor, having just escaped from a burning farmhouse rescues Ian, Barbara and Susan who are sentenced to death under the blade of the guillotine. This was followed by *Juke Box Jury*; Nick liked this programmes as he was keen to keep up with the latest releases.

WEEK 2
Sunday 16 August - Saturday 22 August 1964

Sunday 16 August

Nick had arranged with Keith to spy on Don after Family Mass, which started at 9.30am. Although he would be attending with his parents Nick wanted to make sure that Don didn't volunteer for any after-Mass activities. As it was a clear, bright, sunny day the pair had decided to walk, leaving their bicycles in the builder's yard next to *Heading and Watts* paper-shop and they arrived at the church about 10.30am. They sat on a garden wall opposite the church and waited. Nick pulled a *Toffee Crisp* and a *Mars Bar* out of his pocket and gave the latter to Keith. As the enjoyed their chocolate bars Keith asked, 'what are you expecting to gain from this?'

'I'm not sure,' replied Nick, licking his lips and wishing he had another. 'But I want to make sure that Don doesn't stay behind after Mass and I also want you to see this Father John bloke.'

After a while the church doors opened and Father John walked out with another priest, followed by the congregation, who shook their hands and paid their compliments.

'Which one is he?' asked Keith.   'The slightly bald one with the beard,' replied Nick.

'Don't like the look of him.'

'No, he's a nasty piece of work.'

'Will Moira be here?' asked Keith, noticing one or two very attractive girls appearing.

'Yes, she normally goes along with her friend Dympna. You should know that.'

'Of course, I'd forgot; she's nice, Dympna, quite fancy her, myself.'

Nick shook his head, 'you fancy anything in a skirt. Anyway she's not your type; her tits aren't big enough for you.'

'Yeah, perhaps you're right, but she's got a nice slim figure, so that would suit you. Anyway, look, here comes Don with his parents.'

The boys watched as Mr and Mrs Patrick exchanged pleasantries with Father John. Don just walked by, looking down at his feet. A few seconds later Moira and Dympna appeared, both looking gorgeous, dressed in the best Sunday dresses.

'Are you going to speak to them?' asked Keith.

'No I don't think so; we'll keep this investigation to ourselves.'

As the congregation dispersed, Nick noticed one boy saying goodbye to his mother and smiling from ear to ear. He made his way back to the church and was greeted by Father John who took his hand and disappeared into the church.

'Looks like Father John has chosen a new special one,' said Nick, before adding, 'bastard.'

Nick and Keith quietly left the church without being seen by either Moira or Don.

'What are you up to, today?' asked Keith.

'Not a lot,' replied Nick. 'We're going to my Uncle Albert and Auntie Betty's for tea this afternoon.'

'That's nice.'

'It's okay, they are a lovely couple and it gives me chance to play with my cousin David.'

'But what are we going to do about the cases?'

'Well I'm meeting DI James tomorrow and find out what he knows about Eddie Reynolds, then we need to find out from Don what that priest is up to.'

Monday 17 August

Nick couldn't stop thinking about the events of Saturday afternoon; Moira's mum had grabbed his dick. She had squeezed it and said 'not bad.' Well if she wanted it, she was going to get it, good and proper. There was nothing wrong with an older woman fancying a younger lad. Okay, so he was only fourteen, but he would be fifteen in four months' time. He had recently read a book entitled *A Cold Wind in August* by Burton Wohl, in which a young man had an affair with an older woman and he was only seventeen years old. As he walked towards Moira's house he thought, a man's got to do what a man's got to do. He was wearing his best trousers and a clean, crisp, white shirt with the top three buttons undone and the collar turned up. He pulled out a cigarette from the packet of *Peter Stuyvesant* he had nicked from the paper-shop this morning. He lit it up and let it hang from the corner of his mouth. He knew she would be alone, Mr Harris would be at work and Moira was taking her little sister Elizabeth shopping this morning. Mrs Harris didn't work Mondays. He knocked on the front door and waited. After about thirty seconds the door opened slightly.

'Who's there?' asked Mrs Harris in her smooth, seductive, Irish accent.

'It's me,' answered Nick, nonchalantly.

The door opened and Mrs Harris said, 'I was hoping it would be you, I'm so glad you've come.'

Nick took a long drag on the cigarette, and then slowly exhaled. He then flicked it over the hedge into the next-door-neighbours garden. He walked through the front door and made his way straight to the living room. Mrs Harris closed the front door and followed him. They stood there facing each other. She was wearing a pink housecoat with lovely water lilies embroidery. She slowly untied the sash and allowed the housecoat to fall slowly to the floor. He admired her perfect 36-26-36 figure. She stood there wearing only her underwear, a black bra that was straining to hold in her magnificent bosom, black lacy knickers, a black suspender belt and black stockings. She walked over to him, threw her arms around his neck and kissed him passionately. He felt her tongue dart about his mouth, she tasted of strawberries. He put his arms around her waist, feeling her silk-like skin, before squeezing her firm buttocks. He could feel his manhood straining to be free.

'Have you done Dalton yet?' a voice boomed in his ear as Nick awoke from his daydream.

Disoriented, Nick looked around to see that the Dalton paper round was still on the floor, unmarked.

'I'll do it next,' Nick shouted out.

'What's up with you this morning?' asked Ron Hart, manager of Heading and Watts newsagents. 'You're not normally this slow.'

'Sorry, boss. I've got a lot on my mind.'

'Well get a grip… …..Caroline's waiting,' replied Ron in a slightly creepy tone.

Caroline Harvey was a new papergirl and a few days ago Nick had teach her the paper- round. It was one of the duties that he had to perform. Nick didn't mind, it was nice to get out of the shop for a while. Dalton was an easy round that took about twenty-five minutes and you didn't need a bike. Nick, being a perfect gentleman, had carried the bag for Caroline whist she delivered each of the papers in their respective letter boxes. When they had finished Nick gave half of his *Toffee Crisp* to Caroline, which they consumed as they walked back to the shop. Caroline had obviously taken this gesture as sign that Nick fancied her. Although she was reasonably pretty, she was a year younger than Nick and he already had a girlfriend. But this did not stop her making eyes at him every time she came into the shop. And everybody knew that she fancied him like mad. Nick finished the round that he was marking, put it on the floor and picked up Dalton round. Nick really enjoyed marking the papers in the morning. They had a good system; Ron would pull together the rounds on the front counter, and then pass them to Nick, who worked in the back room. He operated on the ice-cream fridge which was covered by a large piece of ply-wood.

He would write the numbers and the streets on the papers as well as inserting the weekly and monthly magazines. Normally he would place the finished round on the shop floor but this time he had to pass it over to Caroline.

'Hello Nick, how are you today?' said Caroline, her face, a picture of happiness.

Nick, feeling his face redden replied, 'I'm fine, all the better for seeing you.'

Caroline beamed back, 'perhaps I'll see you later.'

'Maybe,' replied Nick and quickly disappeared into the back room.

Nick finished his shift at 8.00am, said goodbye to Ron and went to collect his bike from the builder's yard next door. He had just finished unlocking the chain when he heard a voice say, 'hello Nick.' It was Caroline.

Nick, still feeling frustrated from his earlier daydream, put the chain into his saddle-bag, turned walked towards Caroline. Without stopping he grabbed and started kissing her passionately. After the initial shock, Caroline flung her arms around his neck and enjoyed the experience. After a minute Nick pulled away, gave Caroline's little arse a gentle squeeze and said, 'sorry love, got to see a man about a dog.'

With that he mounted his bike, rode off, leaving Caroline stunned and grinning from ear to ear.

Nick spotted DI James straight away, this time he was more soberly dressed in a nice pair of blue slacks and a lemon short sleeved shirt. After acknowledging him, Nick ordered a mug of tea and a bacon roll, before joining him at his table. Nick could hear a radio playing in the background; he recognised the programme – *Morning Music* with the BBC Midland Light Orchestra.

'Good morning, Nick.'

'Good morning, Sir.'

DI James took a sip of his tea and asked, 'how is the

investigation going?'

'Should have it cracked by the weekend.'

'Really?' replied DI James, looking surprised.

'No, but it's going well. But we need your help once again.'

'Okay, tell me what you have got.'

'Well, you were right about Billy Watkins, he was definitely involved. We can't prove it, but we think he was the driver.'

'Did he lose his temper?' asked DI James; suppressing the urge to smile.

Nick did laugh, 'how did you guess? He threw a bucket of water over me.'

'No surprise there, what else did you find out?'

'We think we know the name of one of his conspirators. His name is Eddie Reynolds. Eddie was Billy's best friend at the time Peter went missing; they were inseparable. Also, Eddie was the best man at Peter's parents wedding, so that's a connection.'

DI James was impressed and added, 'and you want me find out about this Eddie Reynolds.'

'That's the idea.'

'So you haven't spoken to him yet?'

'Bit difficult really, didn't I mention? Eddie committed suicide round the time of Peter's disappearance. Our theory is that, after whatever happened to Peter, Eddie was so full of remorse that he topped himself. So, can you look into his suicide; see what was recorded and any contacts that we may talk to.'

'No problem, I don't remember the suicide, but I'll check it out and let you know what I find.'

'Thanks,' said Nick, at the same time as he heard John call out, 'one bacon roll.'

Nick had decided to stay in and have a quiet night watching one of his favourite detective programmes, *No Hiding Place. Coronation Street* had just finished when there was a knock on the front door. Mrs Allen opened the door and ushered DI James through to the living room. No introductions were needed as DI James had called many times on the Allen household.

'I'll make some tea then,' said Mrs Allen.

''That would be very nice, thank you,' replied DI James.

DI James made himself comfortable, and when the tea was served he dunked his *Digestive* into the tea and took a bite. Nick watched him intensely and thought, a man after my own heart.

'I've looked in the files about your suspect Eddie Reynolds and you were right, he did commit suicide.'

Nick gave DI James his I already know that look.

DI James pretended he didn't see it. 'Anyway, it all looked pretty straight forward, hanged himself by tying a rope to a rafter in the loft and jumping out. His landlady found him when she came home from shopping. Bit of a shock for her, opening the front door looking up the stairs and seeing him hanging there. There was an inquest and they gave the verdict as suicide due to depression.'

Nick thought for a moment, and then asked, 'I know he was an only child and both his parents are dead; so is there anyone who could help us?'

'Apparently he had a fiancé, she gave evidence at the inquest; her name is Dorothy Whitehouse. We had an address and I checked it out for you, but she's moved and gave no forwarding address, sorry.'

Nick sighed, 'no worries, thanks for that. I'm sure I'll think of something.'

DI James smiled, and said, 'I'm sure you will.' He finished his tea, said his goodbyes and showed himself out.

Mr Allen, who was now getting used to the CID popping in, drinking tea and eating his biscuits, commented, 'so Nick, what do you intend to do now?'

'I need to find Dorothy Whitehouse, any suggestions?' asked Nick.

Mr Allen thought for a while, before saying, 'just a thought; they may have reported the suicide in the local paper, it may be worth a look. They might have mentioned something that's not in the police file.'

Tuesday 19 August

Sandra Boyd was in a foul mood as she made the twenty minute walk to the St. Albans City library. At 27 years old she was single and still living at home with her parents and her life was going nowhere. In the beginning, being a librarian was her dream job, she loved books and the English language. She had gained a first class honours degree in English Literature and her dissertation on the works of Thomas Hardy had been well received. Sue Bridehead[4] was her all-time favourite heroine. Many a time she had spoken to her parents about buying or renting a place of her own, but they wouldn't hear of it. What would the neighbours think? No, they would say, not until you're married. She was engaged once; to an English teacher. They had met at university, fell in love and planned to live in a nice village somewhere in the Cotswolds. Then out of the blue, he told her that he'd met someone else and she hasn't seen him since. What really annoyed her was that she was born ten years too early. How she envied the youth of today; she loved the colour and style of the clothes. She loved the music, especially the Rolling Stones. How angry was she when she found their latest LP in the dustbin last night. Now she was stuck in a dead-end job and having to deal with either screaming kids or smelly tramps sheltering from the rain.

Nick decided to visit the public library straight after breakfast. Situated in Victoria Street the public library was opened in 1911, a fine building with an ornamental carved lintel above the door. His shift at the paper-shop was uneventful and he managed to avoid Caroline. He knew kissing her yesterday was a mistake and he would be in deep trouble if Moira found out. But sometimes he felt so frustrated he wanted to kiss every girl that he came in contact with. At 9.30am he entered the library and made his way to the reception desk. Nick hated this public library; for some reason he always felt uneasy, as though everyone was looking at him and just waiting to say ssshhh if he made a noise. At the information desk sat a stern looking woman dressed in a grey two piece suit with a white high necked blouse and a string of cheap pearls. Her mousey coloured hair was tied in a bun and she wore thick horn-rimmed glasses. She looked up at him with an expression that could turn milk sour and said, 'can I help you?'

Forcing a smile, Nick replied, 'Good morning to you, I was wondering, do you keep back copies of the *Herts Advertiser?*'

Still looking at him, her brown eyes penetrating his brain, making him want to run a mile, she said, 'yes we do.'

'Err....where are they kept?'

'In the backroom.'

'May I see them?'

'Why?'

Nick was now getting very agitated but somehow he resisted the urge to say something extremely rude. He took a deep breath and counted to ten before saying, 'I'm on a research project for the St. Albans Police; I need to see back copies of the *Herts Ad* from May 1959 till the end of the year. If you don't believe me, why not pop along to the Police Station, it's only a few doors down and ask for Detective Inspector Philip James. I think you will find he can back up my story.'

The librarian stood and said, 'there's no need for that tone, I have to be careful who I let in the backroom. There are some funny people about. Follow me.'

Nick followed the librarian into the backroom. It was a dingy room with shelves full of bound back copies of local papers and periodicals. In the centre there were two long wooden benches surrounded by chairs.

'Sit there,' said the librarian, as she quickly found the bound copies for Nick. As she reached up, Nick couldn't help noticing that from behind the librarian was quite shapely.

'I think this is what you are looking for,' said the librarian, slamming the large bound volume down in front of him.

Coughing and fanning away the dust Nick looked up to her, 'thank you, you're so kind.'

The librarian just stood there, arms folded, looking down her nose at Nick.

'I think I'll be alright now, you can go back to your desk, and this could take some time.'

'That's okay; I'll stay for a while.'

That's all I need, thought Nick, but trying to turn a negative into a positive, he said,' that's great; perhaps you can help me. You must have more experience at this than I have.'

The librarian thought for a while before saying, 'okay, just for ten minutes. Now what exactly are we looking for?' She sat down beside Nick, giving him a little nudge and said, 'more over.'

'Right, well sometime in May 1959 a man called Eddie Reynolds committed suicide; I'm hoping that there was a report on the inquest.'

The librarian frowned, 'surely you friend in the police could tell you all about it?'

'He has, but I'm trying to trace his fiancé. It's a long shot but the paper may say something the Police didn't know.'

This seemed to satisfy the librarian and together they trawled through the editions. They started at June and it was nearly an hour before they found what they were looking for. The librarian, whose name, Nick found out, was Sandra, spotted the headline "Depressed Mechanic Commits Suicide". Nick quickly read aloud the report of the inquest which stated that Eddie Reynolds, 27, took his own life, due to depression. It was towards the end of the article that Nick found what he hoped he would find. "Mr Reynolds' fiancé, Miss Dorothy Whitehouse, who works in the Millinery department at *Green's* Department store in Chequer Street, said… ….."

'That's it,' cried Nick, grabbing Sandra and giving her a big kiss on the lips. 'Oh, sorry,' Nick pulled away.

Waiting for a slap round the face or the cry of rape, Nick braced himself for the worst.

'Oh,' said Sandra, blushing from ear to ear. 'That was fun, so glad I could help.' Closing the binder, she picked it up and returned to the shelf.

'Well,' said Nick, visibly relieved, 'thank you for your help, but I must be on my way now.'

'No problem,' replied Sandra, whose cheeks were now glowing. 'Anytime you need help, just ask and I'm here every day except Thursdays.'

Nick had arranged to meet Moira, Don and Keith in Sally's Inn café at 2.00pm. All three were sitting there when he arrived. A strawberry milkshake was waiting for him; Don and Keith were drinking cokes and Moira a cup of tea. After telling them about his library visit Moira said, 'listen, I haven't done much for this investigation, let me sus out this Dorothy. I've got a friend who works at *Greens*; and if she still works there she could introduce me.'

Nick thought for a while before saying, 'okay, good idea. I think it might be a bit insensitive for all of us to walk up to her and ask why her ex-fiancé topped himself.'

'I'll pop down there now, the sooner we sort this out, the better.'

Moira finished her tea, said goodbye and made her way to *Green's* department store in Chequer Street.

Nick watched as the girl he loved left the cafe and then said, 'she'll be a little while, so we'll need some sounds to keep us going,' before digging out some change and approaching the Jukebox.

'What have you put on?' asked Keith, as Nick returned. 'I hope it's not all soppy love songs.'

'Just wait and see,' replied Nick, shaking his head

As it happened Keith was happy, Nick had chosen the following songs – *Can't Buy Me Love*, Beatles, *Bits and Pieces*, Dave Clark Five, *Not Fade Away*, Rolling Stones, *Here I Go Again*, Hollies and the compulsory Cilla Black song, *You're My World*.

'So,' said Keith, bluntly. 'What have you been up to, Don, with this priest?'

Don didn't answer; he just gave Nick a dirty look.

'Don't look at me like that, mate. We're just concerned about your welfare,' replied Nick.

Again, no response from Don.

'Listen mate, we just want to help you; your mum said you were unhappy and you've hardly said a word all day.'

'No-one can help me,' mumbled Don.

'Just tell us how it started and we'll be the judge of that. Remember, we're your best friends. If anyone can help - we can.'

'Okay,' said Don reluctantly, 'but don't judge me; these things happen.' He took a large slurp of his coke. 'It all started just after my mum stopped me seeing you. She suggested I got myself another hobby and suggested joining the scouts. I thought – why not. It was okay, I enjoyed some of the things we did, but compared to our previous adventures it was a bit boring. And, because I joined when I was thirteen and most boys started when they were eleven, I was two years behind and I found most of the tasks quite easy. Anyway, Father John, who's the Scout Master, suggested that I should stay back after the meetings and he would help me to catch up. That was okay for a while, and then he asked me if I played football and if so, would I be interested in playing for the Scout team. Of course I was interested and told him so. We started talking about football and he mentioned how he used to manage an Army team when he was doing National Service. He also told me that he was a medical orderly and he learnt how to understand a man's development in relation to his sporting performance. He explained that the techniques he used enhanced the performance of the scout team and that's why they were unbeaten for the last two years. It sounded like bollocks to me, but I went along with it. Anyway, he said that if I wanted to play for the team, I would need to have my physical details recorded. I said "what does that mean?" He said that he would need to measure and record my development. I agreed, but then he asked me to strip off down to my underpants. He said all the other players did it. Then he started measuring me, first my height, the width of my shoulders, the distance between my elbow and wrist and elbow to my shoulder. Then he measured the distance around my calves, biceps and thighs. All this he recorded on a chart. Then just when I thought it was all over, he asked me a strange question.'

Keith jumped in, 'what sort of question?'

Don blushed, 'he asked me if my testicles had dropped. I didn't know what he meant. As far as I'm aware they've always been there.'

'I don't understand,' said Keith, looking confused. They both looked at Nick, who always seemed to know a lot of useless information.

Nick gave a little cough and was glad that their favourite waitress, Anna, wasn't working today. He could imagine her reaction if she overheard them talking about their testicles. Today's waitress was Judith and if anyone could make your balls disappear, she could. She was overweight, wore glasses, had a very bad case of Acne and Halitosis; and obviously had a chip on her shoulder.

'As far as I'm aware, a boys balls appear just after they are born. They are quite small at first, but get bigger when you reach puberty. Don't ask me what that means, but I think that it's when they fill up with spunk. Sometimes, one or both fail to appear, but a doctor would have checked for that when you are quite young.'

'How do you know all this stuff?' asked Keith.

'Well,' replied Nick, 'it just happens that one of my cousin's balls failed to drop and he had to have an operation.'

There was a brief moment of silence before Nick continued, 'I just remembered, when we were in our first year we all had to see the school doctor and he had a feel to see if I was alright down there.'

Keith laughed, 'of course, it's all coming back now. I remember my mum insisting she came with me and kept going on about having clean underpants on. I told her that I put clean ones on every day, but she wouldn't give up.'

Nick continued, 'I remember that Richard Martin got a hard on and the doctor had to hit it with a pencil.'

They all laughed and said how embarrassing it must have been. Then a serious look came on Nick's face and he said, 'Did Father John examine you?'

Don's face went crimson as he looked down at the table. At

the same time Judith appeared, 'can you keep your smutty talk to yourselves, or I'll have to ask you to leave.'

Keith looked at her and said, 'go away Judith, you're making Nick's milkshake curdle.'

'Well?' asked Nick.

Don gave a small nod of the head.

'The bastard,' screamed Keith, as the other customers turned and starred at him. 'Sorry.'

'Do you want to talk about it?' asked Nick, not wanting to upset Don any further.

'It was awful, he seemed to hold them for ages, he only let go when I asked if they were alright.'

It was very clear that Keith was getting extremely worked up, 'Nick,' he said 'I don't care what else we have got to do; we've got to stop this bastard. How many others has he interfered with?' At that point Moira appeared.

'How did you get on?' asked Nick, as Moira re-joined the boys in their booth.

'Well, she still works there, but we have a small problem,' replied Moira. 'My friend told me that Dorothy goes a bit funny when Eddie's suicide is mentioned. Well, to be honest, she said that Dorothy was a bit funny anyway. Actually, what she said was that Dorothy Whitehouse was a very strange woman. She totally changed after Eddie's death, never goes out and has alienated all her friends. I'm not sure how we are going to sort this.'

'Sounds to me like she needs to see a trick cyclist,' said Don, who was feeling a little better after his confession.

'Yeah,' agreed Keith. 'She certainly needs some sort of help.'

'That's it!' exclaimed Nick. 'You two have cracked it; she needs help and we'll provide it.'

'How?' asked Don.

'Grief Counselling!'

'What's that?'

'Well, grief counselling is a form of psychotherapy that aims to help people cope with grief and mourning following the death of loved ones, or with major changes that trigger feelings or grief.'

'And what do you know about grief counselling, Nick?' asked Keith.

'Absolutely nothing, but I'm sure my contact in the library will find a suitable book for me,' said Nick, grinning from ear to ear.

'I get the idea,' enthused Moira. 'I'll have a word with my friend and get her to persuade Dorothy to see you. But we need a good cover story - I know, you could be a trainee counsellor.'

'Great idea,' replied Nick. 'I could say the church sent me, but I better use an alias, just in case it all goes wrong.'

'And you'll need a disguise.'

'There's usually a Jumble Sale somewhere on Fridays, we should be able to find you something there,' added Keith.

'I'll try and get my friend to make the appointment for Monday evening, oh, and don't forget I'm going on holiday with Dympna on Saturday.'

Nick wasn't sure how he felt about Moira going on holiday. Was it jealousy he felt or loneliness? Would she meet someone else - he had; although technically he hadn't started going out with Moira when he was snogging Suzanne. He was just being silly; of course she'll come back to him. What was that saying? "Absence makes the heart grow fonder", that was it. Straight away he thought of another, "out of sight, out of mind".

Wednesday 19 August

With nothing planned, Nick was glad when Don phoned him, saying he was going up the town to buy a new pair of football socks and would he like to join him; Keith was busy today. The best sports shop in town was *Wrens* in Chequer Street and having purchased a nice pair of red football socks they decided to have a wander around the Wednesday market. They were just admiring the Guinea Pigs on the pet stall when Nick noticed two girls walk by.

'Look, Don,' said Nick, 'see those two girls; well the one on the right is Jennifer Hewitt. Come on lets follow them.'

They followed the girls through the market until they reached the *ABC* café.

'Fancy a cup of tea?' asked Nick.

They followed the girls into the café and ordered two cups of tea. They sat a couple of tables away and Nick said, 'this is what I'll do. I'll go over and say how much you fancy her, but you're shy and ask her if she will go out with you.'

'What if she says yes,' asked Don, with a look of terror on his face.

'I haven't thought of that, oh, just play it by ear.'

Nick stood up, walked over to the girls' table and sat down opposite them.

'I'm sorry to disturb you, but my friend over there finds you very attractive and would like to ask you out, but he's never had a girlfriend before and he's a bit shy.'

Jennifer looked over at Don, smiled and then said, 'he's very sweet but I already have a boyfriend.'

'Oh, that's a shame,' replied Nick.

'But you both look nice boys so why don't you join us and we can just have a little chat while we drink our tea.'

Nick beckoned Don over and indicated to bring the teas. When they were seated, introductions were made, Jennifer friend's name was Linda Mardling. Linda was reasonably pretty, with straight, shoulder length brown hair. She was wearing a white knitted polo neck jumper with a knee length black and white check skirt. Jennifer looked like her photograph, very plain and was wearing a grey skirt and grey 'V' neck jumper over a white blouse. Nick thought she was still wearing her school uniform.

'So tell me about this amazing boyfriend you have, I mean, he must be special if you prefer him to my friend Don,' said Nick.

Don was blushing and looking down at his tea cup.

Jennifer smiled, and said, 'I agree that Don is very handsome, but beauty is only skin deep and my Christopher is so sweet. I call him my Chrisy Wissy and he calls me Jenny Wenny.'

Nick noticed Linda look towards the heavens.

Jennifer continued, 'he's just perfect and I think that one day we'll get married and have lots of children.'

'No one could be that perfect, he must have some faults,' said Nick.

'Well, if I'm honest he does talk a lot, I love listening to him, but it would be nice to get a word in edgeways.'

They stayed there for about another ten minutes making polite conversation, but Nick was now getting bored with Jennifer's babbling. He stood up and said, 'it's been a pleasure ladies but we must leave you now, things to do.'

Linda stood up and gave Nick a kiss on the cheek and slipped a piece of paper into his hand. Outside Nick looked at the note – it was Linda's phone number.

Mrs Allen had made Toad in the Hole for their evening meal and as Nick tucked in his father asked, 'what are you up to tonight, Nick?'

'Nothing planned at the moment, why?' replied Nick.

'Can you take some runner beans round to your uncle John's?'

Nick sighed, 'if I must; but you know that if my cousin Gwendolyn's in, I'll get lumbered playing Monopoly with her. So don't wait up.'

Thursday 20 August

Nick had invited Keith and Don over for breakfast as they both wanted to be present for the meeting with Christopher Wright. Mrs Allen was very happy to entertain Nick's friends and cooked for them fried eggs on fried bread which was smothered with *Daddies* sauce. Suitably refreshed they retired to the living room and waited for their 9.30am appointment. They were just thinking that he wasn't going to show, as it was at least ten minutes past the appointed time, when Mrs Allen shouted out, 'is that your boy sitting on the front wall, crying.'

The boys rushed to the front window to take a look and there was Christopher sitting on the wall, head in hands.

'Mum, can you bring him in, you're good at the sympathetic stuff,' asked Nick.

Within a few minutes Mrs Allen escorted a red-eyed Christopher Wright into the living room. He sat down in an empty chair, tears still trickling down his cheek.

'I'm sorry,' sobbed Christopher. 'I shouldn't have come; I know what you're going to say.'

'What makes you say that?' asked Keith.

'I saw her yesterday, bold as brass, walking down the High Street, hand in hand with another boy.'

'Are you sure?' asked Nick sceptically.

'Don't you think I don't know my own girlfriend,' shouted Christopher.

Nick shrugged his shoulders. Christopher stood up to leave.

'Sit down, Mr Wright and listen to what we have to say. Jennifer Hewitt is not cheating on you; in fact she thinks the world of you … … … Chrisy Wissy.

Christopher's jaw physically dropped and both Keith and Don starred at Nick.

'Let me explain; yesterday Don and I just happened to meet Jennifer and her friend Linda Mardling. We tried to chat her up but she politely declined but invited us to join them for a chat and I must say that she is a very nice girl. She told us how happy she was and even talked about marrying you and having children. Slightly weird I thought. But she did say that you do talk too much.'

'I know; it's a fault of mine. I talk when I get nervous and I'm always nervous when I see Jennifer, she's just too good for me.'

Keith and Don were struggling to stop themselves laughing.

Nick continued, 'when I had my first girlfriend my father gave me some advice, he said "It is important to listen, girls are often very self-centred and like to talk about themselves." Now if you had listened, you might have found out a little more about her sister.'

Christopher looked confused, 'what about her sister?'

'Do you know her name?'

'No.'

Nick smiled, 'her name is Janette and she is Jennifer's TWIN sister.'

'I never knew that.'

'Obviously; and they are two sides of the same coin.'

'What does that mean?'

'They are like chalk and cheese. Yesterday I spoke to my cousin, who just happens to live round the corner from the twins and she knows them well. Apparently Jennifer is the sweet one and Janette is a man-eater. They fell out because Janette always used to pinch Jennifer's boyfriends when she brought them home. They are identical and the only way to tell the apart is by their clothes; Jennifer always wears a dress or skirt whilst Janette prefers slacks or jeans. So unless the girl you saw yesterday was wearing a skirt, you should be very happy.'

Christopher looked relieved and the colour was coming back to his cheeks. 'I don't know how to thank you.'

Keith lent forward and handed him a piece of paper. 'I think this will help, it's our expenses. It's mostly bus fares and refreshments, which we incurred following the WRONG girl. You have seven days to pay.'

'Thank you, you've been most kind.' He took the invoice, shook each boys hand and the turned to leave.

'I'll see you out,' said Nick and escorted Christopher to the front door.

Friday 21 August

There was a mad scramble at exactly 7.00pm when the doors of the St. Luke's Church, in Camp Road were opened. Nick had to hold on to Moira as the hoard of elderly women rushed into the hall, all desperate to grab that elusive bargain. Mrs Allen had often taken Nick to Jumble sales, but this one was too far away and both Nick and Moira had to cycle there. Most of the crowd were rummaging through the Women's Clothes stall, which allowed Moira to take Nick to the Men's Clothes stall. It wasn't long before she found a suitable disguise in the form of a country cardigan in a manly cable and rib pattern. It reminded Nick of the sort of cardigan Roger Moore used to model in knitting patterns; it was a perfect fit. Moving on to another stall, Moira then located a bow tie in London bus red with a bright circle pattern, this was followed by a pair of heavy horn-rimmed glasses. Having purchased all the items for a very reasonable price, they were back outside in fifteen minutes flat. They didn't want to hang around because tonight they were off to the Market Hall to see a fab new local group called the Vincents. They had just recorded their first record entitled *Lonely Little Girl*. The vocalist was a lad called Dave Webster whose stage name was Rae Vince. The other members of the group were Alan Walton, lead guitar, Ken Hardman, bass guitar, Dave Lickman, rhythm guitar, Colin Shipton, Drums and Harvey Dunstan on the organ.

Saturday 22 August

Today was the start of the football season and Nick and Keith were off to London to see their favourite team Tottenham Hotspur, play their first match – a home fixture against Sheffield United. They walked up to the bus garage at the top of St Peter's Street, purchased their Red Rover tickets and waited for the 84 bus. Don, who was a Manchester United fan, had declined an invitation to join them, preferring to take part in a friendly scout game.

The journey was uneventful and the boys arrived in plenty of time and took their favourite position at the Paxton Road end of White Hart Lane. A crowd of 45,724 cheered on the Spurs to a 2-0 victory; the goals coming from Nick's favourite player Jimmy Greaves and Frank Saul. The boys were also impressed with Spurs two new signings, goalkeeper Pat Jennings and left back Cyril Knowles.

After the match they made their way back to Arnos Grove to catch the 84 bus. When he had finished reading the match programme from cover to cover, Keith said, 'just think, if the girls weren't on holiday we would have had to take them to the Grand Fete at Sandridge. Did you know that it was being opened by Keith Fordyce[5]?'

'Just as well they were then; as much as I like Mr Fordyce he doesn't hold candle to the mighty Spurs.'

'Absolutely, so what are we going to do about Father John?' asked Keith.

'Difficult; we can't just go to the police, they wouldn't believe us and we can't go to the church, because they wouldn't believe us either,' replied Nick.

'We need more evidence. If we can find other boys that he's abused, someone has got to listen to us. Your mate DI James, he'll listen to you.'

Nick had never seen Keith so worked up about a case before, but he knew that he was right. Finding out what happened to Peter Waller was important, especially to him, but, if young boys were being abused, then that must take priority and once again it was up to him to stop it.

'You're right of course. We need another plan of action, but we need to keep the girls out of it, at least for the time being. It's lucky they're both on holiday this week; it'll give us time to investigate it without fibbing to them. When is Brenda back?'

'She's flying back next Sunday, I'll expect I see her on Monday.'

'Moira's back late on Saturday, so I won't see her till Sunday. Hopefully we should have something to go on by then.'

'That's good, so what's the plan?'

Nick thought for a while; how do you go about asking someone if they've been groped by their scoutmaster? 'Okay, I've an idea. Don's got a freaky friend called Algernon, god, you would love him. I thought I could pay him a visit. He doesn't have many friends but he seems to know a lot of what's going on. I'm sure with a little persuasion he could give us a few names.'

Keith nodded his head, 'sounds like a plan.'

They sat in silence, looking out of the window, as the 84 bus made its way through South Mymms heading towards London Colney.

'I've had a thought,' said Nick. 'I know we said that the downfall of Father John is our main priority, but we mustn't lose sight of our other case. I would like to have them both wrapped up before we go back to school.'

'Can't see that happening, can you? I don't see how we are going to find out who the third man was. You got any ideas?'

'You're right of course; but we need to put a bit of pressure on Billy Watkins. So listen carefully, this is what I propose.'

For the rest of the journey Nick outlined his ideas. As the bus turned into St Peters Street, Keith said, 'excellent, I'll have a word with Don and we'll see what happens.'

It was a bit of a rush, but Nick was in luck, a 330 bus had just pulled in at the St. Peters Street stop when he alighted from his bus. A gentle jog from the bottom of Folly Lane and he was settled in front of the television with five minutes to spare. Tonight was the first ever showing of *Match of the Day* on BBC2. Nick sat glued to the television as Kenneth Wolstenhome said, 'Welcome to Match of the Day, the first of a weekly series coming to you every Saturday on BBC2. As you can hear we're in Beatleville for this Liverpool versus Arsenal match.' After looking at graphic captions of both teams, Ken was joined by his summariser, Wally Barnes, who previewed the game. Liverpool were the defending champions, the ground was full and the first ever Match of the Day goal came when Ian Callaghan crossed to Roger Hunt who hooked the ball into the top left hand corner with a right-foot volley. Liverpool won 3-2, Barnes gave his views at half-time and at the end of the game, Wolstenhome provided a news round-up.

WEEK 3
Sunday 23 August - Saturday 29 August 1964

Sunday 23 August

'What do fancy doing this afternoon,' asked Don. He was sitting on the back lawn of Nick's house listening to *Radio Caroline* with Nick and Keith.

'I don't know,' replied Keith. 'I'm not in the mood to do much today.'

'I hope you two aren't going to mope around all week, just because both of your girlfriends are on holiday,' added Don. 'Come on, let's have a wander round the lake, something's bound to happen, it always does.'

Keith slowly stood up, 'if we must.'

'Are you coming, Nick?' asked Don.

Nick jumped to his feet, 'you're right, we can't sit around all-day feeling sorry for ourselves. What we need is excitement, thrills and adventure.'

'And we're going to find it down the lake?' commented Keith, shaking his head.

'Of course we are, it's our destiny. The world is waiting for us.'

'I know you are my best friend but sometimes you do talk a

load of bollocks. Do you want to ask your mum if she got any stale bread? Feeding the ducks may be the highlight of the afternoon.'

'Okay.'

As usual, on a Sunday afternoon, Verulamium Park was very busy and it gave the lads a buzz just being there. Straight away they headed for the boating lake where a group of men were showing off their radio controlled model boats. A large crowd had assembled to watch them and the boys had to push their way to the front to get a better view. Totally enthralled, Nick had failed to notice the boy standing next to him.

'I say old chap, are you not speaking to me today,' said the boy.

Nick looked round, smiled and replied, 'sorry Sebastian, didn't see you there. How the devil are you?'

Spiffing, absolutely spiffing; really enjoying the ol' school hols.'

Sebastian Fellows was a very posh boy, with a pleasant face, who attended Nick's Grammar School and lived in a very large house in St. Michaels Street.

'So what brings you to the lake and mixing with the proletarians?' asked Nick.

Although Sebastian had a very upper-class upbringing, he had a great sense of humour and never took offence when being ribbed about his poshness and he always gave as good as he got.

'It's nice to mix with the serfs now and again and Ma and Pa are out for the afternoon, so I was at a loose end.'

'Well, it's your lucky day; you can rough it with us. You know Keith and this is my other friend Donald,'

Sebastian shook Don's hand and said, 'awfully nice to meet you, ol' chap.'

'The pleasure's all mine,' replied Don. 'Should I bow?'

'Normally, but I'll make an exception this time,' laughed Sebastian.

After a while the boys left the boating lake and took a slow walk towards the *Tominey's* ice-cream van which was situated at the other end of the main lake.

'How are you feeling now, Nicholas, I heard you nearly met your maker the other week?' asked Sebastian.

'A lot better thanks,' replied Nick. 'It is just one of the hazards of being a consulting detective.'

'I heard that you're just and an annoying busybody,' said Sebastian, with a smirk on his face.

'That has been said a few times.'

'I'll tell what ol' boy, I'll treat you all to an ice-cream, and then I shall test you deductive powers with a little mystery that has occurred at the ol' homestead.'

Sebastian purchased four 99s and the boys found a nice patch of grass and made themselves comfortable.

'Right chaps; let us see just how good you are. A few days ago a valuable painting that was displayed on the wall in the dining room, mysteriously disappeared. It was there when we breakfasted, then half an hour later it was gone.'

'The butler did it,' said Don.

'No, I don't think so. Old Jenkins has been with us for donkey's years, he's part of the family.'

Don chuckled, 'you mean you actually have a butler.'

Sebastian pretended to be shocked, 'of course, doesn't everyone; who's going to serve the jolly ol' breakfast?'

'Okay,' interrupted Nick, 'let's have the facts; who were in the house at the time and why do think you weren't burgled?'

'At the time there were five of us at home; apart from me, there were Ma and Pa, Jenkins and the cook, Mrs Wilson. The dining room windows were locked and no one could have walked out with it without being seen, it's a rather large painting.'

'Did you call the police?' asked Keith.

'Of course, Pa phoned 999 straight away. They were here within ten minutes, but totally clueless.'

'Who was the investigating officer?' asked Nick.

'A DC Higgins; nice chap, but not the brightest button in the box, do you know him?'

'Our paths have crossed a few times.'

'Tell us about the butler, I still think he did it,' asked Don.

'It's a nice story. Jenkins was my grandfather's Batman during the First World War. When the war was over Jenkins fell on hard times, so grandpa hired him as a Butler. When my grandfather died and Pater inherited the house he kept Jenkins on. He's retiring next month and going to live with his sister in Herne Bay.'

'Does he live with you,' asked Keith.

'Yes, he has two rooms at the top of the house, he wants for nothing.'

'Still think he done it,' said Don.

'What else can you tell,' asked Nick. 'Has anything else gone missing?'

Sebastian thought for a while, 'we did have a break in, a few months ago. Professional job, they said. They came through the French windows, took quite a bit of silver and somehow cracked the safe, and took grandfather's war medals, the scoundrels. Again the police were clueless, so we changed all the locks, made the windows more secure and had a burglar alarm fitted.'

'And none of the stuff has been recovered.'

'Afraid not.'

The boys sat there for a while, deep in their own thoughts. Then Nick said, 'we'll take the case.'

'Will we?' asked Keith.

'I'm telling you, the butler did it,' said Don.

'Of course he did,' replied Nick. 'We just have to prove it.'

'Do you really think so?' asked Sebastian. 'Why would he do such a thing? And what has he done with the painting, I think one of us would have spotted him walking out with it. And the police searched his room.'

'That my friend is the mystery and we shall do our best to solve it. Is he in the house at the moment?'

'No, he takes Sunday afternoons off, I think he plays bowls. But he's always back by seven to serve tea. My parents will also be home by then.'

'Would it be alright if we come round and have a look at the crime scene?'

'Absolutely, I thought you'd never ask.'

William Jenkins was feeling rather pleased with himself as he cycled the short distance from the Townsend Bowls club in Waverley Road to St. Michael's Village. His team had just beaten St. Albans Bowls club by 4 ends to 2 and he had won his triples game by 25 points to 18. He would just have time to pop in the *Six Bells* for a quick pint before returning home and serving tea to the Fellows family. It wouldn't take long; Mrs Wilson would have prepared the sandwiches and cakes and once he had cleared up he should be back in the pub before 9.00pm. He had been butler to the Fellows family since 1920. Following the war, he had struggled to find employment and it was only by a stroke of good fortune that he bumped into Captain Fellows. It was a cold miserable December afternoon when Captain Fellows somehow spotted him in a queue outside the Mission Hall. The Captain took him home, gave him a hot meal and offered him the job as butler. It was a good job and he was always kept busy looking after the large family. The pay was nothing to write home about, but he was given free accommodations and three meals a day. When the Captain died ten years ago his son inherited the house and it was stipulated in the will that he was to be kept on. But it wasn't the same any more. Is there really a need for a butler in this day and age and with only three members of the family in residence, there wasn't that much for him to do. He smiled to himself, thinking, things are going to get better. He had handed in his noticed and would be retiring soon to live with his sister in Herne Bay. Dolly, his only living relative, had recently been widowed and had begged him to live with her. She had a nice bungalow by the sea and plenty of room for the two of them. He had a nice little nest egg stashed away; plenty for them to live out the rest of their lives in comfort.

It came as a bit of a surprise to Mr and Mrs Fellows when they walked into the dining room to find their son, Sebastian sitting there with three other boys. It was also very disconcerting to see them all with supercilious grins on their faces.

'What's going on?' asked a confused Mr Fellows.

'I've invited some friends back for tea,' replied Sebastian. 'Hope you don't mind Pa; they are awfully good chaps. This is Nicholas; he in my class at school, as is Keith and this is Donald, he's a Catholic.'

All three boys, in unison said, 'pleased to meet you.'

Mr Fellows, felt a little uncomfortable as the boys continued to gaze at him, still smiling.

'Darling,' said Mrs Fellows, who was tugging at her husband's jacket.

'Just a moment dear; is there something you want to say, boys?' asked Mr Fellows.

Nick had noticed that Mrs Fellows wasn't looking at them, but at the wall where the missing painting was now hanging.

'Darling, look,' said Mrs Fellows, with a little bit more urgency.

Mr Fellows followed her gaze and exclaimed, 'oh my giddy aunt, where did that come from?'

The smiles on the boy's faces widened even more. Mr Fellows turn to his son and asked, 'Sebastian, explain.'

'Well father, it's like this. Nicholas, here, is a consulting detective, you know like Sherlock Holmes and these are his associates. I hired them to find the missing painting – and they did. So as a reward I invited them to stay for tea. It was the least that I could do.'

Mr Fellows was a little shaken but he managed to pull himself together before saying, 'who stole it?'

'It was the butler,' replied Don.

Nick stood up; this was the moment he was waiting for. 'Let me explain; after listening to Sebastian's version of events I quickly concluded that if there was no way that the painting could have been removed without someone seeing, so it makes sense that the painting must still be in the room. As Sherlock would say, "when you have eliminated the impossible, whatever remains, however improbable, must be the truth." So where does one hide such a large painting? The first thing that struck me was that it seemed odd to have a single bookcase in the dining room; it looked out of place.

On further inspection I noticed some scuff marks on the floor by the right-had side of the bookcase.' Nick indicated where. 'Then I noticed something else strange. This book on the right doesn't have a title on the spine, but if you pull it, this happens.'

Nick pulled the book towards him, this was followed by a large click and the right hand side of the bookcase moved forward.

'Well I never,' exclaimed Mr Fellows. 'I never knew that was there.'

Nick pulled the bookcase to reveal a secret compartment which was full of objects that had also mysteriously disappeared.

Mr Fellows looked a Nick, before asking, 'and you think Jenkins is responsible?'

Nick answered, 'who else? I think he was stealing these things and was going to use the proceeds to fund his retirement. As you know, he's leaving your employ at half-term. This just happens to coincide with you taking young Sebastian on holiday to France. With the house empty he could remove the loot without anyone knowing.'

'I think we should call the police, darling,' said Mrs Fellows.

'He would just deny it,' replied Mr Fellows.

'I sure the police would find his fingerprints all over the stuff, we only touched the painting,' said Keith.

'If I may make a small suggestion; let us continue as normal and see Jenkins' reaction when he serves tea. He'll give himself away. Then sack him. As nothing now is actually missing I don't think the police need be involved. Also, we don't get on very well with DC Higgins,' said Nick.

Mr Fellows agreed and took his usual place at the head of the table; Mrs Fellows sat next to him. After making small talk for a few minutes the door opened and in walked Jenkins carrying a large platter of sandwiches. After placing the platter in the centre of the table, Jenkins could feel six pairs of eyes staring at him. As he looked up, out of the corner of the eye, he could see the missing painting. The look on his face was the look of a guilty man.

'Something you want to say?' asked Mr Fellows.

Jenkins was speechless.

'Case closed,' said Nick.

'I'm very disappointed, Jenkins,' said Mr Fellows. 'My family have looked after you for over forty years and this is how you treat us. I suggest you back your bags now and leave before I call the police.'

Once the boys had finished their sandwiches and consumed numerous cakes, they said their farewells. Mr Fellows was more than grateful and slipped a £10 note to Nick. As they walked home, Nick said, 'well, I asked for excitement, thrills and adventure, I suppose that was a good substitute and we've made a few bob,' waving the £10 note in the air.

'You know what should happen now?' said Keith. 'After solving an important case like this, we should return home and ravish our girlfriends.'

Nick agreed, 'absolutely, how I would love to frolic naked with Moira on large, King size, double bed; heaven.'

'Shame,' replied Keith. 'You'll just have to fantasize over your secret Cilla Black scrapbook.'

Nick gasped, 'how do you know about that.'

Keith smiled, 'you're not the only detective on the block.'

Monday 24 August

Dorothy Whitehouse was cursing herself; what possessed her to agree to talk to a grief counsellor. She was well over Eddie; after all it had been five years. Yes, she may not have had a boyfriend since, but that was because she hadn't met the right man. She had moved on, she had moved into this flat, left all memories of Eddie behind and was getting on with her life. If only people would leave her alone and now she would have to invite a complete stranger into her home. He could be anybody, a rapist, a murderer, or worst of all a Jehovah Witness. What time was he coming? 7.00pm, hopefully he'll be gone before *Coronation Street*.

At 7.00pm exactly, Nick Allen knocked on the door to Dorothy Whitehouse's flat. He was feeling slightly uncomfortable wearing a cardigan, bowtie and glasses. He had also re-styled his hair with a large dollop of his dad's Brylcreem to give him a sharp parting. Not knowing what to expect, he took a deep breath and feared the worst. The door opened and standing there was a reasonably attractive woman, dressed in a smart blue dress with contrast check trimmings and pointed collar with bow. It had a full skirt with two pockets and three-quarter length sleeves and an all-round belt. She had shoulder length auburn coloured hair, which had recently been styled. Nick thought the whole look was a bit fifties. She had a nice smile but he thought she had scary eyes.

'You must be Ronald Henry,' said Dorothy. Nick had decided to use an alias; he was using the name of the left back in the 1960/61 Tottenham Hotspur double winning side.

Dorothy showed Nick into the lounge, which was unremarkable and doubled up as a dining room, Nick felt a little nervous as he made himself comfortable sitting at her dining table. He took a notebook out of his briefcase and laid it on the table then fumbled around to find his fountain pen. The room was pretty stark, an old two-seater settee which had seen better days and a wooden sideboard. In the corner stood a Pye 14 inch television and a Champion three-speed portable record player sat on the floor next to a pile of 45 and 78 rpm records. *Magic Moments* by Perry Como was playing.

Dorothy bent down and turned the record player off; Nick couldn't but help notice her shapely rear. 'That was our song, me and Eddies.' But before he had a chance to speak Dorothy said, 'you're a bit young to be a grief councillor?'

Nick forced a smile, 'well actually, I'm just training to be one.'

'I know that,' replied Dorothy. 'I mean normally grief councillors are older, you know, more experienced in life.'

'Ah, yes,' said Nick, thinking I thought I supposed to be asking the questions. 'Well it's like this, the church thought that…' Nick's mind was racing. I should have had this all thought out before I came here. 'It's not only old people that lose loved ones, sometimes youngsters do. They may lose a parent or a grandparent or even a close friend. So the church in its infinite wisdom thought these unfortunate souls would respond to someone nearer their own age. So I volunteered for the training programme and here I am.' Smiling to himself and thinking, I'm good.

'Which church?'

Not wanting to incriminate his own church, he replied, 'St Stephens; the Reverend Hart-Synott, it was his idea, he's a friend of mine.' Which was partly true; the Reverend was a football mad vicar and mad as a box of frogs and had on many an occasion taken Nick and a few of his friends to Sally's Inn Café after a game of football.

That seemed to pacify her for the moment, 'Okay, where shall we start?' said Dorothy as she sat opposite Nick.

'Good; let's start at the beginning, what was Eddie like leading up to his demise?' Nick thought that sounded better than suicide.

'We were very happy, life was great. I used to see him about four or five times a week. We would go to the pictures or to a dance. Sometimes just for a quiet drink at the Farmers Boy. We would plan our wedding; discuss how many children we would have and what their names might be. Life couldn't have been better.'

'Then what happened?'

'All of a sudden he seemed to go a bit cold, sometimes I might only see him once or twice a week.'

'Did you mention this to him?'

'Oh yeah, he just said he was busy.'

'And you had no idea what caused this change?'

'No; but after nagging him for over an hour one evening I finally broke him. He said he was seeing someone else. I was just about to wallop him one when he said it was a man. Well I was shocked; I didn't think he was a bloody poofter. Then he explained; he'd met an old friend from the Army, errr, Michael - that was his name. He told me that he had just moved into the area and he was showing him around. Helping him settle in and introducing him to the faces and make some new friends. Well I thought if that was all, why couldn't he just tell me?'

This was just the information Nick wanted, but he needed to tread carefully. 'Sounds a bit fishy to me, what was Michael's other name?'

Dorothy was deep in thought, 'he never said. But you are right there was definitely something not quite kosher. You know, before this Michael appeared, Eddie and I used to have sex quite regularly.'

Nick wasn't sure he liked where this was going. She seemed to go into a trance and a smug look came over her face

'On my half days he would finish early and come round to my flat. He would knock on the door, I would answer it and he would say, "The car is all fixed." and I would say, "That's great, what was wrong with it?" He would then say, "The big end had gone." "Oh," I would say, "that sounds expensive, how much?" Then he would make up some extortionate price and I would say, "That's more than I expected, I don't think I can afford it." Then he would pretend to get annoyed and shout "I want my money and I want it now." and I would pretend to cry and sob, "I haven't got that much money." Then he would force his way in and say, "If you can't pay with cash then you must pay in kind." "I don't know what you mean," I would say. Then he would approach me, slowly undoing his overalls and then take me, there on the kitchen table. It was fantastic. I used to love the smell of oily overalls, it always turned me on'

Now Nick, who had never heard a women talk so openly about sex, was getting a little hot under the collar. Although he was clearly embarrassed, he had to admit to himself he was feeling a little horny.

Dorothy continued, 'and then it just stopped, and I haven't had sex since.'

Nick was puzzled, 'you mean you haven't got a boyfriend?'

'No I haven't been out with a boy since Eddie died. In fact you are the first male to set foot in this flat since I moved here three years ago.'

'Well that is definitely something we need to work on,' replied Nick confidently, as he pretended to make notes in his notebook.

Dorothy smiled, 'you know, this is really helping. I feel much better already; you're so easy to talk to.'

Nick smiled, 'that has been said before.'

Dorothy stared at Nick strangely, and then commented, 'you know you're not a bad looking lad and if you didn't wear those awful glasses and silly cardigan, you would be quite attractive.'

Nick blushed, 'it's my parents; they are quite old fashioned. They make me dress like this.'

Dorothy stood and stared before walking towards Nick. She then bent down and removed his glasses.

'Now what else can we improve?' said Dorothy, before lifting up his shirt collar and removing his bow-tie. She then undid the top two buttons on his shirt before brushing his hair with her fingers into a more natural style. 'There, that's much better.'

Nick was getting more than a little flustered and was worried about where this was going, he had to change tack. 'Do you have any photos of Eddie?'

'Do you think that would help?' asked Dorothy, a little put out.

'I think so; by putting a face to the man, it should help get into his mind, try and work out what was going on.'

'Maybe; I've got a tin somewhere,' said Dorothy, as she disappeared into her bedroom.

Nick was frantically thinking what to do next, this was definitely not a good idea. At least Little Nick was behaving. Dorothy returned carrying an old Queen Elizabeth II coronation biscuit tin. Have a browse through these, they might help. I'll get us some refreshment; would you like tea or I think I've got some sherry left over from Christmas?'

'Tea will be fine.'

Dorothy disappeared again into the kitchen; Nick opened the tin and started browsing through the photographs. The photos where unremarkable, just the usual array of holiday snaps and studio portraits. He was just about to put them all back into the tin when one caught his eye. It was a 6 by 4 inch photo of Eddie posing in his swimming trunks. After studying it for a while he slipped it into his note-book.

'Everything okay?' asked Dorothy as she returned carrying a tray with two cups of tea and a Battenberg cake.

'Thank you,' said Nick, as Dorothy placed the tray in the centre of the table and passed one of the cups to him. Nick was a little concerned about the size of the knife Dorothy had brought in to cut the cake. It had a nine inch blade.

'How many sugars?' asked Dorothy.

'Two please.'

Dorothy spooned the sugar into Nick's tea and gave it a stir. She then cut two slices of cake; passed one to him, then devoured the other in three mouthfuls. 'I'm really glad I found you, it's been a great help to me. Will you need to see me again?'

Nick thought for a minute before answering, 'See how you feel tomorrow, then if you think you would like to see me again, give me a ring, I'll leave you my phone number.' But it won't be the right number, he thought.

Nick finished his tea and cake, which he enjoyed; Battenberg being one of his favourites. As he stood up to go Dorothy rushed over to him and frantically started kissing him. Her hands were wildly pulling the shirt out of his trousers and then Nick could feel her fingernails digging into his back. Nick was in shock, one second she was passionately kissing his lips, the next second, biting his neck. Her breathing was getting faster, her hands were everywhere; was she turning into an octopus, thought Nick. Now her hands were now desperately trying to undo his trouser belt. It was clear that Little Nick was up for this as he strained to be free. Then as quickly as it started, it stopped. Dorothy turned away, buried her face in her hands and wept hysterically. Nick used the time, before she calmed down, to smarten up. He heard her sobs subside and before turning to face him she took a deep breath.

'I'm sorry, but I don't think this will work; it's too soon. I find you very attractive and I know you love me, but it wouldn't be fair on Eddie.'

'I understand,' replied Nick. 'You need time to grieve.' With that,

Nick grabbed his fountain pen and notebook, making sure the borrowed photo didn't fall out, stuffed them in his briefcase. As he opened the door to leave he turned and said, 'I'll leave you the bow-tie and glasses… …a reminder of what could have been.'

Tuesday 25 August

Nick, Don and Keith were sitting on the lawn in Nick's back garden discussing the case; the Beatles were singing *Anna* on Nick's new transistor radio.

'How did you get on with Miss Whitehouse yesterday?' asked Keith.

'She's a total nutcase, she almost raped me,' replied Nick, giving a little shiver.

Keith and Don both starred at Nick before Don said, 'what do you mean?'

Nick explained in detail the events of last night.

'Wow,' gasped Keith, 'and all you found out was that he had a mate called Michael.' Nick had not mentioned the borrowed photograph.

'I know it's not much but it's still a lead, I'm sure we can use it.'

'Don't see how; who do we ask that knows the surname of a friend of a man who's been dead for five years. That was a mouthful - you know what I mean.'

Nick looked forlorn, 'when you put it like that.'

Don, who so far had remained silent said, 'what we need to do is find the connection between our three suspects. What stands out to me is that both Billy and Eddie worked for *Marlboro Motors*. What's to say that this Michael doesn't work there to?'

'Don's got a point,' added Keith. 'I think we should check it out.'

Nick wasn't sure, he thought that would be too easy, but was happy to go along with them. It was as this point that Mrs Allen appeared from the kitchen.

'Nick, there's someone to see you,' she said, with a mischievous grin on her face.

Behind her was a rather plain looking girl, Nick guessed she must be about the same age or slightly younger than himself. She had long straight, mousey coloured hair, slim, with what one could only described as a pleasant face. She was wearing a pair of pink shorts, short sleeve white blouse, white ankle socks and a pair of white plimsolls. She was definitely not Keith's type, knowing his penchant for large breasted girls and too prim and proper for Nick. Don's taste in girls was still unknown.

Nick smiled and asked, 'what can we do for you?'

'I believe you are an investigator and I would like to hire you,' she replied confidently.

'Actually, I'm a consulting detective and these two gentlemen are my associates. So, how can we help you?

'My cat has gone missing and I need you to find it.'

Holding back the urge to laugh Keith was first to answer, 'I'm afraid that at the moment we are in the middle of two very important investigations and I don't think we have the time to help you.'

The girl looked disappointed.

'I'm sure we could fit you in,' interjected Don. 'If you would care to give us your details we shall do our best to find your pet.'

'Thank you, my name is Linda and I live at number 32 across the road.'

'Do you have a phone number?'

'No, we don't have a telephone.'

Don looked disappointed but continued, 'no problem; now can you tell us all about the missing cat.'

Linda sat down on the grass opposite the boys and carried on with her narrative, 'her name is Holly and she is black and white.'

'When did you last see her?' asked Nick.

'Two days ago; normally she is very friendly, but lately she's been very restless and not eating. She normally plays in the garden and always comes in for her tea, but this time she didn't and we haven't seen her since.'

'Okay, just let me take all this down,' said Don, picking up his notebook and pencil. 'Is there anything you would like to ask us?'

Linda thought, 'what are you fees?'

Don was quick to answer, 'for this type of case we charge a standard fee, dependant on results, of course. It would normally be half a crown, but as you are a neighbour we can offer a twenty percent discount. So we'll say two shillings plus expenses.'

Nick and Keith looked at each other, mouths open.

'Thank you that will be acceptable. When can you start?'

Nick cut in, 'we'll be over this afternoon to have a look round and I just have one question. Have you noticed if Holly has put on any weight recently?'

Linda though for a while before answering, 'now I come to think of it, yes. But she is still growing and she has a healthy appetite.'

'Thank you.' Nick stood up, held out his hand and said, 'we'll see you later,'

Linda stood up, shook Nick's hand and replied, 'thank you, you have been very kind.'

Keith followed suit and shook Linda's hand. Don also stood up and shook Linda's hand but held on to it a little longer than necessary. This was noticed by both Nick and Keith. Once Linda had retrieved her hand she said goodbye, turned and walked away.

When she was out of sight both Nick and Keith said, 'you fancy her.'

Don blushed, 'no I don't.'

'Of course you do, and there's nothing wrong with that,' laughed Nick. 'In fact, it's about time you got yourself a girlfriend, and you have got to start somewhere. Just think, once we've located her cat, you'll be her hero....putty in your hands.'

'Exactly,' said Kim. 'Then ask her out, yeah, take her to the pictures on Saturday.'

Don frowned, 'I do like her, but what if she turns me down, I'd feel such a fool.'

'Let's be honest, I don't expect she gets many offers,' said Keith, forgetting his sensitivity.

Don ignored Keith's remark and continued, 'but how the hell are we going to find the bloody cat?'

Nick smiled, 'trust me we'll have the case cracked by tea-time and you will have your first date.'

It was mid-afternoon when Nick, Keith and Don walked across the road to number 32. They knocked on the front door and it was answered by a stern looking women with rollers in her hair and wearing an apron. She folded her arms, looked down her nose and said, 'can I help you?'

'Good afternoon Mrs err….?' said Nick.

'Bryce,' replied the woman.

'Mrs Bryce pleased to meet you. My name is Nick Allen and these are my associates Keith Nevin and Don Patrick. We are here to investigate the disappearance of a cat called Holly.'

Mrs Bryce frowned, 'Oh yes, Linda told me to expect you. How much is she paying you?'

Nick and Keith turned and looked at Don, who replied, 'two shillings'.

'Well I'll pay you two and six not to find the damn thing.'

Linda appeared smiling, from behind her mother. 'Oh there you are, come on in. Don't listen to mother, she's only joking, she loves Holly really.'

The boys squeezed their way passed Mrs Bryce and Linda led them through the house to the back garden.

'I'll put the kettle on then, shall I? Expect its thirsty work looking for cats,' said Mrs Bryce sarcastically.

Nick turned round and noticed half a smile on Mrs Bryce's face.

'Take no notice of mum, she's an angel really,' commented Linda. 'Now where do you want to start?'

Nick looked around; the garden was reasonably large and well maintained. The first half was a neatly manicured lawn with a well-stocked flower border; the second half was devoted to vegetables. Nick noticed that the runner beans looked exceptionally good. At the far end of the garden was the customary garden shed.

'I expect you have searched the house,' said Nick. 'But would it be alright if Keith has another look, especially in the cupboards and quiet corners?'

Linda said that would be okay and Keith disappeared into the house via the back door.

Nick said that he would like a closer look at the garden shed and they made their down the garden path. Standing outside the shed, Nick tried the door but it was locked.

'I don't think Holly is in there, dad always keeps it locked' said Linda.

Still smiling Nick replied, 'when was the last time the shed was open?'

Linda thought for a while before answering, 'I'm not sure.'

'Never mind, just get the key and we'll have a look.'

When Linda returned, Nick took the key and slowly unlocked the shed door. Inside the shed was the usual array of garden implements. To the left of the shed, a workbench littered with different sized flowerpots, bags of compost and things Nick didn't have a clue about.

'What's that noise?' asked Don. They listened.

'Sounds like a mouse,' replied Linda.

'Or a rat,' added Don. 'I bloody hate rats.'

Nick took another look at the shed, and then asked, 'what's in that wooden crate in the corner?'

Linda looked, without entering the shed and replied, 'my dad keeps his old rags in there.'

'Okay, stay here while I have a look.' Nick crept in and inspected the box. What he saw brought a lump to his throat. Looking up him was the missing cat Holly and snuggling into her underside were three gorgeous balls of fur. He turned and beckoned Linda to have a look.

'Oh my word,' gasped Linda. 'Look, three kittens; aren't they lovely.'

Don rushed in to have a look as Nick stepped aside.

'I'll leave you to it and I'll go back to the house and tell the others.'

Nick found Mrs Bryce in deep conversation with Keith.

'Any luck? enquired Mrs Bryce.

Nick bit his lip to stop himself laughing, 'well I have some good news and some very good news.'

'You've found the cat and it's dead,' stated Mrs Bryce, with that half smile on her face.

'Close, but no coconut; we have located Holly and … … …her three kittens.'

'Holy mother of Jesus, that's all I need.'

'You've had a shock,' added Keith. 'Sit down, the kettles boiled and I'll make you a nice cup of sweet tea.'

Keith made the tea and the three of them sat round the kitchen table to enjoy their drink along with a packet of *Rich Tea* biscuits.

It was a good ten minutes before Don and Linda appeared. Linda was carrying the box to show her mother. Don followed with a large grin on his face and looking rather flushed. The boys stayed in the kitchen for another twenty minutes laughing and joking with Mrs Bryce who, behind her stern exterior, had a wicked sense of humour.

On the way back to Nick's house, Keith asked Don if he had made a date with Linda.

'I think so,' replied Don.

'What does that mean?'

'I can't actually remember what I said.'

In unison Nick and Keith said, 'explain!'

'Well,' replied Don, blushing again. 'She was so excited about the kittens; she just grabbed me and snogged my face off.'

'Lucky you,' exclaimed Nick.

'Fantastic, added Keith. 'It's always the quiet ones.'

'Well,' said Nick. 'Perhaps we should become 'Pet Detectives', just think of all those gorgeous birds out there that will do anything for someone to find their lost pets.'

Feeling really pleased with themselves, the three boys walked back to Nick's house.

'So what are we going to do about finding this Michael bloke?'

asked Keith as they walked into the kitchen; Mrs Allen was preparing the evening meal.

'How did you get on?' she asked.

'Well,' chuckled Nick, 'we actually solved a case without anyone getting hurt or police involvement.'

'Miracles will never cease.'

'Is it alright to use the phone, we might have a lead on the Waller case.'

'Of course you can; as long as you put a couple of pennies in the box.'

The boys went through to the hall where the phone was situated and closed the door behind them.

'Who are we phoning?' asked Don.

'*Marlboro Motors* of course. Let's see if anyone called Michael works there,' replied Nick.

'And they are just going to tell you,' said Keith sarcastically.

'I'll put on a deep voice and pretend to be the police.'

'Good idea; you can say you're that pratt DC Higgins,' laughed Don.

Nick quickly found the number in the local telephone directory and dialled it. Keith and Don huddled round to listen to the conversation. After three rings a woman answered.

'Good afternoon, *Marlboro Motors*, how can I help you?'

'Good afternoon, my name is Detective Constable Higgins from the St. Albans Police and I was wondering if you could help us with our enquires?' said Nick, trying to make his voice as deep as possible.

'Of course, ask away,' the woman sounded excited.

'Thank you; can you tell me if you have an employee called Michael working for you?'

'Well, we have three, can you be a bit more specific.'

'Yes, sorry,' Nick was thinking fast and it didn't help that Don and Keith were breathing down his neck. 'He would be in his mid to late twenties and started working for you round about 1959.'

'Oh yes, I know exactly who you mean - Michael Brown. Nasty

bit of work, it doesn't surprise me you're asking after him.'

'What can you tell us about him? Anything you say will be treated in absolute confidence.'

'He works in the stores and you will often find him serving on the spare parts counter. I'm sure he's on the fiddle and he's a dirty ol' sod, always making crude remarks about my tits. And he always slaps my arse when he walks past.'

'Have you reported him?'

'I did once, but my boss said not to be silly and if I couldn't take a little bit of fun, I should get a job in a convent.'

'Well thank you Miss… … sorry I Didn't catch you name.'

'Woodstock, Ruth Woodstock.'

'Oh, just one more thing, do you know where he lives?'

'Springfield Road, not sure of the number but it will be in the phone book.'

'Thank you, Ruth. You have very helpful and don't worry, I'll make sure that your delicate backside will not be molested again.' With that, Nick replaced the phone.

'You'll make sure her delicate backside will not be molested again,' said Keith, looking at Nick in amazement. 'We're trying to track down a kidnapper and maybe a potential murderer and all you're interested in is protecting her delicate backside.'

Nick looked sheepish, 'just being a gentleman.'

'And how do you intend to do that? Start some sort of arse-watch?'

'No, I'll just get Digger Barnes and his mates to pay him a visit.'

Keith mellowed and said, 'yeah, that might work.'

Nick put his hand in his pocket, found two pennies and put them in the small wooden box that was situated on the small table that housed the phone.

'What's out next move?' asked Keith, as they walked back through the kitchen.

'A glass of orange juice I think, then tomorrow I'm going to visit Don's friend Algernon. Not sure what to do about Michael, arse-grabbing Brown yet. But I'm sure something will come to me.'

Having filled their glasses with orange juice they ventured into the living room and found Nick's brother engrossed watching the *Five O' Clock Club* on the television, starring Ollie Beak, Murial Young and Fred Barker.

'How's it going bro, still lusting over Muriel Young[6]?' asked Nick.

'Huh, we're not all sex maniacs like you three,' replied Richard.

'Perhaps not, but she's a bit mumsie for my taste.'

'Is this your favourite programmes, Richard?' asked Don.

'No it's not my favourite and I've told you, call me Dick. My favourite is *Noggin the Nog*[7], but it's not on at the moment.'

'I like that one, perhaps you should have Noggin as a nickname as no one ever calls you Dick,' said Keith.

Richard thought for a while before replying, 'good idea but not Noggin, Nogs. That's it from now on I shall be known as Nogs.'

Wednesday 26 August

Algernon Teggegh sat in his bedroom, bored to tears. He was still without a girlfriend and no-one to play with and he hadn't seen his friend Donald since that football practice ten days ago. He didn't like that boy that took Donald away that day, he was a bully. But, he had to admit that he did give him some good advice about getting a girlfriend. He was now growing his hair and trying different styles, also it was his birthday soon and he had asked his parents for a guitar. As for his other problem, he had found a house brick in the garden and along with a ball of string; he was hoping for a quick result.

Nick stood apprehensively at the end of the drive that led to Algernon Teggegh's house, it was massive. He estimated that it must have been built at the turn of the century and he wouldn't be surprised if they had servants. A nice Jaguar XJ6 was parked in front of the garage. Nick took a deep breath before pressing the doorbell. As the door opened Nick's jaw fell at the sight of the imposing figure of Algernon's father. There could be no mistake, even in the crowd at a North London Derby you would still recognise Algernon's father. He stood at least six feet two inches high, had a mop of ginger hair and stick out ears. No wonder little Algernon was worried.

Mr Teggegh gave Nick the once over before speaking in a very deep voice, 'Can I help you?'

'Is Algernon in?' replied Nick, managing just a little smile.

'And you are?'

'The name's Allen, Nick Allen, it's very important.'

'Are you a friend of Algernon; he's never mentioned you?

'More a friend of a friend, but we have met before.'

But before Mr Teggegh could speak a young girl, about ten-years old, appeared by his side; again, easily recognisable, this must be Algernon's little sister. She had the customary red hair, tied in two bunches and the hereditary stick out ears, which didn't look too bad on her. She gave Nick a big smile which made her look quite attractive. As mentioned earlier Nick had a thing for freckles and this little girl had an abundance of them.

'He's upstairs, I'll take you,' she said before grabbing Nick's hand and tugging him towards the stairs. 'My name is Rudbeckia, but you can call me Becky. Do you have a girlfriend?'

'As a matter of fact, I do,' replied Nick, as he started to ascend the stairs.

'Is she as pretty as me?' asked Becky, in a matter-of-fact tone.

Without thinking, but trying to be nice he replied, 'of course not. I don't think anybody could be prettier than you.'

'Good, then you can chuck her and go out with me.'

I don't believe this, thought Nick, before saying, 'it doesn't work like that, I love my girlfriend and we're very happy. Anyway I'm much too old for you.'

Becky seemed a little upset and replied, 'I bet you don't fancy me because I don't have any breasts, but I will have next year; my mum says I will.'

What is it with this family? thought Nick, as they reached the top of the stairs.

'That's Algernon's room,' said Becky in a sulky tone. She opened the door and shouted, 'someone to see you.'

Nick entered the bedroom; it was a lot bigger than the one he shared with his little brother. He was slightly envious; it had a massive bookcase which covered the whole of one wall. About half of the shelves had books whilst the other half housed all sorts of model cars, aeroplanes and various souvenirs. Algernon was sitting on the edge of the bed dangling a house brick from a piece of string. As he looked up at Nick his face visibly turned the brightest shade of crimson.

'What are you doing?' enquired Nick, resisting the urge to burst out laughing.

'Errm, well I .... I'm doing an experiment, yes, science homework. I have to find the density of a house brick.'

'Of course, silly me,' replied Nick, knowing full well he was lying. Nick remembered this experiment and to find any density you first have to weigh the object – no scales visible. Then find its volume by displacement – no water visible. Of course he could just measure the brick to work out the volume and there was a ruler on the bed; although Nick thought Algernon might have been using it to measure something else.

Pulling himself together Algernon said, 'what are you doing here, what do you want?'

'Information, just some information; tell me what I want to know then I'll be off.'

Algernon smiled, 'information is power.'

Nick shook his head, 'what are you talking about?'

'My dad said, "Information is power. But it is what you do with it that either makes you great or diminishes you".'

'For Christ's sake, I only want to ask you a few questions,' replied Nick, suppressing the urge to give this kid a slap.

'What's it worth?'

Nick counted to ten as he scanned the room and noticed a small pile of rope in the corner. 'How's your knot tying going?'

'Okay, why?'

Nick smiled, 'well I thought, if you were struggling I could teach you how to tie a few. I'm excellent at tying knots.'

Algernon thought for a while before saying, 'okay, you teach me to tie a few knots, and then I might answer your questions.'

Nick walked over and picked the rope up and threw it to Algernon, 'okay, show me what you can do.'

For the next hour Nick immersed himself in teaching Algernon to tie various knots including a Timber hitch, Highwayman's hitch, Bowline and a Sheepshank. The only knots that he could tie before were the Reef Knot, Clove hitch and Round turn and two half-hitches. Despite his reservations, Nick thoroughly enjoyed himself and found Algernon a willing and capable student.

'I think you are a great teacher,' said Algernon after tying a Highwayman's hitch with his eyes shut. 'You should become a teacher when you leave school.'

'Why thank you, the pleasure was all mine. Now it's your turn; tell me the names of the other boys who have been Father John's "special one".'

'Why do you want to know?' asked Algernon.

'Algernon!' said Nick, giving him his best - you don't want to mess with me - look.

'Okay, as far as I can remember there were three before Donald; Patrick Sinclair, Robert Byrne and Paul Logan.'

Paul Logan,' gasped Nick.

'Do you know him,' asked Algernon.

'His name is known to me,' said Nick, not wishing to give anything away. 'Well, thank you Algernon, you've been most helpful.'

'You can call me Al, Ginger Al. Do you get it? Good isn't it?'

Nick chuckled to himself and thought, he's learning. Just as he opened the bedroom door he turned and asked 'has it grown much?'

'Piss off,' replied Algernon, before chucking a copy of *Treasure Island* at Nick's head.

As he reached the bottom of the stairs he noticed Rudbeckia

standing there, arms folded and a face like thunder. He walked over to her, bent down, cupped her face in his hands and gave her a big kiss on the lips and said, 'when you're sixteen, I'll take you out, you beautiful creature.'

With that he opened the front door and left, leaving another girl grinning from ear to ear.

'I didn't know Paul Logan was your cousin,' said a surprised Keith, as they sat in a quiet booth in *Sally's* Inn Café. *You're No Good* by The Swinging Blue Jeans was playing on the Juke Box. 'Why haven't you told us?'

Nick shrugged, 'never really came up, did it.'

'He plays in goal for the scout football team, he's very good,' added Don.

'Of course he is; he's my cousin.'

'So why didn't you mention it?' screamed Keith.

'It's a long story; we don't get on.'

'Well, I think you better tell us now. If we're going interrogate him it would be helpful.'

'Okay. It's a bit like the War of the Roses really, you know, feuding cousins. It's always been like it, as long as I can remember. All I know is that my dad doesn't get on with my uncle Bill and my mum's not too keen on my auntie Anne, that's my dad sister. So it follows that I don't like my cousin Paul. Which is funny really because I get on really well with my other two cousins, Joan and Beth; they're Paul's sisters. I remember when we were young I would be walking towards his house and he would be walking towards me. Then as soon as we met, we would start fighting and then we'd both run home crying to our mums; happy days.'

Keith sat there shaking his head, 'nothing's ever straight forward with you, is it?'

Nick smiled, 'I know, I'm a complicated fellow.'

'So how are we going to approach this?' asked Keith. 'Do you think he'll talk to us?'

'I think this is one interview I need to do on my own and I'm dreading it.'

'Fair enough, but is there anything we can do to speed up the investigation, we're running out of time.'

'You're right of course, let me think. I know, while I'm seeing my estranged cousin why don't you two go and have a chat with Patrick and Robert. You know where they live Don, don't you?

'Of course,' said Don excitedly. 'They both live on the New Greens Estate, should be easy to find. Yeah, leave it to us.'

Excellent, so hopefully by tomorrow we'll have enough evidence to bring this rampant priest down.'

'So, changing the subject,' said Keith. 'Have you heard from Moira?'

'Funny you should ask that, I received a letter this morning.'

'Where did you say she went?'

'She's staying in a caravan at the St. Osyth Beach Estate in Clacton.'

'Is she having a nice time?'

'I think so; she said she's missing me ....'

'Of course.'

'.....but she had another row with Dypmna. She said she was sitting on one side of the bed writing this letter, whilst Dympna was on the other playing Patience.'

'Huh, why can't a woman be more like a man?'

'Good title for a song.'

'Have you heard for Big Brenda,' asked Don.

'Yeah, I got a postcard this week, She's having a nice time, said she went on a trip to Pompeii. It was quite enjoyable, but a bit boring at times. She said there were parts that her parents wouldn't let her see for some unknown reason and the House of Faun didn't have any amusements, just mosaics and statues.'

Nick laughed and then he noticed that someone had put *Hey Paul* by Paul and Paula, on the Juke Box. 'Listen they're playing our song.'

'I didn't know we had a song,' replied Keith.

'Not you, you pratt, Moira. It's our song; we change the names and sing it to each other.' Nick started singing – '"Hey, hey Moira, I wanna marry you. Hey, hey Moira, no one else will ever do. I've waited so long, for school to be through. Moira I can't wait no more for you. My love, my love." And then she would sing the next verse using my name.'

Keith was shaking his head, 'God that is sooo soppy.'

'What do you sing to Brenda, then Keith?' asked Don. 'I've got a lovely Bunch of Coconuts.'

'I don't think coconuts grow that big,' laughed Nick.

At that point Anna walked over to clear their table.

'Hello, Anna,' said Nick. 'Can I say how beautiful you look today?'

'That's very sweet of you,' replied Anna, in an unusually friendly tone. 'Actually Nick, I dreamt of you last night.'

'Did you?' replied Nick, getting a little excited.

She leant forward a little, and whispered 'oh yes, I dreamt of your body.'

Nick was now speechless.

She leant forward even more; Nick could smell her perfume, *4711 Eau de Cologne,* and then said 'I dreamt the police asked me to identify it.' With that she walked away laughing.

'Stupid cow,' remarked Keith.

Nick smiled to himself, turned his head to look at Anna. As he caught her eye she smiled and with a single finger, blew him a kiss.

Nick turned back to his friends and said, 'she's just playing hard to get.'

Thursday 27 August

Nick had instructed Keith and Don to search out Robert Byrne and Patrick Sinclair after lunch; he thought there would be a good chance to catch them before they go out for the afternoon. He would do the same for his cousin.

Paul Logan lived in the same road as Nick; actually it was only twelve doors away. Thinking of the best way to approach his estranged cousin, he failed to notice Paul as he walked mindlessly towards him. Paul mumbled 'hello' as their shoulders brushed.

Coming to his senses Nick shouted, 'Paul, have you got a minute, I need to ask you something.'

Looking down his nose, he replied, 'I'm in a hurry, make it quick.'

'There's no need for animosity, I just want to help you.'

Looking confused, Paul said, 'who says I need help?'

'Where are you off to?' asked Nick, trying to break the ice.

'If you must know, I meeting some mates up the town, then we are going to the flicks.'

'That's nice, what are you going to see?'

'633 *Squadron*, it's showing at the Odeon.'

'Good film, I'll walk with you.'

Paul gave a sigh, 'if you must, but what's this all about?'

'It's a bit sensitive, but I've been told that you used to be Father John's special one.'

This stopped Paul in his tracks, 'how do you know that?'

'I have my sources.'

'Anyway what's that got to do with you,' replied Paul as he started walking again.

'Did anything happen?'

'I don't know what you mean.'

Nick grabbed Paul's shoulder and said, 'I think you know exactly what I mean. Did things happen that shouldn't have happened? I want to help you.'

Paul went very sheepish before saying, in a low voice, 'no one can help me.'

'Maybe, maybe not, but whatever happened to you was wrong, very wrong. And I want to see that bastard punished.'

Paul started to walk away, 'what can you do?'

'Obviously you don't know me as well as you should.'

Paul thought for a moment, 'I have heard rumors, but they all sounded a bit far-fetched to me.'

'Look, just tell me what you can; I'm the soul of discretion. I just need to know what we are dealing with.'

They walked a little way before Paul stopped and sat on the wall of Moira's front garden. Nick sat down beside him, but said nothing.

''It was awful,' Paul was fighting back the tears. 'At first everything was fun, I felt special. Father John would give me sweets and small presents; I would help around the church doing little jobs. Like tidying up the prayer and hymn books and making sure the flowers were okay. But then he started touching me. At first he said he was checking my development, measuring my thighs and calves; then it was other parts. After one particular scout football match I was covered in mud. There were no changing facilities; we just turned up in our kit. Well, he said I couldn't go home like that and suggested I went back to his place for a bath. Thinking nothing of it I agreed. Anyway while I was in the bath he came in and offered to wash my back. I said I was okay, but he insisted and grabbed the sponge. He then told me to stand up so he could wash me properly.'

Nick could tell Paul was struggling; he gave him a gentle hug and told him he was doing well. Paul continued, 'When he had finished I got out of the bath and he fetched a towel and insisted that he wiped me dry. Then I asked him "where are my clothes"? Father John said they were too dirty to put back on, but he had some spare ones downstairs. Then he said that he fancied a bath and it was only fair that I washed him down. It was horrible; I had to wash every part of him. Then he appeared to slip into a trance, and then he said, "I've been talking to Jesus." and he says "Would you like to go to heaven?" Then he asked, "Do you love your mummy?" Yes Father, I replied. "Do you love your daddy?" Yes Father. "Do you love me? Because this is our secret and you mustn't tell your mummy or daddy or you will go to the burning fire."'

Paul stopped, dropped his head into his hands and wept. Nick could feel to rage burning inside of him and vowed to himself that he would take this priest down, if it was the last thing he ever did.

'Okay Paul, wipe your eyes and go and meet your mates and leave Father John to me.'

Paul stood up, managed a small smile, said 'thanks' and walked off.

Friday 28 August

'I'm looking forward to this,' said Nick, as the three boys walked past the *Jolly Sailor* public house and crossed the road to Sandpit Lane.

'Yeah, it could be fun,' replied Keith. Don didn't comment.

They had heard, through the grapevine, that the St. Saviour's Youth Club was holding a dance in the parish hall in Culver Road. With Moira and Brenda both due back from holiday this weekend the boys had decided to enjoy their last nights of freedom. After paying a small entrance fee the boys walked through to the small hall. There was a reasonable crowd; most of the boys were standing in small groups, chatting away, whilst a few girls danced in circles around a small pile of handbags. *It's All Over Now* by the Rolling Stones was playing on a turntable situated on the stage and monitored by a rather young looking vicar. For a few minutes they just stood there taking in the surroundings, before they were approached by a rather attractive girl. She was of medium height, pretty, with straight shoulder length blonde hair, parted in the centre. Nick thought she looked nice in her short tartan skirt and plain yellow long sleeved, round neck jumper.

'Haven't seen you here before,' she said, in a slightly squeaky voice.

The three boys all smiled before Nick said, 'no, it's our first time.'

'That's nice; we like to see new members. We do lots of wonderful things; the vicar here is very progressive, not starchy like other vicars. He cares about the youth of today.'

'Is that him playing the records?' asked Keith.

The girl looked up at the stage, 'yes, that's him; isn't he wonderful. He buys all the latest records.'

'He certainly does,' replied Nick, as the Manfred Mann blasted out *Do Wah Diddy Diddy*.

'Wonderful,' beamed the girl. 'How rude of me, I haven't introduced myself. My name is Sonia, and you are?'

'My name is Nick, this is Keith and he is Don.'

'Wonderful; well I hope you have a lovely time,' she smiled and walked away.

'I'm sure we will,' replied Nick.

'Wonderful,' said Keith and Don in unison.   Nick burst out laughing.

'Cor, she's a bit of alright,' said Keith.

'I think she's wond… ….,'

'Don't say it,' laughed Nick and Keith.

'Well if all the girls are that friendly we should have a wond.., sorry, great time,' said Don.

The boys decided to check out the rest of the building; there was a room where a couple of boys were playing table tennis and a kitchen where another attractive girl was serving soft drinks.

'I fancy a coke, anyone else? My treat,' said Keith.

Before either Nick or Don could answer Keith had pushed his way to the counter. It didn't take a genius to figure out why. The girl serving was small in stature with blonde, piled up hair and wearing a very low-cut dress. A fair amount of cleavage was on show; an excellent way to increase sales. Nick thought that Keith was taking rather a long time and was about to join him when a sharp-suited bloke in a button-down collared shirt approached Keith. His greasy hair was in a Tony Curtis style, a relic from the fifties. After a brief conversation Keith returned with three bottles of coke.

'You okay, mate?' asked Nick.

'No problem; I was just chatting to that bird and that thug said I was holding up the queue.'

'But there was no-one behind you,' said Don.

'He obviously fancies her,' said Nick. 'I think we might have to be a little careful who we talk to. Don't want to upset the natives.'

'Might be difficult,' added Don, as he noticed the buxom serving girl smiling at Keith. 'They're all so friendly.'

They finished their drinks and left the kitchen.

'I wonder what's in this room?' asked Don, as he opened the door to a dimly lit, very smoky room. The boys looked in; the room was illuminated by candles. A group of youths, a lot older than them, about eighteen or nineteen years old, were sitting on old, battered sofas; others were sitting on rugs on the floor. Boys and girls all smoking, there was a strange, unfamiliar smell.

'Hey man, wanna join us,' said a male voice from the crowd.

'You can sit with me, gorgeous,' said a sultry female voice.

Don started coughing; Keith pulled out his handkerchief and covered his nose and mouth.

'Thanks,' said Nick, 'another time, perhaps.' With that the three boys left the room.

Don still coughing, walked towards the exit, stuck his hand out for the attendant to stamp it and ran out into the fresh air. Nick and Keith followed him. Outside Nick and Keith waited for Don to stop coughing, before Keith asked, 'what were they smoking?'

'Reefers, I think,' replied Nick.

'I thought a reefer was a type of jacket,' said Don.

'I thought it was a type of ship,' added Keith.

'Yes, yes, you're both right; but a reefer is a slang term for marijuana. I can't believe they were smoking dope in a church hall. What would the vicar say?'

Keith chuckled, 'well Sonia said the vicar was progressive.'

'Well you'll never get me taking drugs. That's for sure,' added Don.

'No, nor would I,' said Keith, as he looked at Nick, who was deep in thought, 'Oh no not again.'

'What is it?' asked Don.

'Look, Nick's thinking. That means only one thing.'

Nick smiled, 'I wonder where they get the drugs from. Who's their supplier?'

'Dare I ask, why do you want to know?'

Nick was now grinning from ear to ear, 'DI James said there was a drugs problem in St. Albans. Maybe we can help him find out who the supplier is.'

'You mean, flush out Mr Big,' enthused Don.

'I don't know about that, but I'm sure we could give him a lead or two.'

'And how do you propose to do that?' asked Keith.

'We go back in there, talk to the natives and see what they know.'

'That could be dangerous, that teddy-boy didn't look too friendly.'

'I agree, but the crumpet in there seems very friendly. I suggest we put ourselves about, chat up the girls, have a few dances, you know how girls love to talk. By the end of the evening we should have enough information to take to the police.'

'Great idea,' said Keith. 'And think of all the fun we'll have getting it.'

With renewed vigor the boys returned to the hall to the sounds of Chuck Berry singing *No Particular Place to Go*. Nick was pleased to see so many kids dancing, he also noticed Sonia dancing with three other girls.

Nick whispered to Don and Keith, 'listen, when the next slow record comes on, we'll ask those girls for a dance.'

Don said, 'but there are four of them and only three of us. One of them will be left out.'

'Does it matter,' said Keith. 'The ugly one must be used to it.'

'Actually if you look, there isn't an ugly one,' said Nick.

Taking a second look, Keith said, 'you're right, that's a problem.'

'I know,' said Nick. 'Let's do it the other way. Which one is the best looking?'

The group consisted of Sonia, who Nick was definitely going for; the busty girl from the refreshment stall, an attractive girl wearing a dark blue sleeveless dress with a high collar, but the one standing out was the fourth girl. Nick thought she looked a bit like Mandy Rice-Davies, blonde, immaculate make-up, a white mini dress and white boots.

'Right,' said Nick, 'this is the plan. I'll take Sonia, Keith, the refreshment girl and Don you take the girl in the blue dress.'

'Sounds good,' replied Keith.

'So what's the theory behind this?' asked Don.

'The one's we've chosen would have expected at least one of us to have asked the other girl first. This will make them feel special and be flattered that we chose them instead of her.'

The boys didn't have to wait long, the vicar, who seemed to be enjoying himself, announced that it was time to slow things down. The boys moved in and before Eric Burdon could sing the first line of *House of the Rising Sun*, all three boys were in the arms of their chosen girl. The Mandy look-a-like seemed stunned, standing alone, but was soon snapped up by some spotty youth wearing thick glasses and sporting a Val Doonigan type jumper.

The *House of the Rising Sun* was over four minutes long which gave the boys plenty of time to chat-up the girls. All three were in deep conversation when, all of a sudden the lights went out. Simultaneously the girls started snogging the boys; this went on for about thirty seconds before the lights came back on and the girls pulled away. The boys had just about composed themselves and re-ignited the conversation when the lights went out again with the same result. When the record finished the girls pulled away, said thank you and rejoined their friends.

The boys found three empty chairs and sat down.

Don was the first to speak, 'that was different.'

'Did you find anything out about the drugs?' asked Nick.

'Bugger the drugs; I could get high on her kisses. She must be the world's best kisser,' gasped Keith.

'What?' asked Nick, pretending to be surprised. 'You actually like a girl for something else apart from her tits.'

'Maybe; but I could still feel them pressing into my chest, and she smelt like heaven.'

'How was it for you, Don?' asked Nick.

'Much better than a Catholic youth club; can you imagine the Nuns allowing that? They would throw a bucket of water over you and all the girls would be sent off to the workhouse.'

There was a silence for a few minutes, each boy lost in his own thoughts. It was only when Nick recognized that another slow record was playing, that he jumped up and said, 'kissing time.'

As Jim Reeves started singing *I Love You Because* the boys noticed that their last dance partners had been taken. Looking around they also noticed that most girls were paired off. Out of the corner of his eye Nick noticed three girls standing by the stage looking in their direction. Don had also noticed.

'What about those three?' asked Don.

'No chance,' replied Keith, 'I have standards.'

Nick had to admit that these girls weren't in the same class of their last partners. Although he couldn't clearly see their faces, they were definitely not 'followers of fashion'. Nick guessed that they were the ones that actually went to church as they were dressed in very dull conservative clothes.

'I have an idea,' said Nick, indicating that they should sit down.

'We missed out there,' said Keith.

'Listen, we'll wait till the next slow one, and then ask those three by the stage.'

'Surely we could find better ones,' commented Keith.

'Trust me; remember what I said earlier, these girls will be really grateful, especially if we ask them first. Also they may not want to let us go and they may tell us a few things. One thing I've learnt about church going girls – they love to gossip and they are usually very randy.'

Reluctantly Keith agreed. Don was happy as he preferred nice girls. It seemed ages before the next slow record hit the turntable. It appeared that the vicar was definitely a big Rock 'n Roll fan. Nick was just about to have a word with him when he recognized the opening bars to DIonne Warwick's *You'll Never Get To Heaven*.

'Let's Go.'

The girls looked both surprised and delighted as the three boys approached them and didn't need to be asked twice. In fact they didn't really need to ask once as they were up and in the arms of their chosen beaus before the end of the first line. Nick's had noticed that his chosen girl was actually quite pretty beneath her National Health glasses and rather old fashion hair style. It was difficult to start a conversation as the girl had wrapped her arms around him and buried her head deep into his shoulder. Then the lights went out. Nick braced himself. In a micro-second the girls lips were glued to his, her tongue was darting in and out of his mouth. Her hands grabbed his bottom as she thrust her hips into his. The lights went on, she released him – slightly. Instead of burying her head again, she looked him in the eye and smiled. Nick kissed her on the forehead. As Nick had predicted, when the record ended, the girls didn't walk away; they grabbed the boy's hand and sat them down, then sat on their laps.

Nick's girl was called Nicola Swallow and attended the Girls Grammar School; she was smart, funny and very good company. After about ten minutes of general conversation Nick just happened to mention the smoking room. Nicola was very forthright in her views on that subject. She was dead against drugs of any kind and was appalled that the vicar allowed them to smoke those things in the youth club. Nick asked her who those boys and girls were. She told him that they all attended the College of Further Education and she didn't know who supplied the weed, but it definitely wasn't the vicar. Concluding that Nicola had told him all she knew, he decided that what he needed was a bit more snogging.

At 9.50pm the vicar announced that the evening was about end and if the boys would grab their partners he would play the last record. Nick was delighted, his favourite singer Cilla Black was to sing *Anyone Who Had a Heart*. It had been a pleasant evening and Nick tenderly held Nicola in his arms before saying goodnight and joining Keith and Don for the walk home.

They stood outside for a while, taking in the cool night air.

'I fancy a bag of chips,' said Don, 'with lots of salt and vinegar.'

'I think my lips have gone numb,' replied Keith. 'Boy; was she a kisser.'

'Was I right or was I right,' said a smiling Nick.

The boys walked in silence to the end of Culver Road and turned right into Sandpit Lane. At the junction with Sandridge Road they crossed the road and turned left towards the *Jolly Sailor* public house.

'I think we're being followed,' whispered Nick. The three boys suddenly stopped and turned around. He was right, only a few yards behind were four boys. Nick recognized the leader, the

Teddy boy who didn't like Keith. He may have seen the other three at the dance.

'Can we help you?' asked Nick.

'I don't like your face,' said the Teddy boy.

'Then don't look at it,' replied Nick.

'Don't get smart with me sunshine, just stay away from the club.'

'It's a free country and God welcomes all to his church … … … and his church hall.'

'I think he's jealous, he thinks we'll pinch all the girls. Not our fault that the girls find us more attractive than him,' said Keith, mockingly.

'Who dresses like him, so yesterday,' added Don, sarcastically.

Nick thought, are they trying to wind him up, because if they are, it's working. He was also worried because he had heard that Teddy boys always carried knives. He was right; the boy pulled out a flick-knife. Nick took one step back, and then allowed the Teddy boy to approach. Nick kept an eye on the knife, waiting for the right moment. He was holding the knife in front of him, but quite low, at waist height; perfect. Then without warning he took a kick that connected with the boy's hand sending the knife spinning into the air. The boy turned his head to follow the flying knife; big mistake as Nick sent a thumping right hand which connected square on the boy's chin. The other three boys just starred open-mouths, then turned and ran away as the Teddy boy hit the ground. As the boys turned away to continue their journey to *Warwick's* Fish and Chip shop in Catherine Street they were surprised to see that a small group of drinkers had gathered to watch the rumpus.

'Nice punch,' said an old man, puffing on his pipe.

'Well done,' said another. 'I can't stand Teddy boys.'

Suitably embarrassed the boys' mumbled thank you and walked quickly away.

Saturday 29 August

The boys had decided to have a wander round the market before their de-briefing in *Sally's Inn* Café later in the morning. Their favourite stall was situated outside *W.H.Smith's*. The stall holder sold a vast variety of household goods. He would shout out the price and say how wonderful the items were to the small gathered crowd, before reducing the price again and again until someone purchased it. He would moan to the crowd, telling them how they couldn't recognize a bargain if it bit them on the nose. If sales were slow he would bellow at his assistant, a puny boy in glasses; could it be his son? They stayed there for about fifteen minutes; Nick purchased a tin of *Cussons Imperial Leather* talcum powder. Keith needed a new shirt, so they made a quick visit to *Jefferson's* Clothes Shop before making their weekly visit to the Record Room. Nick wanted to buy Bob Dylan's *The Times They Are A-Changin'*. On their way back, as they walked past *Burtons* the tailors, they bumped into Nick's friend Ernie Tomkins, 'Hi Nick, what are you up to?' 'Oh, the usual Saturday morning shopping spree,' replied Nick. 'What are you doing? Not buying another suit?

'As it happens, I've just been measured up for a new one; navy blue, three buttons, side vents and sixteen inch bottoms; the business.'

'It's alright for some, wish I could afford a made-to-measure suit,' said Nick, feeling slightly jealous.

Ernie smiled, 'how many times have I told you, dump the schooling and get a job. I'm quids in.'

'Yeah, but a new suit will still knock you back a few bob.'

'No problem, they let you pay it off; thirty bob a week. No sweat.'

'There are two things my mum disagrees with, one, buying things on the never-never and two, me leaving school early.'

'Shame, because the birds really go for a smartly dressed bloke. I'll be fighting them off.'

'I can't argue with that. I'll just have to rely on my sparkling personality and my big knob.'

Ernie burst out laughing, 'must have grown a lot since the last time I saw it.'

'He's been looking at it through a magnifying glass,' added Keith.

Nick blushed and laughed with his friends, before saying goodbye to Ernie. They proceeded through the market until they reached the flower stall. Nick bought a bunch of flowers for his mum, before visiting their favourite coffee bar. After purchasing their usual milkshakes they sat in a booth to discuss last night events.

'Well that was certainly a great night, I think I've doubled my kissing minutes in one evening,' said Don, still grinning from ear to ear.

'And what are your views, Mr Nevin?' enquired Nick.

'There maybe something said about small breasted girls. I definitely think they are much better snoggers; I expect they practice more. I've actually heard that they practice on each other,' replied Keith.

'So, you three have actually managed to find a girl to kiss, then. Where did you find these unfortunates?' asked Anna, the waitress, who was just passing and overheard their conversation.

'We went to a dance last night and they were queuing up to kiss us,' said Don.

'And where was this, at the Blind school? laughed Anna.

'Jealousy is such a sad emotion, now go away and clear some tables,' added Keith.

Anna shrugged her shoulders and walked away.

'She's gagging for it,' continued Keith. 'Have you noticed how she's always hanging around our table when we come here?'

'She just doesn't know which of us she fancies most,' added Don.

'You may be right Don, but let's get down to more important stuff. Keith, did you get anything out of your girl last night? What was here name? asked Nick.

'Pauline, her name was Pauline and yes, I have some useful information.' Keith paused.

'Go on then, tell us.'

'Well, according to Pauline, all those druggies, including the girls attend the F.E. College.'

'I know that, anything else?'

Slightly put out, Keith continued. 'But more importantly, they are all on the same course. They are all studying Economics.'

'That's progress; so is there a link between Economics classes and the dope?' pondered Nick.

'Actually, there is,' said Don. 'My little beauty, her name is Barbara, told me her brother was in that room. She said that they nicked the weed from their teacher. Apparently, he's a bit of a lad and he invites the students round to his house for social evenings. He always has a cupboard full of booze, but the other day when they were round there; they found a stash of weed hidden under a sofa. So they nicked it.'

'Did she tell you the teacher's name?' asked Nick.

'Actually they're not teachers, they are Lecturers,' said Don.

'Whatever, did she give you his name?'

'Yes.'

'And?'

'Oh, yes, his name is Julian Harrison and he lives in Charmouth Road.'

'Fantastic, well done, Don, we'll give this information to DI James and then he'll owe us a favour; and I hate that name.'

'What, Harrison?' asked Don.

'No, you pratt, Julian. Always makes me think of in-breds with no chins from Harpenden, or as we say in St Albans – Luton South; they're always called Julian.'

'Bit hard, but true' agreed Keith.

'Who are Spurs playing this afternoon?' asked Don, changing the subject.

'Away to Everton, hard game, I'll settle for a point,' replied Nick.

'Talking of football, don't you think we should join a youth team? Otherwise we'll just be playing school matches,' said Keith.

'Yes, you're right. I've been so wrapped up in our investigations I've overlooked that. Did you have any team in mind?'

'Not really, what teams are available?' replied Keith.

'Let me think; the obvious one is Carlton Youth.'

'I had thought of them, but it's a bit of a clique, being connected to St Albans City F.C.'

'I think Townsend Rovers would be our best bet. Others that spring to mind are Welwyn Garden City, Ludwick and Bennetts End. But that means travelling out of town.'

'Okay, that's settled. When we've solved these two cases, and we will solve them, we'll put ourselves first for a change.'

'Right, now let's get onto the important stuff. I had no problem locating my cousin, he literally walked into me.' Nick then proceeded to convey the information gained, and then asked, 'how did you get on?'

Keith answered, 'no problem, we visited Patrick first, he lives in Frances Avenue. He was reluctant at first to speak, but we eventually managed to persuade him to open up.'

'Only after you threatened to tell his schoolmates that he was a homo,' said Don.

Keith just smiled, Nick said, 'you learning.'

'Anyway,' Keith continued, 'once we got him alone and explained that we were just trying to help, he eventually told us everything. I think he was relieved after telling us.'

'It was like a weight had been lifted off his shoulders,' added Don.

'But what did he say?' asked Nick.

'Very much the same as your cousin said. It seems that the priest has a thing for bathing with young boys. '

'What about Robert?'

'Again, very reluctant to talk, but once we mentioned Paul and Patrick, he spilled the beans.'

'Well, that's it. I think we have enough evidence to be rid of this turbulent priest.'

Don said, 'are you sure we are doing the right thing?'

Nick shook his head before replying, 'of course we are. We can't allow Father John to continue whatever he's doing to young boys. Look how it affected you. Anyway, any sort of sexual act between men is illegal and bloody disgusting.'

'Suppose, when you put it like that.'

'Well, boys, we seem to have fallen upon evil days.'

There was a pause for a minute while the boys digested the information. It was Nick who broke the silence, 'Did you hear about the fete at Sandridge last week? They reckon over 1000 people attended.'

'I heard that,' replied Keith. 'I also heard that there was a kissing tent and some girl was selling kisses for 1/- a time.'

Don laughed, 'just think, if those girls last night were charging for their kisses, we would be bankrupt '

'Also,' Nick continued, 'they had some kind of beauty contest to find the Youth Club Queen. Some girl called Lynda Reynolds won it and if my memory serves me correct, Anita Westrope came second and Sandra Jelly came third.'

'Do you know any of them? asked Keith.

'No, but I know Sandra's Brother Dave. Anyway I think we should start attending the Sandridge Youth Club; could be fun.'

WEEK 4
Sunday 30 August -
Saturday 5 September 1964

Sunday 30 August

Nick was not in a good mood as he read, for the second time the Spurs match report in the *News of the World*. How the hell had they lost 4-1 away to Everton. Three games played and only 3 points out of a possible six; just not good enough. A knock on the front door instantly raised his spirits; Moira was back from her holiday. He rushed to open it and was ecstatic to see his girlfriend looking even lovelier than when he last saw her.

'Missed me?' she asked, with a half-smile on her face.

'You'll never know how much,' he replied, embracing her with all the love he could muster. 'Come in, come in, did you have a nice time? Tell me all about it.'

It was another sunny day so the young couple made their way to the back garden and made themselves comfortable on the lawn. After telling Nick all about her holiday, she was keen to enquire on how the investigation was going.

'To be honest, we've come to a bit of a stand-still. I interviewed Dorothy Whitehouse and she told me that for a few weeks before Eddie committed suicide he was hanging out with a chap called Michael. She never saw him and she didn't know his surname. Don thinks he's someone who worked with him at Marlboro Motors. We have a name but haven't got round to checking him out yet. We'll have to soon; we're back at school next week.'

'So what was she like?'

'Bloody scary; she only came on to me. I couldn't get out of there quick enough.'

'You mean to tell me that the sex-mad Nick Allen spurred the advances of an older woman, what is the world coming to?'

Nick wasn't sure if she was joking or not and decided to play it safe, 'why would I look at another woman when I have you?'

Moira laughed and said, 'right answer,' as she gave him another cuddle. 'Now I'm back, where are you going to take me this afternoon?

'I thought you might ask that, so as a special treat we are going to see the much anticipate film, *A Hard Day's Night.*'

'Oh,' exclaimed Moira 'that's fantastic, but we'll need to go early to make sure we get in.'

'No problem, it's showing at the *Odeon* at 4.00pm, so if we get there at 3.00pm we should be okay and you can tell me all about your holiday.'

'Good idea, but I want to see this film, so don't expect me to start snogging you as soon as the lights go out.'

'Message understood.'

'I love you, Nick Allen.'

Monday 31 August

Michael Brown looked into the mirror and gave his hair a final adjustment. Big date tonight, he thought to himself. He had arranged to take a girl, Sally Ridgeway, to the pictures and he was definitely on a promise. Unfortunately it would have to be in the back of his car which could be a bit uncomfortable. His favourite spot was the car park behind the *Chequers* cinema, next to the public baths. He really wished he had a place of his own, being 28 years old and still living at home with his parents was a bit embarrassing. Although he never had a problem pulling the birds, he'd never found one that he wanted to settle down with. Except Ruth Woodstock; she was perfect, but for some unknown reason she couldn't stand him. It baffled him, he was always friendly towards her and for some strange reason she had made a complaint about him. To this day he didn't know what he had supposed to have done. He could have really treated her well, especially with all the extra dosh he was pulling in from his little sideline.

'You haven't told us how we are going to handle this,' said Keith, as they dismounted their bicycles at the entrance to Springfield Road. 'We can't just knock on his door and ask him if he kidnapped a boy five years ago,'

'I know that; that's why it's taken me a few days to think this out. Ruth reckoned that he was on the fiddle, so how?' replied Nick.

Don was the first to answer, 'if he works in the stores he must be nicking parts and selling then on the quiet.'

'Exactly; that's what I thought. So I phoned Ruth again for some extra information and she told me that Michael drinks at the *Camp* pub. Well he would, it's only across the road. As it happens my dad was playing darts at the *Camp* on Thursday night and he made a few discreet enquires. Apparently it's an open secret that Michael sells car parts on the side.'

'So,' said Keith, exasperated, 'we're going round to his house to buy car parts.'

'Exactly.'

'I hope you know what you are doing,' replied Keith shaking his head.

They quickly found Michael's house, an unimpressive 1930s pebble dashed three bedroom council house, which was painted white. Nick felt nervous as they walked down the unkempt front garden and knocked on the tired looking front door. Within a minute a smart looking man who the boys presumed was Michael Brown answered.

'What do you want?' said Michael, looking down his nose.

As it turned out, Michael was a good looking man and reminded Nick of the villain Charlie Richardson. Not someone you would mess with.

'Sorry to bother you sir, but a friend told me you might be able to help me. I need a starter motor for a 1955 Vauxhall Velox.'

'You're not old enough to drive,' replied Michael.

Nick laughed, 'no flies on you, sir. It's a long story, but my granddad died recently and he left his car to me. It's in a bit of a state so I'm doing it up. I save up my pocket money to buy parts. It's an expensive hobby, but a friend of mine said you may be able to help me.'

Michael thought for a while before saying, 'well it's a bit inconvenient, I was just going out, but if we're quick. We'll need to have a look in my shed.'

Michael opened the wooden side gate and led them down the garden path to a large corrugated shed. He took a key out of his pocket and unlocked the padlock. Inside the shed were shelves and shelves of car parts. Compared to what he had seen so far, this shed was the tidiest part of Michael's house. After a few minutes of searching Michael had to admit that he didn't have that particular part. This came as a surprise to Nick as he thought that there were enough parts to build a brand new Vauxhall Velox. Nick was disappointed, but then remembered that he didn't actually want a starter motor and almost certainly not enough money on him to buy one.

Putting on a brave face Michael apologized and said that he could get one by the weekend. Nick thanked him and said he would call back next week. It was now time for Keith to act. As they left the shed he said, 'my dad used to have a friend who worked at *Marlboro' Motors*. Eddie Reynolds, do you remember him?'

'Oh yeah, I remember him, topped himself. Weird bloke, bit creepy, couldn't stand him,' said Michael.

'Not a friend of yours, then,' replied Nick.

'Certainly not, he used to hang out with another weird bloke at work, Billy Watkins. They were a very strange couple. It wouldn't have surprised me if they weren't bum-bandits.'

'I thought Eddie was engaged to be married,' said Keith.

Michael laughed, 'I think if I was engaged to her, I'd turn queer; very strange girl, why all the questions?'

'I was just interested when my dad mentioned suicide, can't understand why someone would do that.'

That seemed to satisfy Michael and the boys said goodbyes and promised to call back next week

As they cycled home, Keith said, 'I think we can rule him out,'

A despondent Don replied, 'sorry, I just thought....'

'Don't be silly,' interrupted Nick. 'It was a good call; we have to check out every lead. We can't expect to get it right first time.'

'Suppose not.'

'But, look on the bright side we have uncovered a crook.'

'You're not thinking of reporting him, are you?' asked Keith, suspiciously.

'Did you see how many parts he had in that garage, he obviously nicked them?'

'So he's a little light-fingered, but think of all the money he's saving his mates. Times are hard; he's the new Robin Hood, stealing from the rich to help the poor.'

'You're joking, what did Macmillan say, "Indeed let us be frank about it - most of our people have never had it so good." He's a crook and he's going down.'

They cycled for a while, and then Keith said, 'you're doing this in spite, just because he slapped that girl's arse.'

Nick mumbled, 'might be.'

'Have you seen her arse?' asked Keith, and then shouted 'you bloody well have, haven't you?'

'Not in the flesh, she was wearing a skirt, 'replied Nick sheepishly.

'You don't miss a trick, do you?'

'I like to know if it was worth protecting.'

'How did you know it was her?'

'There's not many women working in the garage, it didn't take much to find her.'

'What's she like then?'

Nick perked up, 'bloody gorgeous, dark blonde, almost golden wavy hair, nice arse and a fine pair of tits; definitely worth protecting.'

'Okay, do your worst. I'll leave this one to you,' sighed Keith.

Tuesday 1 September

Having no luck with Michael Brown, the three boys decided to have a meeting at Nick's house to discuss their next move. Mrs Allen had made a pot of tea and was busy buttering toast and smothering it with marmalade.

'Okay lads, time is running out and we are nowhere near identifying the illusive Michael,' said a despondent Nick. 'We need to put our heads together and have a really good think. Who would know who he is?'

It was Mrs Allen who broke the silence, 'the way I see it, the only person who knew him, apart from Billy Watkins was his fiancé. She must have said something to indicate where they went or who they hung around with.'

Nick thought for a while before saying, 'she did say they used to go to the *Farmer's Boy*, he may have gone there with Michael.'

Keith nodded and said, 'good point, I think we should pay the pub a little visit. I like going to pubs, we always have laugh.'

'Not until I finished my toast, absolutely delicious, Mrs Allen,' remarked Don.

The boys arrived at the *Farmers Boy*, a 'spit and sawdust' public house in London Road at 11.30am and confidently walked into the bar. The landlord, a pleasant looking man smiled and said, 'you're a bit young to be frequenting public houses.'

'This is not a social call, Sir but we'll have three lemonades if that's alright?' replied Nick.

The landlord smiled, 'never turn a customer away, so what can I do for you?'

'We need to ask you a few questions, but first, were you working in here five years ago?

'Yes I was; I'm the landlord and you can call me Mr Roach,' said the landlord as he unscrewed the top off a bottle of R White's Lemonade.

The boys each took a sip of their lemonade before Nick asked, 'do you remember a customer called Eddie Reynolds?'

Mr Roach frowned then answered, 'I remember him; he used to come in quite regularly with his girlfriend. He's dead now, why are asking?'

'It's a bit of a delicate matter, but we are trying to locate a friend of his called Michael, would you remember him? asked Nick, hopefully.

Mr Roach scratched his head, the said, 'can't say I remember him. The only friend he had that I remember was a chap called Billy Watkins. He comes in here sometimes at lunchtime, you could ask him.'

Keith gave a little cough, 'I think we'll give him a miss, we have spoken to him, and he wasn't very cooperative.'

'Yes I've heard he's got a bit of a temper, said Mr Roach. 'I'm sorry I can't help you, but go and sit in the window, drink your lemonade and I'll get on serving the next customer.'

The boys made themselves comfortable, before Don said, 'I like it here, nice and friendly, just as a pub should be.'

'Before the war, my dad used to come in here Sunday lunchtimes and play darts,' said Nick. 'I've lost count how many times he's told me this story. They used to get a lot of top players in here and they used to play for half a pint of beer. You would put your name up on the board and when it was your turn, you would play the winner of the last game. The loser had to buy the winner a beer and the winner stayed on. Well, my dad and his mate put their names down; they played pairs, 301, double on and double off. There were about five or six names down after theirs, when it was their turn. Anyway, my dad's mate threw first and he got double eighteen, triple twenty, triple twenty; that left my dad 145. With his first dart he hit the treble seventeen, which left him 94. Is second dart scored 54, treble eighteen; which left him 40, double top. As you guessed, he hit the double top with his third dart. A six dart finish. All of a sudden, all the names were rubbed off the board, no one else would play them; classic'

The boys were enjoying themselves so much that they failed to notice any of the lunchtime crowd that had assembled. It was only when the landlord came over and recommended that they left did they noticed Billy Watkins standing at the bar.

'I don't want any trouble,' said Mr. Roach.

'Nor do we,' replied Nick.

'I'm surprised you let him in here' said Don.

'You wouldn't if you knew what he was really like,' added Keith.

At that point Billy just happened to turn round to see who the landlord was talking to. It took him a few moments to register who the boys were. Nick finished his drink and stood up, Keith and Don followed suit. It was reminiscent of a scene from the film High Noon as Billy stood there staring at the three boys. With the confidence of safety in numbers the boys didn't flinch. It was Billy who cracked; he turned and ran out of the pub.

'What was that all about?' gasped the Mr. Roach.

'We may be young,' said a confident Don, 'but you don't want to mess with us.'

'Thank you for your hospitality landlord, but we must take our leave,' said Nick, as the three boys exited the pub.

'Well that didn't lead to much,' sighed Keith, as the boys mounted their bicycles.

'But it was fun, are there any other pubs we should visit?' remarked Don.

'In St. Albans?' replied Nick. 'There are loads of them; when we are older we'll make it a project to visit every one of them. But now I think we need to sort out Father John. I have a plan, so let's go back home and start planning.'

Mrs. Allen had offered to make the boys fish finger sandwiches for lunch and by the time they walked into kitchen they were famished.

'They won't be long,' said Mrs. Allen, as she buttered the bread. 'Go in the living room and talk to your brother, something's wrong with him and he won't tell me what it is.'

They found Richard sitting at the dining table with a blank piece of paper in front of him and chewing the end of a pencil.

'What's up Nogs, still trying to write your name?' asked Nick.

'Piss off,' replied Richard.

'Only joking, bro. Mum's worried about you, what's the problem?'

'If I told you, you would only laugh.'

'Of course I wouldn't laugh,' replied Nick, pretending to be hurt. 'The boys and I solve problems, it's what we do. Am I right?'

Keith and Don nodded in agreement.

'Well,' said Richard, 'I'm in love.'

'Aren't you a bit young to be in love?' asked Keith.

'Love doesn't have age boundaries, when she decides to strike; there is nothing you can do.'

'He's got it bad,' said Don. 'Who is the lucky girl?'

'Her name is Kimberley, she is an angel and all the boys are besotted with her. They worship the ground she stands on. Every boy in the school has asked her out and she turned them all down.'

'Have you asked her out?' asked Nick.

'Of course I have, but she turned me down as well.'

Keith looked confused, 'so what's the problem and why are you sitting their staring at a blank sheet of paper?

Richard bucked up a bit, 'well, there is a small chance that she will go out with me.'

'Explain.'

'Well, just before we broke up at school, Kimberley said that she would go out with one of the boys in our class. So all the boys that wanted to go out with her had to write a declaration of love for her and put it a small box that she had provided and she would choose one.'

'Obviously she didn't choose you,' said Keith.

Richard sighed, 'well yes and no. I've just heard that she has chosen three and I've been short-listed.'

'That's good, isn't it?' asked Nick.

'Not really. She wants each of us to write a poem and read it to her on Friday afternoon, and then she will choose the best. Also one of the other boys is Peter Sargent.'

'So?'

'Well you know that in every class there is that one boy who's good at everything. Good at football, good at cricket, fastest runner and always top of the class. Peter bloody Sargent is that boy. He's good looking and his parents are loaded and to make matters worse, we had a poetry competition last term and he won it.'

'Where did you come?' asked Keith.

'Second.'

'That's good,' enthused Don.

'From last,' added Richard. 'And he's a bloody Arsenal fan and a season ticket holder.'

'Well in that case we better make sure that you win the girl,' said Nick.

Wednesday 2 September

DI James looked at his watch, 2.45pm, plenty of time for him to walk through the town for his meeting with Nick Allen at 3.00pm. Why on earth did he agree to meet him? It was bound to be trouble and that was the last thing he needed. He was hoping for promotion to Chief Inspector, but things weren't going well. There had been no major crimes for a few weeks now and he had been lumbered with chasing drug dealers. This had been more difficult than he had expected and he had nothing of any significance to report. His meeting with the Chief Superintendent this morning was nothing less than a disaster.

Nick, Keith and Don sat anxiously in a booth in *Sally's Inn* Café waiting for DI James. The Juke box was playing *Tobacco Road* by the Nashville Teens as all three boys eyed up the shapely figure of Anna the waitress as she wiped down the empty tables.

It was 3.10pm before the inspector entered the café. After ordering a double espresso, he sat down next to Keith.

Looking at his watch Nick said, 'nice of you to join us.'

DI James sighed, 'don't start, I've had a crap day and now I have to listen to you lot.'

'Well if you help us out, you could be in line for promotion,' replied Nick in a reassuring manner.

'Whatever, just tell my why I'm here?'

'We have information that a certain Catholic Priest is abusing young boys.'

DI James let out a big sigh, 'are you sure?'

Nick gave DI James a detailed account of their interviews with Paul Logan, Robert Byrne and Patrick Sinclair. Don sheepishly told him his story.

'You realise what you're asking? And the church have some powerful friends within the force,' said DI James.

'Are you saying you don't want to help? asked Keith.

'I didn't say that,' replied DI James. 'But if what you say is true, then the man must be brought to justice, it's just that ....'

'Just what?' said the three boys in unison.

'Well, it's you lot. I've been warned to stay away from you.'

'By who?' asked Nick, mockingly. Doesn't your mum like you playing with us?'

DI James ignored the sarcasm and replied, 'no, the Chief Superintendent. He calls you my irregulars. It's a reference to....'

'We know what the irregulars are. Actually, I think that's a compliment,' said Nick. 'But why would he warn you off? We've only ever tried to help you.'

'More like solve half your cases for you,' added Keith.

'Well, apparently there has been a complaint. Somebody or bodies have been harassing Billy Watkins.' DI James looked at the three boys, all sitting there looking as if butter wouldn't melt in their mouths. 'Don't play the innocent with me; his mother was in the station yesterday complaining. She's said that her poor Billy is so traumatised that he can't leave the house.'

'He can't be that traumatised, we saw him in the *Farmer's Boy* yesterday,' remarked Don.

'And what makes him think it's us?' asked Nick, looking the picture of innocence.

'Well somehow he's found out that you're looking into Peter Waller's disappearance and he doesn't want me involved. He said that Billy Watkins has a legitimate alibi and had no involvement in the disappearance.'

'Huh, well we know different, so what's he intending to do about it?'

DI James smiled for the first time, 'he's put DC Higgins on to investigate.'

The boys started laughing. 'Then there's nothing to worry about, he's useless,' said Keith.

'Just be careful,' said a concerned DI James.

What DI James suspected but wasn't sure of, was the details of Nick's plan to harass Billy Watkins, hoping that he might crack. Every day over the past week he had phoned Billy's place of work and asked to speak to him. Then putting on a deep voice he said he was Eddie and told Billy to tell the truth. Keith, who delivered newspapers for *WH Smith's* in St Peters Street, would, once he had finished his round, cycle down London Road and wait for Billy outside his place of work. When Billy turned up, he would attract his attention and give him the, I'm watching you sign, by pointing to his eyes, then pointing to him. Don's job was to send poison pen letters to him. Each day he would look through the previous day's *Daily Mail* and cut out words and letters to make up his threats.

Things like TELL THE TRUTH, WE KNOW YOU DID IT and WHERE'S PETER'S BODY?

'Anyway, putting that to one side, what about this pervert priest?'

'We have a plan and we need your help,' said Nick. 'And I guarantee you'll get promotion.'

'And if it doesn't, I could get the sack,' added a despondent DI James.

'If you help us out, we have information that will help you with your drugs investigation,' smirked Nick.

'You're unbelievable, do you know that?' replied DI James, secretly hoping that they did have something as his investigation was going no-where.

'Do we have a deal?'

'Tell me what you know and we'll see.'

All three boys looked at him and in unison said, 'I think not.'

'Okay, okay.' DI James put his hands to his head and said, 'what's the plan?'

'Well, the 15th Scouts group have a football match on Saturday against the 4th Scouts at Cunningham Hill playing fields. We reckon that after the match Father John will take his new 'Special One' back to his digs. We follow him and catch him at it.'

'Where are his digs?' asked DI James sceptically.

'All the priests live in a building next to the church in Beaconsfield Road; Don has drawn a plan of the building.'

Don quickly pulled out a sheet of foolscap paper from his pocket and laid it flat on the table. Pointing to the various rooms on the map, Don said, 'as you enter the front door you have the office to the right and next to the office are the stairs. On the ground floor you also have a kitchen, dining room and lounge. Upstairs there are five bedrooms and a bathroom. He normally takes the boys to the bathroom; that's where we'll catch him.'

'Okay,' replied DI James, trying not to sound too enthusiastic, 'how's this going to work?'

Nick continued, 'the match kicks off at 2.00pm and should be over by 3.30pm. We reckon by the time they get changed and sort themselves out, Father John should be back at the earliest 4.00pm. Don's playing in the match, so he'll follow him back and Keith and I will hang around outside the church. When they arrive I'll phone you from the phone box outside the post office. By the time you get here Father John should be up to his old tricks. Then we nab him.'

'So how are we going to get in; knock on the door and wait till he answers?'

Shaking his head, Nick replied, 'the front door is not locked, they keep it on the latch during the day. It makes it easier for the priests who are coming and going all day.'

'Okay, but what about the bathroom, that's bound to be locked.'

Keith butted in, and said in a deep voice, 'we kick it down and shout, "You're nicked".'

'And just supposing it's not Father John and it's some other priest having a nice relaxing soak in the bath?'

'Then we leg it.'

Nick understood DI James' concern, but added 'our intelligence is reliable and this after-match ritual is a regular thing. I know you're looking at the worst scenario, so this is what we'll do. When we break the door down, Keith and I will enter the room first, you stay at the top of the stairs. If we find what we expect to find, we'll call you. If not, you scarper and no one will know the police were involved.'

DI James thought for a while before replying, 'it sounds risky, I must be mad but we'll take the chance.'

'Will you come alone?'

'Just to be on the safe side, I'll bring a partner.'

'Obviously not DC Higgins, we don't want him anywhere near us.'

'Good point, no I'll bring PC Adams; he seems a good sort.'

'Excellent,' beamed Nick. 'Can I get you another coffee?'

DI James stood up and said, 'as much as I would like to sit here with you and fantasize over Anna, I do have work to do. I'll wait for you call on Saturday.' He got up to go, then said, 'do you really have any information on the drugs or are you just winding me up?'

'We have a little bit, but it can wait till after the raid,' replied Nick.

'I think we ought to tell him now, because I got some more information,' said Don.

Both Nick and Keith looked at him.

'Over to you then,' said Nick.

Don felt very important and gave a little cough before starting his narrative. 'Last Friday, my friends and I met some very friendly girls who gave us some useful information about a Lecturer at the F.E. College who smokes dope. Well the other day I just happened to bump into Barbara in the town and she told me something very interesting.'

'Go on then,' urged Keith

'Well she said that the Lecturer, his name is Julian Harrison, attended the London School of Economics and was very friendly with Mick Jagger, you know, the lead singer of the Rolling Stones.'

'We know that,' said Nick.

'Well, I have it on good authority that he's going to see the Rolling Stones at the *Astoria* Theatre in Finsbury Park on Saturday and he has a back stage pass. I put it to you, that's where he'll pick up his next stash. It's well known that the Stones are druggies and I bet their supplier will be there as well.'

'Thank you for that Don,' said DI James, trying to suppress a laugh, 'But as I'm busy on Saturday either nabbing a rouge priest or picking up my cards, but I'll pass your information over to the Met's drugs squad and let them deal with it.'

With a big smile on his face Don said, 'another case cracked.'

'Before I go, how are you getting along with finding Peter?'

Nick gave out a big sigh, 'not good; we know the name of the third person, Michael, and we suspect he is the ring-leader, but we have no idea who he is or where to find him. Do you know any perverts called Michael?'

'I'll look in my files.' With that DI James, said his goodbyes and left.

'So, back to tomorrow I think we are in for a bit of excitement,' exclaimed Nick.

'So much for you promise not to get me into trouble again,' said Don.

'You'll thank me in the end,' replied Nick.

'What are we going to do now that the cops have twigged operation Annoy Billy?' asked Keith.

Nick thought for a minute, and then said, 'Keith, cancel the morning visits and pop along for a couple of afternoons. It'll take DC Higgins at least three days to notice we've changed track. I'll keep up the phone calls, I use a different phone box every day and at different times, so I should be okay. How are you doing Don?'

'I continue with the hate mail,' replied Don. 'I'll put all the used newspapers on the fire, so if they did raid my house, there'll find nothing.'

'Do you still have a fire on during the summer?' asked Keith.

'Of course, we need it for the hot water and someone always need a bath.' Don has two brothers James, 17 and Stephen, 11 and a sister Jean, 9.

'Sorry I forgot; we have an Ascot 709 water heater that supplies hot water to all the taps.'

'That's a bit technical for you,' said Nick.

'It's just that we had it serviced last week and the gas man explained it to me. Apparently the pilot was blocked and that was what was making bang every time it lit up. It was so bad sometimes it would blow the case off.' The boys all laughed. 'Yeah, and my dad recognised the gas man; he's a famous local footballer; plays for Barnet and England's amateur team.'

'Wow,' said Don, what's his name?'

'Roger Figg.'

At that point the waitress Anna appeared and started to clear the boys table. The boys just stared, sitting there with their mouths open.

'Is that *Chanel number 5* you're wearing today, Anna?' asked Nick.

'I wish,' replied Anna. 'Perhaps you could buy me a bottle for Christmas. You could just about afford it if you save up all your paper round money for the next four months,'

'She's a sarcastic cow,' said Keith, when Anna had disappeared.

'Na, I keep telling you, she's just playing hard to get,' smiled Nick.

'Okay,' said Keith. 'What is the first thing you look for in a girl? Are you a leg person or a breast person?'

'Huh,' sniggered Don. 'There's no need to ask you, what you are.'

Ignoring the remark, Keith said, 'Nick?'

Nick gazed at Anna as she re-appeared, 'I'm a bottom man.'

'Explain!'

'If a woman's body was the universe, then her bottom would be the centre of that universe; everything would evolve from it. Just by looking at her bottom you can tell the shape of her legs and the size of her breasts. It's all about proportion, I'm sure that they are mathematically connected; something about the 'Golden Ratio'. If she has a nice pert, small to medium bum then her legs will long and slender and her breasts will be just bigger than a handful. Her waist will be slim and her cheek bones will be prominent.'

'What a load of bollocks,' interrupted Keith.

'I go for the smile,' said Don, as he slurped the last of his milkshake, 'and the eyes; they are the windows to the soul.'

'Are you going to order any more drinks or are you going to sit here all-day?' asked Anna, standing there hands on hips.

'What do you look for in a man, Anna,' asked Nick, staring at her with doleful eyes.

'Good question,' she replied. 'I know; the size of his wallet.'

'Surely not,' chuckled Nick. 'I think you would fall for someone with twinkling blue eyes, a captivating smile and a taste for adventure.'

'Or a tall good-looking lad with a slight oriental look, who is full of charm,' added Keith.

Don just said, 'or me.'

Anna thought for a while before saying, 'no, a big fat wallet. Now would you like another drink?'

'No thanks, we've off now,' said Nick, as he nodded to his friends. They all stood up and exited the café.

Thursday 3 September

Nick was deep in thought as he marked the papers in the back room of *Heading and Watts* paper-shop. So much could go wrong with his plan, he could get into a lot of trouble and DI James could lose his job. But he had thought it through thoroughly and it had to be done. As he went over it again in his head he was unaware of a person standing behind him.

'Hello, Nick.' It was Caroline Harvey.

'Oh, hello Caroline; what are you doing back here?' replied Nick, who was very surprised to see his visitor.

'Mr. Hart said I could come round, I need to see you. It's very urgent.'

'Okay, what's the problem?'

'I think I'm pregnant.'

'Bloody hell,' gasped Nick. 'Who's the father?'

Looking rather despondent, she replied, 'you are of course.'

Nick laughed, 'don't be silly, I've only kissed you once and you can't get pregnant by kissing.'

Still looking upset, Caroline said, 'I know that, but you used your tongue. You can get pregnant if a boy uses his tongue.'

Nick put down his pencil and looked a Caroline. 'Caroline, you are a very sweet girl, but you cannot get pregnant by kissing, with or without tongues. Hasn't your mum told you about the birds and bees?'

'Not yet, but she keeps meaning to.'

'Well I suggest that as soon as you have finished your paper-round you sit your mum down and demand that she tells you the facts of life. If she tries to fob you off again, tell her you think you're pregnant – she'll listen to you then.'

'Nick Allen, I think you are wonderful,' said Caroline, before grabbing Nick and passionately kissing him.

Nick thought about pushing her away, well for a micro-second. Instead he wrapped his arms round her and enjoyed the sensation. She had a lovely trim body and a perfectly formed bottom which he squeezed gently. Little Nick was showing his appreciation.

'When you've finished, there's a boy out here waiting for his paper-round,' shouted Ron Hart, from the front of the shop.

Nick released Caroline, gave her a nice smile and said, 'come and see me tomorrow and let me know how you get on.'

With that she turned and left allowing Nick to concentrate on his marking up. He had just got back into his rhythm when Ron stuck his head round and said, 'I had a friend who could make a girl pregnant just by looking at her.'

Nick, who was now used to Ron Hart's awful jokes, just replied, 'and how did he manage that?'

'He was cock-eyed.'

Nick continued with his marking. When he had finished and all the paper-rounds were lying nicely on the floor he picked up a copy of the *Daily Express*, took it to the back room and quickly read the report on last night's game between Spurs and Burnley. After Saturday's defeat he was thrilled to read that Spurs had won by four goals to one.

Friday 4 September

When Nick placed the last paper-round onto the shop floor he noticed that Dalton round had gone. Caroline had sneaked in, taken her round without Nick noticing.

'Did you see her?' asked Nick.

'She was in and out quicker than a Bishop in a brothel,' replied Ron.

'Strange, I thought she would have told me how she got on with her mother.'

'I'm surprised her mum let her continue working here, now she knows you're lusting after her daughter.'

'Let's just put the record straight, she lust's after me. Is it my fault I'm a babe magnet?'

'You just be careful, young Nick. We don't want the shop to get a reputation.'

'You never know, it might increase business.'

Caroline was waiting outside the shop when Nick finished his shift.

'Hello, Nick,' said Caroline. ''Will you walk me home?'

'Of course I will,' replied Nick, as he collected his bicycle from the Builders yard next door.

'I feel such a fool not knowing where babies come from.'

'We all have to learn sometime,' replied Nick in his most sensitive voice. 'Now tell me what happened'

'You were right; when I asked her she made some excuse that she was busy, so I told her I was pregnant. She burst out crying. That seemed to do the trick; she sat me down straight away and asked me how it happened. When I told her that a boy had given me a French kiss she started crying again and then her crying turned into laughter. I pretended to be hurt and then she settled down. She then apologized and confessed that she was scared that I would grow up to soon. Anyway, eventually she told me the facts of life. She was embarrassed at first, then I asked a few questions and she relaxed a bit. In fact by the end of it I think we have become much closer. Now apart from being my mother she now is my friend as well – and it's all thanks to you.'

Nick smiled and said, 'I'm really pleased.'

'The funny thing is that deep down you already know how babies are made and it comes as no surprise when you are told. But it does seem a bit painful and messy; I don't think I'm ready yet.'

Nick gasped, 'I should hope not, after all you're only thirteen.'

'Mum said that the first time isn't very good, but it gets better with practice. She did say that a lot of boys just want you for sex and that to make sure that that when it happens the boy is really special.'

'Sound advice.'

'So I've made a decision, when I'm old enough I want you to be the first.'

Nick was speechless.

'I expect you'll have girlfriend, but that doesn't matter, I know you will be gentle with me and I'll always love you.'

Much to his relief they had reached Caroline's home.

'That's really nice,' said Nick, slightly embarrassed. 'Well, here we are – so just give a call when you're sixteen – and I'll see you tomorrow.' With that Nick gave Caroline a quick kiss on the cheek, mounted his bike and rode off.

'Are you ready yet,' asked Mr Allen, shouting to Nick from the bottom of the stairs.

'Coming,' replied Nick, as he appeared from his bedroom.

Mr Allen had taken the day off work to accompany Nick to buy his new school uniform. Nick had outgrown his school blazer; his trousers had seen better days and his school shoes were beyond repair. Together with a couple of white shirts, it was going to make a bit of a dent in his wallet. The uniform was purchased at *Foster Brothers* and the shoes from *Freeman Hardy Willis.*

As they exited the shoe shop Mr Allen said, 'I could do with a beer.'

'The *Wellington's* just there, can we try it? I've always wondered what it's like,' replied Nick, slightly excited at the thought of going into another pub.

'Why not; as long as they don't mind you coming in.'

The *Wellington* pub was just two doors away and they entered by the side door into the saloon bar. The bar was clean and tidy with embossed wallpaper adorned with framed military prints. Behind the bar stood a plain middle-aged woman who Nick assumed was the landlady.

'Mind if the boy comes in?' asked Mr Allen.

'As long as he behaves himself,' replied the landlady.

Mr Allen looked at Nick and said 'sit there and behave yourself.'

Nick noticed the half-smile on his father's face and replied, 'yes sir.'

'I'll have a light and bitter, a glass of lemonade for the boy and two packets of crisps, plain, not those horrible flavoured ones.'

Mr Allen placed the drinks and the crisps on the table and said, 'just going to point Percy.'

With Mr Allen in the Gents and the landlady serving in the public bar, Nick was all alone. He was just running through the details of tomorrow's operation when he noticed a small boy appear from behind the bar. Nick thought he was the scruffiest boy he had ever seen and was definitely in need of a good meal. He stood by the bar and looked at Nick.

'Hello,' said Nick, 'what's your name?

'Charlie,' mouthed the boy. 'Can you help me?'

'What's the problem?'

At that point Mr. Allen returned. Nick automatically turned is head to look at his dad but when he turned back Charlie had disappeared.

'Who were you talking too?' asked Mr Allen.

'Just some young boy, right state he was in,' replied Nick.

'Perhaps he's the landlady's son.'

'If he is, then she needs reporting, never seen such a scruffy kid.'

Their conversation was interrupted by the sound of a glass breaking. The landlady reappeared. She looked at Nick.

'Wasn't me,' said Nick, holding up his glass.

The sound came of another glass breaking in the public bar.

'That bloody Charlie,' screamed the landlady. 'Why can't he just leave us alone?'

'If he's not yours why do you let him in the pub?' asked a confused Nick.

The landlady looked shocked, 'have you seen him?'

'He was here a minute ago, looks like he hasn't been fed for a month.'

'Oh my God,' said the landlady, turning white. 'You actually saw him.'

Nick, totally confused looked at his dad, 'you saw him, didn't you?'

Mr Allen shook his head, and then they both looked at the landlady.

'Charlie is a ghost; back in the 18th century when this pub was called the *Blue Boar*, a local boy called Charlie was killed by a coach turning into the stable and he's been haunting the place ever since.'

Mr Allen looked at Nick and asked, 'have you seen any ghosts before?'

Nick sheepishly replied, 'one or two.'

'Well, there's your next case, stop Charlie from smashing up the *Wellington*.'

Nick huffed, 'who do you think I am – *Maxwell Hawke*[8]? I'm a consulting detective not a flaming Ghost Hunter. Anyway, when I see them I don't know they are ghosts.'

'Just a thought,' replied Mr Allen, before taking a large gulp of his beer. 'I needed that.'

Peter Sargent looked in the mirror and thought what a lucky person he was. If anyone was born with a silver spoon in his mouth it was him and things were getting better by the day. There was no doubt about it, at ten years old Peter had everything. He was strikingly handsome, with blonde wavy hair, and an aristocratic air about him. Rumour has it that his family were distant relatives of some minor royal. His loving parents were extremely rich and he wanted for nothing. Now he was off to meet his favourite Arsenal player, Joe Baker. Yesterday he received a letter from the Arsenal Supporters Club informing him that Joe Baker would be signing autographs at *Heading and Watts* paper shop in Catherine Street. Also, he would be giving a short talk to twelve local supporters at 2.00pm and he had been selected to attend. Hopefully it wouldn't last too long because he had to be at Kimberley Foster's house to read her his love poem. She had chosen three boys to compete for her affections and they all had to be at her house at 3.00pm this afternoon. Each would read to her their poem before she made her final choice. Was he worried? Not really, the other boys were Clive Wells and Richard Allen. Clive was good at poetry but wasn't the best looking bloke on the block and was extremely overweight. Whereas Richard wasn't bad looking, but he was rubbish at poetry and he had a weird brother. He couldn't see Kimberly picking him. It was going to be an exceptionally good afternoon.

At 2.00pm armed with his autograph book, Peter Sargent walked into *Headings and Watts* paper-shop. He thought it would be crowded, but all he could see was three older boys browsing through the magazine rack. He noticed that they were all wearing red and white scarfs; he approached them.

'Excuse me,' said Peter. 'Are you here to see Joe Baker?'

The nearest boy, who looked vaguely familiar replied, 'yes we are, exciting isn't it?'

'What time is he due? I thought it started at 2.00pm?

'I think he's running late, but he's on his way.'

At 2.15pm a young boy, wearing spectacles, about twelve years old walked into the paper-shop, he was carrying a brown paper carrier bag; his name – Joseph Baker.

'Sorry I'm late,' said Joseph. 'Where are we going?'

'Go through to the back, the manager said we could use the shed. It's been set up all ready for you,' said Nick Allen.

Peter looked confused 'what's going on?'

'That's Joe Baker and he's giving the talk this afternoon,' replied Nick, as he grabbed Peter by the arm. 'And you don't want to miss it.'

Keith grabbed Peter's other arm as they escorted him through the shop and into the back yard where the shed was situated. Joseph stood behind a trestle table and started to empty the contents of his carrier bag. A bench had been erected by placing a builder's plank on two piles of old newspapers. Peter sat in the middle with Nick; Don and Keith sat either side.

Joseph smiled and said to his audience, 'thank you for coming, todays lecture is about *Brooke Bond* Tea Cards. Before the war, cigarette cards had been collected in their millions – small rectangles of coloured pasteboard inserted in cigarette packets. The tobacco manufacturers had not reintroduced the cards after the war. Now *Brooke Bond* inaugurated 'picture cards … … …...'

It was the longest hour of Nick's life as Joseph explained the history of *Brooke Bond* picture cards and insisted that they look at his complete collection of cards all neatly stuck in the appropriate presentation book. They eventually allowed Peter to go, but only after making sure that he had obtained 'Joe's' autograph. Before they left, Nick thanked Joseph and slipped him two shillings.

Nick was looking forward to his tea tonight, fish and chips. As he tucked in to his meal he noticed the smile on his brother's face.

'Nogs, how did it go this afternoon?' asked Nick.

'Okay,' replied Richard. 'I'm going to the pictures tomorrow with Kimberly and her parents.'

'Excellent, she must have liked your poem.'

'Didn't really need it, the other two didn't turn up.'

'Why was that?' asked Nick, trying to keep a straight face.

'I knew Clive was on holiday, but have no idea what happened to Peter.'

'He must have had a better offer. So let's hear your poem.'

'Roses are Red
Violets are Blue
I made you this poem
Because I'm in love with you
I am very pleased
That you didn't run away
So I don't have beg
To make you stay'

Saturday 05 September

Nick and Keith cycled to Beaconsfield Road and parked their bicycles next to the telephone box outside the post office and waited. At 4.15pm a blue 1955 Morris Minor fitting the description of the car described by Don, drove past them and pulled into the church car park. The two boys casually walked past the car park and discretely observed the occupants. As expected Father John was the driver and a young boy-scout in the passenger side. Nick recognised him, his name - Mark O'Gorman. Confident that they had not been seen they turned round and made their way back to the phone box to wait for Don. It was only a few minutes before he appeared frantically pedalling away.

Breathing heavily, Don asked, 'have they arrived?'

'It's all going to plan,' replied Nick. 'I'll phone DI James now for back-up, then it's all systems go.'

It was a good fifteen minutes before DI James and PC Adams appeared. Nick was getting worried in-case Father John had finished his vile deeds. DI James parked his car next to the Morris Minor and joined the boys along with PC Adams, who Nick noticed was in plain clothes.

'All set then?' he asked, with a nervous look on his face.

Nick could feel the excitement rising inside of him, 'everything is fine, now listen carefully, we will stick to the original plan. Keith and I will approach the bathroom first and if we find what we think we should find, we'll call you.'

'What about me?' enquired Don.

'I think you should stay down here, just in-case Father John starts his Catholic mumbo-jumbo on you.'

Feeling slightly left out Don mumbled, 'okay.'

All five walked to the front door of the Priests accommodation, Nick gently gave the door a gentle push – it opened. Nick looked in, empty. He quickly turned right, past the office and ascended the stairs, two steps at a time; Keith was close behind. Once they reached top, they quickly located the bathroom, it had a sign half way up the door. Nick looked round and observed the two policemen waiting at the top of the stairs. DI James nodded, Nick gave a 'thumbs up'. He took a deep breath; he could feel his heart pounding in his chest. He delicately tried the door handle and was surprised to find that the door was unlocked. Then he burst through the door with Keith close behind. The scene was almost as he had expected, the boy-scout, naked as the day he was born, was standing in the bath; his small penis fully erect. Father John was sitting on the bath edge in just his underpants, holding a large, soaking wet sponge. But hovering in the corner, looking on, was another priest; this one fully clothed.

Father John instantly recognised Nick and screamed, 'what the hell are you doing here?'

A wave of calmness came over Nick as he announced, 'Father John, I'm arresting you for indecent acts against under-age boys; anything you say will be taken down and ....'

'You can't arrest me; you're not a policeman.'

'But I am,' said DI James, walking in, holding his warrant card.

'I'm getting out of here,' said the other Priest, who was a good six foot tall and quite young. Nick estimated he must be about twenty-five years old.

As he started to move Keith jumped on him, screaming 'no you're not.' At the same time, Father John stood up and hurled a bar of soap at DI James, which missed him by six inches. Nick stepped forward and pushed Father John on the chest and he fell back into the bath. As DI James stepped forward he stood on the bar of soap that had rebounded off the back wall and stopped just in front of him. For the next minute the scene in the bathroom was reminiscent of a Laurel and Hardy film. The result of DI James stepping on the soap, as Nick would describe later, he fell Arse over Tit. Every time Father John managed to scramble out of the bath Nick punched him in the face and he fell back into it. Mark O'Gorman, whose penis had now almost shrivelled to a non-existent state, had stepped out of the bath, crying hysterically, and frantically searching for his clothes. The other priest, who had managed to overpower Keith, tried to leave the bathroom but was apprehended by PC Adams. DI James, although a little dazed after his fall, had regained his feet was frantically trying to stop Nick landing yet another blow to the very swollen face of Father John. Unbeknown to our group of vigilantes another priest, alarmed by the fracas had dialled 999. Whilst DI James held Nick back, Father

John had managed to get to his feet and holding on to his sodden under-pants had made it to the bathroom door. But as he tried to make his getaway he tripped over the outstretched leg of Don Patrick. Standing on the back of the fallen priest he turned to PC Adams and shouted, 'cuffs, please.'

The uniformed police arrived a few minutes later to see Father John, still in his sodden under-pants and sporting a collection of red marks around his eyes standing hand-cuffed next to the other priest, also hand-cuffed, with blood trickling down from his nose.

'Take 'em away,' ordered DI James, to the very confused police constable. Turning to Nick, he smiled and said, 'I've got no idea how I'm going to explain this. But, we did well, now go and take care of that young lad.'

'Don't you think this one should put some clothes on, Sir?' asked the policeman.

Still rubbing the back off his head DI James said, 'yes, sorry, find him a cassock or something to put on.'

In the excitement Nick had totally forgotten about Mark O'Gorman. Turning to Keith he asked, 'where did he go?' Keith just shrugged his shoulders.

'He's in there,' replied Don, pointing to one of the bedrooms.

They found Mark almost dressed, sitting on a bed pulling his socks on. He had stopped crying but his eyes were red and his cheeks still wet. He looked up when he heard the boys, his face changed from fear to relief.

'Thanks for saving me,' said Mark, as he rushed over and gave Nick a big hug.

Mark was a nice looking lad with dark eyes and dark brown hair. He was thirteen years old and lived in the same road as Nick.

'No problem, mate,' replied Nick as he gently pushed Mark away.

'I didn't want to be here, but Father John said it was God's will.'

'We understand.'

'And please don't tell anyone I had a stiffy,' pleaded Mark.

'Of course not.'

'It's got a mind of its own, always goes hard when you don't want it to.'

'Don't worry mate,' said Keith, 'it happens to all of us. Mine even gets excited when I see a naked female mannequin in a shop window.'

The other three boys all burst out laughing.

Keith went bright red before saying, 'I'm only joking, of course.'

When they had composed themselves Mark asked, 'what will happen now?'

'For one thing, you won't be seeing Father John again, he'll be going down for a long time. I expect the police will want to interview you; but only talk to DI James. They'll probably keep this very low key. Who was that other priest? Did he touch you?'

'That was Father David, he's new. No, he didn't touch me; he was too busy touching himself.'

'Errr, that's disgusting; did you know that wanking causes blindness and epilepsy… … I read it in book,' added Nick.

'How long have you been the special one?' asked Keith.

Mark thought, 'I think I came after Don. I'm sure he chose me because of my good-looks. My mum always said that they will be a blessing and a curse. I understand what she means now.'

'If you say so,' said Nick. 'But now, let's get you home.'

Nick offered to walk Mark home then thanking and congratulating Keith and Don on their efforts, he told them to cycle home and he'll see them tomorrow.

It was 11.00pm before Nick finally got to bed that evening. Before closing his eyes he reflected on the calm and pleasant evening he had just experienced. His father had taken him along with Mrs Allen and Moira to the *Tudor Tavern* in George Street for a steak meal. Nick had only been there once before and he had always been envious of the diners when passing the establishment and peering through the windows. Mr Allen thought it would be a nice treat for him before going back to school. It also coincided with him winning the jackpot on the one-armed bandit at the *Waverley Club*. Before the meal they had a pre-dinner drink in the cellar bar.

Mr Allen had a glass of light ale whilst Mrs Allen had a schooner of cream sherry from the wood. Nick asked for a cider and Moira settled for lemonade.

As they were shown to their table, Nick admired the 15th century timber framed building with exposed oak beams. His father had told him that present building was made up from two medieval Inns called the *Swan* and the *George*. Not being too experienced in ordering food in a posh restaurant, both Nick and Moira followed his parents and ordered Prawn Cocktail, followed by Rump Steak and Black Forest Gateaux. Nick was a little embarrassed by their waitress who was known to him. Her name was Veronica Goldberg. About six months ago Nick had rescued Ronnie, as she liked to be called, from a gang of white slave traders. Throughout the evening she was very attentive to them but especially to Nick. It seemed that every minute she came to the table checking that everything was okay and giving Nick a quick cuddle and the occasional peck on the cheek. Everyone noticed that the portions on Nick's plate were much larger than everyone else's. He was also aware that Moira was getting slightly jealous, which stopped him enquiring about Ronnie's sister Jane. Although Jane was about five years older than Nick, he really fancied her and often popped in to *Kings* Gift shop in St Peter's Street, when he was alone, for a chat.

WEEK 5
Sunday 6 September - Saturday 12 September 1964

Sunday 6 September

Moira had instructed Nick to come to her house in the afternoon and bring his transistor radio. It was another glorious day with the sun shining and not a cloud to be seen. After enjoying his Sunday roast, lamb this week, he grabbed his radio and strolled the two hundred yards to Moira's house. After knocking on the front door and waiting an abnormally long time, Moira eventually answered the door.

'Sorry,' said Moira. 'We're in the garden.'

Nick stood there totally stunned; Moira was wearing a skimpy pink bikini. He had never seen so much of her before, everything was there, on display, for him – legs, tummy, arms, and skin everywhere.'

'Close your mouth, Nick,' said Moira. 'Haven't you seen a girl in a bikini before?'

Nick mumbled something totally incomprehensible.

'We're sun-bathing this afternoon; hope you've brought your swimming trunks.'

'You never said we were sun-bathing,' said Nick, as he followed

Moira through the house towards the back garden; never taking his eyes off her delightful bottom and resisting the urge to give it a squeeze.

'Men,' gasped Moira. 'You're hopeless, what else would we be doing, that's why I asked you to bring your tranny.'

Totally confused, Nick followed Moira into the garden. Forcing himself to look up from Moira's bottom, he was not expecting to see the sight that was before him. Sitting on a blanket, sipping a glass of orange squash through a straw was Moira's little sister, Elizabeth. Elizabeth was a year younger than Moira. She looked up, smiled and said, 'hello Nick.'

To Nick, Elizabeth was just a younger version of Moira, they looked very similar. Elizabeth was also wearing a bikini; hers was turquoise blue with white polka dots. Although her breasts were not quite fully developed, there was still enough on display to arouse Nick. There were three towels, laid side by side, Elizabeth occupied the one to the left, and Moira took the one to the right, leaving the middle one free for Nick. Making himself comfortable he removed his t-shirt and rolled his jeans up us far as they would go. Elizabeth finished her drink, put on her sunglasses and laid down on her back, Moira followed suit. Nick just sat there, slightly flustered. Why is it he thought, that girls get totally embarrassed if you see them in their bra and knickers but have no problem flaunting themselves in a skimpy bikini? He didn't know where to look, well he did know where to look, it was just where to look first. He needed a distraction. 'How was church this morning?' he asked.

Moira sat up, 'funny you should ask that, it was really strange.'

Nick smiled to himself, 'why was that?'

'Well Father John was absent and so was Father David. Father Michael had to take Mass and he's so old they almost had to carry him in. Rumours were flying around; some said they were taken ill, others say they were arrested.'

'I heard it was a drugs raid,' interjected Elizabeth.

'Don't be silly,' exclaimed Moira. 'Priests don't take drugs.'

'You'll be surprised what priests get up,' said Nick, with a smirk on his face.

'There definitely was a punch up; according to my friend Sally,' added Elizabeth.

'I'm sure it'll all come out in the wash,' said Nick as he lay back on his towel and thinking about yesterday's excitement.'

For the next five minutes the three of them just lay there, basking in the sun's rays. It was Moira who broke the tranquillity.

'I'm just going in for a minute. I've got stomach cramps.' With that she ran back to the house.

'Nick, can you put some sun lotion on my back?' asked Elizabeth as she turned over onto her front.

'No problem,' said Nick, as he picked up a tube of *Nivea sunfilta Cream* and squirted the cream into his hand.

Elizabeth reached round and undid her bikini catch, leaving her back completely exposed. Nick kneeled beside her and gently rubbed the cream into her back. When he'd finished he said, 'there, all done.'

'Can you do my legs as well?' asked Elizabeth.

After pouring some more cream into his hands he started on her calves, and then moved onto her thighs. Her legs were slightly apart which allowed Nick to rub the cream to the very top of her legs. Now this was getting a little too much for Nick; he was now enjoying himself. With each stroke he was getting nearer and nearer to the bottom of her bikini. How close could he get? When his hand reached the top of her thigh he would have sworn her heard her give out a little moan. After putting a bit more cream on his hand, he ran it slowly up the inside of her thigh. Did she open her legs just a little more? Slowly his hand descended and then back again; another moan? A noise behind alerted him to the fact that Moira was returning.

'That should do,' said Nick quickly before returning to his towel.

As Moira returned, Nick noticed that she had put on a pair of shorts over her bikini bottom.

'I'm sorry,' she said. 'My curse has started, and I feel awful. I'm going to lie down. You can stay if you want or you can go off and do your own thing.'

Nick stood up gave her a cuddle, 'don't worry about me darling, you just go and get yourself better. Is there anything I can do?'

Moira managed a small smile; Nick could tell she was in pain. 'No, I'll be alright tomorrow.' With that she turned and walked back to house. Nick sat back down on his towel.

'You can do my front now,' said Elizabeth.

Nick, who had momentarily forgotten about her, turned to see that she was now lying on her back. He couldn't see her eyes due to the dark sunglasses she was wearing. What to do? He grabbed the sun cream. One quick coat, thirty seconds, and then I'm off, he thought. He started on her shins and worked up towards her thighs. It was no good, things were stirring. As he was getting higher he glanced at her face; what was she thinking? Why is she licking her lips? Why is she breathing funny? He picked up the tube again and gave it a squirt, aiming it at her navel. It was a good shot; the white liquid trickled out and made a slow bee-line towards her bikini bottom. Nick put his hand on her tummy and started to rub gently. She twitched and took a deep breath; the consequence of this movement was that her loose bikini top moved to expose her left breast. It was no good, temptation had won. Nick slowly slid his hand towards it and gave it a gentle squeeze. It felt good, so soft, just short of a handful, but perfectly delightful. He bent down and kissed her full on the mouth. Then something strange happened, or didn't happen. She never flinched, no response what so ever. Even her lips stayed completely still. Nick sat up, said, 'I'm sorry,' grabbed his t-shirt and transistor radio and left. As he turned the radio off, Matt Monro was singing *Walk Away*. Nick gave a wry smile. He walked through the house, shouting 'goodbye' up the stairs, before letting himself out off the front door. His head was spinning. What was he thinking, will she tell Moira? He'll deny it; what was she doing? He'd heard the expression – Prick Teaser - now he knew what it meant. Little Nick certainly did - a cold bath was in order

Monday 7 September

'How was school today?' asked Mr Allen, as he made himself comfortable in front of the television. *Coronation Street* had just finished and he was looking forward to a new drama called *The Other Man*, starring Michael Caine, Sian Philips and John Thaw.

'You know, Dad, first day and all that. Didn't do much, but I'm looking forward to it. Need to concentrate a bit more this year, what with GCE 'O' levels next year. Hopefully I'll do well, and then they might let me stay on for 'A' levels, then who knows, university,' replied Nick.

'You know that you could leave at Easter and get an apprenticeship; set you up for life.'

Mrs Allen tutted, 'we've talked about this before, you know I want Nick to stay on. Just because we had to leave school early, what with the war and all, it doesn't mean Nick has to do the same. We should encourage him to do better than we did and hopefully he'll think the same when he has children. By the way how is Moira these days?'

'She's fine, Mum; although she started her period yesterday, so no grandchildren this month.'

'Nick,' shrieked Mrs Allen. 'I hope you're not… ….'

'Don't be silly Mum, only joking.'

'Look it's starting, said Mr Allen, as he took out a Manikin cigar and lit it.

No sooner than the drama started there was a knock of the front door.

'Bloody hell,' swore Mr Allen. 'Who the hell is that, every bloody time I want to watch a programme…

'I'll go Dad,' said Nick, as he rose from his chair to answer the door. Nick had a feeling it might be DI James. He was right. 'It's DI James,' he shouted, 'he wants a word with me. I'll take him in the kitchen.'

'No you don't,' shouted Mr Allen, 'bring him in here.'

'I'll put the kettle on,' sighed Mrs Allen.

'Sorry to bother you at this time of night but I have some important news for Nick,' said DI James, feeling a little uneasy.

'What's he been up to now?' asked Mr Allen.

'Well,' said DI James, looking at Nick, then at Mr Allen. 'I'm not sure how much Nick has told you about the events of Saturday afternoon.'

Mr Allen just stared at Nick, who in turn stared at DI James.

'Well, it's like this,' said Nick. 'And to cut a long story short, on Saturday afternoon DI James and some of his colleagues helped me and the boys save Mark O'Gorman. You know him, he lives across the road.'

'Save him from what?' asked Mrs Allen, who just returned to the living room.

Nick took a deep breath and the said quickly, 'being abused by a perverted priest.'

'I hope there was no trouble, you promised Mrs Patrick there would be no more trouble,' said Mrs Allen.

'It was Don's fault in the first place,' argued Nick. 'Well not his fault exactly, but that's what was making him miserable. He was about to be abused, until I stepped in. It's disgusting, Mum, honestly you don't want to know.'

DI James butted in, 'But it's all okay now, the culprits have been apprehended and it won't happen again.'

'I think the kettle's boiling, I'll make the tea,' said Mrs Allen, as she walked back to the kitchen.

'So what happens now,' asked Nick. 'Do you want a statement, will I have to go to court.'

'No, that won't be necessary, there won't be a trial.'

Nick looked perplexed, 'don't tell me you've let him go.'

DI James looked embarrassed, 'I didn't let him go. If it was up to me, I'd toss him in a cell and throw away the key. It's the church, they said it is a church matter and they would take care of it.'

'So you've released him.'

'I had no choice, orders from above.'

'I can't believe it; so he's out there, walking the streets looking for his next victim.'

'Not exactly, they've taken them both back to Ireland. They'll deal with them there.'

Mr Allen, who was having trouble taking all this in said, 'the Clerical power structure not only protects clergy who are sexually active but sets them up to live double lives.'

DI James, nodding said, 'I'm afraid your father is right.'

Nick was fuming, 'it was a sad day for England when we stopped burning Catholics at the stake.'

'But it's not all bad news,' said DI James, with just a touch of enthusiasm. 'Father John's real name is Michael Flanagan and his best friend is or should I say was, Eddie Reynolds.'

Nick's mood changed instantly, 'that's fantastic, we've found our third man. But why is he called Father John?'

'Well, apparently when he joined the church, they already had a Father Michael, so he used his middle name.'

'So, did you interview him, did he tell you what happened to Peter?'

'Unfortunately by the time I found this information, Father John had been shipped off to Ireland.'

Nick's emotions were in turmoil, 'what put you on to him?'

'Once I realised his name was Michael, I had a hunch. I checked his military service record and cross-referenced it with Eddie's. They were conscripted and de-mobbed on the same day and were both in the same unit. Further digging revealed that they were good friends.'

'So what happens now, can we bring him back?'

'Afraid not, I took my findings to the Chief Superintendent and surprise, surprise he told me to forget it.'

'He's a bloody Catholic, isn't he?'

'You guessed.'

'You'll have to go higher, go to the Chief Constable. You can't let this go.'

'We have no actual evidence it's all circumstantial.'

Nick was pacing up and down, Mr Allen was looking worried.

Mrs Allen returned with her tea tray. The three men were silent as Mrs Allen poured out four cups of tea.

'Not going well then?' asked Mrs Allen.

'You've done well, Nick, but I think you should let it go now,' said Mr Allen. 'You need to concentrate on your school work.'

'Never! I'll never give up until I find that poor boy, and when I do, I'll go to the Chief Constable myself and demand the resignation that tosser.'

'I hope you're not going to do anything silly, Nick,' said Mrs Allen, looking really worried.

'I don't care if it's silly, dangerous, illegal, I'll do what it takes to solve this case and I'll do it on my own. So I'll bid you farewell Inspector, and thanks for your help, but I'm off to my room. I have a lot of thinking to do.' With that he left the three adults and ran up the stairs to his room.

Tuesday 8 September

Nick walked slowly down the Hatfield Road towards the Pioneer Youth club. He had formulised a plan in his head and despite what had been said, it was outrageous, dangerous and totally illegal. But he needed some help and Digger Barnes was the right person to provide the assistance he needed. Hopefully he would be frequenting the youth club this evening. He was in luck; Digger was there, sitting in the corner, accompanied by two, rather attractive girls. Nick wasn't sure how he felt about girls wearing leather jackets, but these two Rockers, both with long blonde hair, white t-shirts and skin-tight jeans looked absolutely stunning.

Digger saw Nick looking over at them and shouted, 'hi Nick, come and join us.'

Nick pretended to be surprised and said, 'thank you.' He walked over, trying to look nonchalant; sat down and said 'hi' to the two girls.

'On your own tonight, where's your mates?' asked Digger.

'Just popped in hoping to see you - bit of business.'

'I see; sorry girls could you just give us a minute.'

The girls seemed a little put out, got up and left. Nick couldn't stop staring at the pair as they made their way to *Ma's Bar*.

Turning back to Digger, Nick said, 'they seem like nice girls.'

Digger smiled, 'they're okay, fix you up with one of them if you like.'

'I'm okay for the moment, but I may come back to you on that one'

'So,' said Digger. 'What can I do for you?'

For the next twenty minutes Nick explained the whole story of Peter going missing and his progress in trying to find him. Then he outlined his plan to find the whereabouts of the missing boy.

'So, let me get this straight,' added Digger. 'On Friday at 5.00pm, you want me to kidnap this Billy Watkins when he leaves work and take him to the backroom in the Alma Road Youth Club where you are going to torture him until he spills the beans.'

Nick took a deep breath, and then said, 'In a nutshell – yes.'

'Sounds like fun, leave it to me.'

With that Nick said goodbye and left. As he walked home, he felt a bit peckish so he treated himself to six pennyworth of chips with scraps from *Warwick's* in Catherine Street.

Wednesday 9 September

'How did you get on with Digger, yesterday?' asked Keith as they sat in a booth in *Sally's Inn* café after a hard day's studying at school.

'All sorted,' replied Nick

'You haven't told us what you have planned'

'I'll tell you more tomorrow when the girls are there, I need them as well, but we're going to kidnap Billy Watkins and torture him. Don, are you up for it?'

'It sounds a bit dodgy to me, but it sounds exciting. Just think I could be the first in our family to go to borstal.'

'I won't let it get that far, I'll take all the blame. I'll tell them I tricked you into helping me.'

'Okay, but I've been thinking,' said Don, with a serious look on his face. 'We've been so engrossed in all these investigations we haven't thought about who we are.'

Keith looked confused, 'I know who I am and Nick certainly knows who he is.'

'No, no, you don't understand – are we Mods or Rockers?' said Don.

'I've never really thought about it, have you Nick?' asked Keith

'Do we have to be one or the other?' replied Nick.

'Of course we do, it gives you an identity. Shows what you believe in and what happens if there's another battle, you'll have to choose then,' said Don.

'So you think that all the Mods and Rockers are going to have a massive punch-up at Verulamium on the next Bank Holiday?' replied Nick.

'And the next Bank Holiday is Christmas Day,' added Keith.

'Listen to me Don; you don't have to belong to either. Answer me this – do you prefer to wear jeans and a leather jacket and ride a motorbike or smart fashionable clothes and ride a scooter? And what about music? Do you like Rock 'n Roll or the new modern music?'

Don looked confused, and then answered, 'well I'm not old enough to have a scooter or motorbike. I like wearing jeans, but I also like to look smart. Anyway, I can't afford to buy the latest gear and with two brothers and a sister, my parents can't either. As for the music, I love it all.'

'Exactly,' enthused Nick. 'We don't have to fall into a particular group, we are our own persons. We appreciate all the good aspects of both groups. We are living in exciting times and there is more to come. Let's just enjoy it; the austerity that our parents experienced after the war has gone, it's a new dawn.'

'Nick's right, we're individuals and we're friends with both Mods and Rockers. Digger Barnes is the archetype Rocker and Nick's friend Ernie Tomkins is the classic Mod with his trendy suits and cash to spend. So we should call ourselves 'Individualists', said Keith, looking rather pleased with himself.

Don thought for a few seconds before replying, 'that's sounds a good idea, but what about those battles on the beaches, do you think it will happen again?'

'Difficult to say, but I do know that the Easter Monday one was blown out of all proportion' replied Nick.

'What do you mean?'

'Well you remember Veronica Goldberg, Jane's sister, the one we rescued before Easter? I saw her the other week in *Kings* Gift shop and she told me that she was there at Clacton on Easter Monday. She was with her boyfriend Jim; they went down on his Lambretta. They had a rotten time, it was cold, wet and miserable, and most places were closed. Basically they all got bored; there were a few scuffles, no more than normal and it got blown out of all proportion.'

'But why?' asked Don.

'Apparently there wasn't much going on for the press to report on, so once they heard the stories they made a meal of it.'

Their conversation was suddenly interrupted by the presence of DI James entering the café. He checked that the boys were there before ordering a coffee, and joining them. Nick was the first to speak, 'what do we owe the pleasure of your visit?'

DI James sipped his coffee, a double espresso. He needed the kick it gave him, before interviewing this lot. 'There have been some recent events, strange events and I just wondered if you knew anything about them.'

The boys shook their heads and looked at each other.

'Sorry,' said Keith. 'Can't think of anything, can you?'

'No,' agreed Don. 'You know all about what we've been up to. After all, you were there.'

DI James noticed that Nick looked a bit sheepish.

'So tell us,' summoned Keith. 'What have we supposed to have done this time?'

Still looking at Nick, DI James started; 'a few days ago we received a call from the manager of *Marlboro' Motors* in London Road. He asked us if we could help him; he'd received an anonymous phone call informing him that a member of staff was pilfering motor parts and they were stored in his garden shed. He asked if we could get a warrant to have a look. This was granted and a couple of uniformed officers along with DC Higgins and the manager went to have a look. The gentleman was not very happy about this and tried to stop the officers entering his premises. After a brief struggle the gentleman was restrained and the shed was inspected.'

'Did they find anything?' asked Keith.

'It was like an Aladdin's cave, car parts everywhere. So he was arrested and taken into custody.'

'That's good, isn't it? Can't see what we've supposed to have done,' added Don.

'It doesn't end there. He was charged then released on bail. Obviously he was sacked but he was allowed to pick up his personal stuff. Apparently he was very popular among the staff, but there was one woman who had a grievance. After collecting his belonging he charged into her office and accused her of shopping him to the police. There was a bit of a commotion and we were called in. He was escorted from the building. I was free, so I popped along to interview the women. Can you guess what she said?'

The three boys just looked at him.

'She said that she didn't shop the gentleman, but she did say that a DC Higgins had phoned her and had made enquires about him.'

'On the ball then, our DC Higgins, your influence must be paying off,' remarked Keith.

'Now that's the funny part; you see, he swears he never made that call. You're very quiet Nick, nothing you want to add?'

'It's a mystery to me, but no harm done. You got your man and everyone is happy,' replied Nick.

'You would think so, wouldn't you? So tell me this, why do you think DC Higgins was ambushed last night. He took quite a beating and spent last night in hospital.'

'Well we didn't beat him up and I can't see why you are blaming us,' said Keith, but was secretly worried about what Nick had done.

DI James sighed, 'this is how I see it. In your investigation both your suspects worked at *Marlboro' Motors*. You're looking for a third suspect called Michael. Bet you can't guess what the thief's name is?'

'George?' asked Don.

DI James shook his head, 'as you well know, his name was Michael. Also the girl, who happened to be a bit of a looker, told me that DC Higgins had promised ….'

'You said DC Higgins didn't make the call,' exclaimed Don.

'Okay, the caller, pretending to be DC Higgins, promised that he would stop Michael harassing her.'

'Sorry, still not with you,' said Keith.

Totally exasperated and shaking his head DI James said, 'a lady in distress, along with the other things I've mentioned, they all point to you.'

Nick had heard enough, 'they had nothing to do with it, it was me and I'm sorry about DC Higgins, but I couldn't have foreseen that. Just a casualty of war; I'll send him some grapes.'

DI James thought for a while. 'So is he your third man?'

'You know darn well he's not. Bloody Father John, come Michael or whatever he's calling himself now is. We were just putting a few wrongs to right – it's what we do. So don't keep going on, no harm's been done, has there?'

'That's the problem, my boss received a letter from his immediate boss congratulating him on the performance of DC Higgins and suggested that he was ready to take his Sargent's exam. Of course DC Higgins is now taking all the credit. So I suppose he deserved a beating. No, we'll keep it between us and I can always use it if I need to.'

'So, what did you think of Miss Woodstock?' asked Nick, trying to lighten the mood.

'Charming, absolutely charming; now promise me that you'll

keep out of trouble and concentrate on you schoolwork.'

'We still haven't found Billy,' said Don, sheepishly.

DI James stood up and walked away muttering, 'I give up.'

'Who's you friend?' asked Anna, as she cleared their table.

'Oh, him,' replied Nick. 'That's Detective Inspector James; we occasionally do some consultancy work for the Police. He just popped in to ask for some advice.'

Anna shook her head, 'just listen to yourselves, you do talk a load of rubbish.'

Ignoring the remark, Nick asked, 'Anna, darling; I was just wondering where we should go for our honeymoon. They say the Isle of Wight is quite nice, this time of the year.'

'In your dreams.'

'One day,' said Nick. 'You'll be sitting in your council flat with your overweight alcoholic husband and three screaming kids and you'll see me on your rented television set; when I'm rich and famous. Then you'll think to yourself, I could have married him.'

Anna looked down at Nick and with a smile that Nick was hoping for, replied, 'you're half right; but I'll be sitting in my Mayfair apartment with my millionaire husband watching *Police Five* and a mug shot of you will appear and I'll think, that's that pervert who used to come in my café and try to look up my skirt.'

Nick loved this banter and replied, 'fair point, but just for interest, and I can't be bothered to look, what colour knickers are you wearing today?'

As she turned away she replied, 'I'm not wearing any.'

Thursday 10 September

Nick had briefly spoken to Moira, who suggested that they all meet at her house as her parents were out and she was looking after her sister, Elizabeth. Reluctantly he agreed; he had not seen Elizabeth since Sunday and was still a little worried in case she said something. At 7.00pm Keith, Brenda and Don had arrived and sitting with Moira in the lounge waited anxiously for Nick to speak.

'Thank you for coming and you are free to leave at any time.'

'As if we would,' commented Keith.

'You may want to, after you've heard what I have planned.'

'Ever the dramatist,' said Keith, before receiving a sharp elbow from Brenda.

Ignoring the remark Nick continued, 'as you know, we have hit a brick wall with our investigation into finding Peter Waller. We have identified the three kidnappers, one is dead, and one in Ireland whilst the other is untouchable.'

'You didn't tell me that you had found Michael,' interrupted Moira, looking extremely put out.

'Ah,' said Nick, momentarily forgetting that he hadn't told the girls about their priest. 'DI James identified your Father John as the third man. His real name is Michael; apparently he'd been up to no good, don't know all the details, but that must have been what all those rumours at your church were about.'

'When did he tell you that?'

Thinking fast, Nick replied, 'yesterday, he popped in *Sally's* yesterday and told us. Anyway, we need to finish this now and I've formulated a plan and I need your help. It will be dangerous and slightly illegal, so I'll understand if you want to drop out.'

'Just tell us first,' said Keith, 'then we'll let you know.'

So Nick outlined his plan to kidnap Billy Watkins, take him back to the Alma Road youth club and torture him until he talks.

'I love dressing up,' said Brenda. 'Do we have to supply our own costumes?'

'No,' replied Nick. 'That's all been taken care of; just make sure that you get there as soon as you can. I suggest you come straight from school. Tell your parents you're going to a friend's for tea.'

'You're enjoying this,' said Keith.

Nick smiled, 'I play the game, for the games own sake.'

'Do you think it will work?'

'We can but try.'

Friday 11 September

It was a strange sight when a single spot-light was switched on in the back room of the Alma Road Youth Club. It shone straight at Billy Watkins who was naked from the waist up and tied to an old wooden chair. Standing in front of him was Nick, still dressed in his school uniform. It reminded Nick of an old war film he had recently watched, where a German officer was interrogating a captured British spy. Nick resisted the urge to say 'Ve have vays of making you talk'.

Billy was still very drowsy from the effects of the chloroform that Digger had used to subdue him during the kidnap. Nick threw a glass of water in his face; this seemed to have the required effect.

Billy looked around and shouted, 'let me go, what you want?'

Nick was the first to respond, 'Billy, you have been a naughty boy. You have sinned in the eyes of God; you will go to hell.'

'I've told you, I don't know what you are talking about.'

'More lies. Now I'm going to tell you what I know, then I'm going to show you what will happen to you if you do not tell me the truth.'

'I'll get you for this.'

Nick ignored the remark, 'On the 3th May 1959, you, Eddie Reynolds and Father John kidnapped Peter Waller. You did something so disgusting that your best friend Eddie committed suicide. Father John threatened you, and told you that you must never breathe a word about what had happened. Now you are going to tell me what really happened to Peter. I know that Father John likes to 'entertain' little boys and that itself is a mortal sin.'

The spotlight was extinguished and the left hand side of the room was illuminated by red bulbs. A strange smell filled the air; Nick recognised it as sulphur. Out of the shadows appeared Digger Barnes, dressed in his customary attire of black t-shirt under a black leather jacket, blue denim jeans and his legendary green hob-nail boots. His face had been painted red with large black eye brows and a small black goatee beard. Behind him followed Don, wearing a complete Devil's costume which consisted of a red cat-suit complete with a hood with horns and a tail. His face was covered by a mask and he was carrying a devil's trident. Nick stepped back as Digger and Don approached. They began to circle Billy; Digger took a large drag on the cigarette he was smoking and blew the smoke into Billy's face; Don, following behind, kept prodding Billy's legs and back with his trident.

Billy was continually coughing, but it didn't distract the pair from their tormenting.

'I need a drink,' Billy shouted, in between coughing fits.

Digger walked away and returned with a glass of yellow liquid. He offered it to Billy's lips and he eagerly took a large sip, but instantly spat it out.

'Ah,' Billy shouted. 'It tastes like piss.'

Nick walked back in front of him, smiled and said, 'that's because it is piss.'

'Please let me go, I know nothing,' cried Billy.

Digger and Don continued to encircle and torment Billy.

'Stop blowing smoke in my face,' pleaded Billy.

This time Digger answered as he cowered over his hostage, 'do you want me to put this fag out?'

'Yes please,' pleaded Billy, as tears rolled down his cheek.

'Certainly,' said Digger as he stubbed the cigarette end into Billy's arm. The following scream was deafening. Nick cringed.

Suddenly the red lights were extinguished and replaced by bright white lights on the right hand side of the room. Standing there was Keith dressed as a vicar, complete with dog collar and holding a bible. Behind him, Moira and Brenda dressed as angels. Brenda was the first to move, she approached Billy with a glass of crystal clear water. She offered it to him and he greedily gulped it down. As Brenda stepped back Moira approached with a tube of antiseptic cream and gently applied it to the cigarette burn. When she had finished Keith approached, his bible open if front of him and in his best vicar's voice said, 'Leviticus, chapter 18, verse 22. Thou shall not lie with mankind as one lies with a womenkind; it is an abomination.

Leviticus chapter 20, verse 13. If a man also lie with a mankind, as he lieth with a woman, both of them have committed an abomination; they shall surely be put to death. Their blood shall be upon them.'

Keith stepped back and the bright white lights were replaced by the single spot-light and Nick standing in front of Billy.

'It's up to you mate,' said Nick. 'You have seen the difference between heaven and hell; you know what God thinks about your dirty little habits. So I'm offering you a chance to redeem yourself, repent now and stop this suffering, because this is what is going to happen to you when you die. You will go to hell, a place where men are tormented with fire and brimstone and the fearful, and unbelieving, and the abominable, and the murderers, and the whoremongers, and the sorcerers, and the idolaters and all the liars, shall have their part in the lake which burneth with fire and brimstone: which is the second death.'

'I keep telling you, I don't know what you are talking about,' sobbed Billy.

'That's a shame, but before my devilish friends return, let me tell you something. Father John has confessed, he's told us everything. Everything except what happened to Peter. Now he's gone and he's not coming back. You're on your own.'

'I don't believe you,' screamed Billy. 'Father John will protect me and you will be cursed forever.'

The white light was extinguished and the red lights returned, along with Digger and Don. Digger had lit a fresh cigarette and continued blowing smoke in Billy's face. Don was enjoying himself as he repeatedly prodded Billy with his trident. Nick noticed that within the scratches on Billy's back a few droplets of blood began to appear. Digger took a long drag on his cigarette then gave Nick a questioning look. Nick reluctantly gave a subtle nod then closed his eyes and waited for the scream. At last Billy cracked, sobbing his heart out he said, 'I didn't do anything, I was just the driver. It was Father John's idea; he had the thing about little boys. Even Eddie just went along to please him.'

'Okay Billy, let's take it from the beginning. Would you like another glass of water?' He asked, as he beckoned to Brenda.

Suitably refreshed and a little relieved he continued, 'Father John liked to entertain little boys; he used to lure them to the vestry and do things to them. I didn't like to watch; actually it made me feel sick. He used to say it was God's work and he was purifying them. Anyway, on that particular day we were driving around, you know, Father John, Eddie and me and Father John sees this kid he recognizes from church. So we pull in alongside and Father John persuades him to get into the car. Then I drive them to the vestry. Once there, I sat in the corner reading a comic and didn't take much notice. Then after about fifteen minutes, the kid was standing there with no clothes on, Eddie flips. Father John couldn't believe it. Eddie is screaming not to touch the boy and gives Father John a hefty punch in the mouth. Father John then goes for Eddie and a right scuffle starts. Eddie shouts at me to get rid of the boy. I quickly help the boy put his clothes on and I rush him to the car. I was driving him home; we got to the bottom of Folly Lane, by the garage. I stopped at the junction and the kid jumped out of the car and ran off. I've never seen him since.'

Nick thought for a while, and then said, 'Did you see which way he went?'

'I think he ran towards where we picked him up, but I turned left and went up Verulam Road.

Nick was satisfied, he turned to Billy and looked him straight in the eyes and said, 'there, that wasn't that bad was it? You could have saved us a lot of time and yourself a lot of pain. '

'Are you going to tell the police about me?' asked Billy.

'They already know you were involved; I just want to find Peter.'

'Will you untie me, please?'

'Certainly,' replied Nick as he pulled out his penknife and started cutting through the bonds.

When Billy's hands were free, he just sat there exhausted. Nick bent down and cut the ties from around his ankles. Nick almost felt sorry for him, that sad pathetic, bedraggled, figure sitting there.

Nick half turned to walk away, then turned back and punched Billy in the face with such force that he fell backwards to the floor.

'That's for throwing water over me.'

Nick waited outside whilst the others got changed into their normal clothes. So what have we learned, he thought. Most of what Billy had told him seemed to tally with his own theory, except they were no nearer to discovering the whereabouts of Peter Waller. Digger Barnes was the first to appear and Nick thanked him for all his help and Digger replied that he had enjoyed himself and wished him luck in finding the missing boy. After a few minutes Keith, Don, Moira and Brenda appeared.

Don was the first to speak, 'that was fun, and don't you think I looked good as a devil?'

'Yeah,' replied Keith. 'That tail really suited you.'

Moira walked over to Nick and took his hand, 'what are thinking darling? You look pensive.'

Nick put his arms around and gave her a gentle hug. 'That went well, but we still don't know what happened to Peter.'

'I know,' replied Moira, desperately trying to think something to say that would help.

Saturday 12 September

Nick was feeling a bit frustrated as he finished off his bowl of *Kellogg's* Corn Flakes and for once is wasn't sexual frustration. What more could he do to find Peter. If what Billy had told him yesterday was true and he was 99% certain it was, then something else must have happened to him. Why didn't he go straight home? Was he abducted again? Surely not; if he was dead, how on earth were they going to find his body. He was totally out of ideas. He would leave it for today, take his mind off it; think of other things. Now he was back at school, he needed to make use of the weekend; enjoy himself. This afternoon he would, along with Keith, go as see

St. Albans City play Tooting and Mitcham at Clarence Park. Don was playing in a Scout football match. Spurs were away to West Ham United, so a double win would go some way to cheering him up. This evening he would take Moira to the *Ballito*[9] to see Linda Laine and The Sinners. If they arrived before 8.00pm it would only cost 4/- for the first hundred, after that it was 5/-.

The day didn't go well; St. Albans lost 0-1 to Tooting and Mitcham. Tooting scored the only goal of the match whilst the St. Albans defenders waited for an offside whistle. It was a very inept performance and only Nick's favourite player Herbie Smith played well. On arriving home he was told that Spurs had lost 2-3, and just to make the day complete Moira was late and they had to pay the full 5/- entry fee for the dance.

WEEK 6
Sunday 13 September –
Wednesday 16 September 1964

Sunday 13 September

Nick was still feeling down as he mounted his bicycle after finishing his shift at the paper-shop. Even after receiving a snog from Caroline when he gave her a box of *Cadbury's Milk Tray* for her birthday did little to raise his spirits. What he needed was divine intervention and he was just in time to catch the Family Mass at St. Michaels Church[10]. Although he found it difficult to concentrate, one passage he heard stuck in his mind – Proverbs 3:5-6 Trust in the LORD with all your heart and lean not on your understanding; in all your ways acknowledge him, and he will make your paths straight. It was another glorious day even though the forecast was rain, and as he exited the church he hoped that the big man upstairs had heard his prayers. During communion he had caught the eye of Mary Hyde, a girl on the estate he had lusted after for some time. He knew Mary was a regular church goer, but whenever he attended, she was with a different boy. Many a time, when he was single, he had planned to ask her out, but every time she was escorted by her latest beau. Oh Mary Hyde, from Batchwood Drive, those pretty eyes, and smile so wide, when will you be mine?

Keith has suggested that the boys take the girls for a nice walk round Verulamium Lake. Don had at last invited Linda, whose kittens were doing extremely well, to join them. After about twenty minutes without mentioning Peter Waller, Brenda said, 'I've an idea, we know where he got out of the car, so if we start there and walk to his house we might find him.'

'After five years,' laughed Don. 'I doubt it.'

'No,' interjected Nick, 'Brenda's right. If we follow his trail, something might, just might come to mind.'

Despite hoping to spend more time enjoying the sunshine and the relaxed atmosphere of the lake, Linda said, 'I can tell you are all tensed up, so the sooner you solve this case the quicker I can enjoy your company.' Don smiled and gave her a kiss on the cheek.

So reluctantly the group left the lake at the St Michaels Street exit and made their way up Branch Road to where Billy Watkins left Peter Waller. They stood at the junction of Verulam Road and Folly Lane.

'So, if Peter was dropped off here where would he go? Surely he would make his way home. What could have distracted him?' Nick was getting frustrated and kept banging his head with his fist. 'Ah,' he screamed, 'what am I missing?'

'I don't think we should hang around here too long, it looks like rain,' said Brenda noticing the sky clouding over.

After a few seconds Nick shrieked, 'that's it; it was raining. I remember now, after a couple of hours looking for him there was a terrific thunderstorm. We had to abandon the search; what if Peter was caught in the rain, surely he would look for somewhere to shelter. Where would he go?'

'He could have gone up the lane. He might have had a camp up there,' said Keith.

Nick thought for a while before saying, 'that's a possibility, but I think it might be something else. There is something at the back of my mind. God, it's so frustrating. What is it?'

The group stood there looking at Nick, willing him to remember. Brenda broke the silence with a casual remark, 'maybe he went into one of those houses.'

Moira cut in, 'I don't think an eight-year-old boy would just knock on a stranger's door and ask for shelter.'

A grin appeared on Nick's face, 'Not unless he knew one of them. It's coming back now; Peter had a friend who lived along here. In the last house I think, yes, number 182.'

'Your right,' gasped Moira. 'Andrew Chambers, I often saw them playing together. How did you know the number?'

'We deliver papers there.'

Without prompting the group they crossed the road, walked about thirty yards and stopped at the garden gate of 182 Folly Lane; a neat, large, 1930s three-bedroomed semi-detached house. It had a good sized front garden with neatly trims lawns either side of a concrete path. Nick led his friends down the path, turned, and looked at them. They smiled, as he turned back and knocked on the front door. After a short period of time the front door opened and a pleasant looking man in his late forties answered it.

'Can I help you?' asked the man, whom Nick assumed to be Andrew's dad.

'We were wondering if Andrew was in, we need to speak to him urgently,' replied Nick.

'Are you friends of his?' asked Mr Chambers.

'Not exactly, but we must see him, it's a matter of life or death,' pleaded Moira.

'Sounds interesting; he's round the back playing in the garden. Use the side gate; I'll inform him that you're here.'

Nick opened the wooden side gate and led his friends to the back garden. Andrew was sitting on a blanket on the lawn with another boy. They were engrossed in a game of *Monopoly*. Their concentration was broken by the approach of the six teenagers. Andrew was the first to speak, 'Hello, you're Nick Allen, aren't you?'

'That's right, and I'm sorry to disturb you game. Are you winning?' asked Nick, as a friendly gesture.

Andrew chuckled and said, 'well I've just bought my first house on Mayfair.'

'But I've got a hotel on Bond Street,' said the other boy.

'And you are?' asked Nick.

'Sorry, this is my friend, Colin,' replied Andrew.

'Nice to meet you,' said Nick

Keith, Don, Moira, Linda and Brenda each gave a little wave and said, hi.'

'So, what can I do for you?' enquired Andrew.

Nick noticed Mr Chambers lurking in the background, listening to every word spoken.

'We're looking into the disappearance of Peter Waller; we believe you were friends with him.'

'That's right, we were in the cubs together and he often came round here to play army games. Sometimes he would bring his soldiers and we would make forts in the garden. We got on really well, he was a nice boy, but I know nothing about his disappearance.'

'So you never saw him on the day he disappeared.'

'No, I remember it well. Peter went missing on the Sunday and we went away for the weekend,' Andrew turned to his dad and said, 'that's right, isn't dad?'

Mr Chambers acknowledged his son's question and joined the group who were all now sitting on the lawn. 'That's right; do you have any idea at all at what happened to him?'

'We know who kidnapped him, we know he escaped and the last place anyone saw him was outside the petrol station. We also know that it was raining quite heavily and we thought that he might have come here for shelter.'

'I can see where you are coming from, but Andrew's right, we went away Friday night. A weekend in Devon, I remember, got a good deal on a caravan. We got delayed and didn't get back till Monday evening.'

There was a pregnant pause before the arrival of Andrew's mother carrying a tray containing a large jug of lemon squash and a stack of plastic beakers.

'Refreshments, anyone?' asked Mrs Chambers, who Nick thought was more than attractive for a lady in her forties.

The lemon drink was sharp, cold and totally refreshing. Nick felt relaxed as he sipped his drink and cast his eye around the impressive garden. It spanned the width of the house and measured at least 100 feet long. The first half was lawn edged with a spectacular array of flowers in full bloom, which unfortunately Nick could not name. The back half of the garden was devoted to vegetables but out of sight due to large hedge.

'Tell me, Andrew, is there anything that you can think of about Peter that might help us understand what happened to him.'

'I don't know, he was just a normal likeable boy. He was fun to be with, although his obsession with playing Army games could be a bit tiresome. He liked to play in the Anderson shelter, which we did when dad was at work.'

Nick looked at Mr Chambers, who raised his eyebrows.

'What's an Anderson shelter?' asked Keith.

Mr Chambers answered, 'during the last war the government issued Anderson shelters to all householders as an air-raid precaution. They were made of corrugated steel panels and dug into the ground. Unfortunately, during the winter they often flooded. Now I had forbidden Andrew to play in there, because the door kept sticking.'

'Sorry dad, but I promise I've never been in there since,' implored Andrew.

As Nick listened with interest his mind was racing. It was like a mental jig-saw, putting all the pieces together. Moira could see what was happening and whispered to Keith, 'he'll have it cracked in a minute.'

Nick stood up, looked at Mr Chambers and said, 'I have a theory which I would like to put to you. But first, one question – did you lock the back gate when you went on holiday in 1959?'

Mr Chambers thought for a while and then said, 'I doubt it.'

'Okay, this is what I think. Peter jumped out of the car ran across the road. It was pouring with rain and he needed to find shelter. So where does he go, straight to his friend's Andrew's house.'

'But he knew we were on holiday,' stated Andrew.

'Good point, but that doesn't matter. He had had a traumatic experience and may have forgotten, either way I think he had already decided to take refuge in the Anderson shelter. I think he's still there.'

Brenda was first to comment, 'he couldn't have lasted five years in there without food, he would starve to death.'

'Precisely,' replied Nick raising his eyebrows and looking at Mr Chambers. 'I think we need to have look.'

'Okay,' said Mr Chambers, visibly shaken. 'But the rest of you kids stay here,'

Someone mumbled, 'not likely,' as all seven children scrambled down the garden and stood gazing at the Anderson Shelter. These shelters were 6 feet high, 4 feet 6 inches wide and 6 feet 6 inches long. They were buried 4 feet deep in the soil and the covered with a minimum of 15 inches of soil above the roof. The earth banks could be planted with vegetables and flowers that at times could look quite appealing. Nick could see that the door was blocked by earth that had been brought down by the rain.

'Andrew, can you fetch me my spade from the shed,' said Mr Chambers.

Andrew quickly disappeared and returned with a fairly new *Spear and Jackson* spade. He handed to his father.

Nick looked at Mr Chambers and said, 'I think I should do it.'

Taking the spade, he climbed down and started digging away at the earth in front of the door. After a few minutes he tried to pull the door open but it wouldn't budge.

Mr Chambers turned to Andrew and said, 'nip to the tool shed and get my crowbar and you better bring my torch as well.'

Mr Chambers joined Nick and together they tried to prise the door open, Mr Chambers at the top with the crowbar, and Nick at the bottom with the spade. Slowly but surely door started to move. When the gap was big enough, Nick took the torch and looked in and there, on the floor in lying in the foetal position was the body of a young boy dressed in an Army outfit; beside him a wooden rifle. Nick turned and looked at Mr Chambers, tears started to run down his cheeks. Brenda grabbed Moira and Linda, then wept loudly, the boys just hung their heads.

Mr Chambers said, 'I'll call the police.'

'No, I'll do it,' replied Nick. 'I know who to phone.'

Mrs Chambers said, 'I'll show where it is.'

Nick followed Mrs Chambers back into the house and she showed him where the phone was. A nice new ivory model situated on a neat table in the hall. He phoned the local police station and asked for DI James. He was told that he was off duty. Nick stated that it was imperative that he contacted DI James and the receptionist promised to call his home number and Nick gave her the Chambers number to call back. Nick waited by the phone until it rang, five minutes later.

'Nick, is that you?'

'DI James, thank God it's you.'

Nick heard DI James sigh before saying, 'what has happened?'

'We've found him.'

'What, you've found Peter?'

Nick, on hearing DI James's voice, felt his confidence returning, 'of course, did you ever doubt that I would?'

'Don't get cocky; just tell me where you are.'

Nick filled DI James in with all the details and was told not to touch anything and wait there till he arrived. Feeling a mixture of sadness and triumph, Nick returned to the garden. Brenda was still sobbing her heart out and Nick suggested to Keith that he took her home. This was agreed and Don said he would take Linda home. Moira approached Nick and gave him a big hug before asking him if he was okay. Mr Chambers then asked him what the police said; Nick repeated the instructions and Mrs Chambers invited them to sit on some garden chairs that had mysteriously appeared. Andrew and Colin continued their game of *Monopoly*. Mrs Chambers returned to the house whilst Nick, Moira and Mr Chambers sat in silence.

The knock on the front door came ten minutes later and DI James was escorted through the house to the back garden. He was then shown the Anderson shelter and after a brief inspection, he said, 'Okay, it looks pretty straight forward. I'll call it in.'

'Someone will have to tell Mrs Waller,' said Nick.

'I'll do it, once I've finished here.'

'Don't forget to tell her it was me who found him. It might stop her throwing stones at me.'

DI James smiled.

'Also,' said Nick, in a serious tone. 'If she wants to know exactly what happened to Peter, I will be happy to oblige; if she can handle the truth.'

DI James sighed, 'always the dramatist.'

Nick gave DI James a dirty look and said, 'do you want to know the truth?

'Sorry, of course I do,' replied DI James, sheepishly.

'Good, then set up the meeting, then we can all move on.'

Monday 14 September

The meeting was arranged for the next day; Nick had suggested that his mum and Mrs Harris should be present. Moira said she wanted to be there to support Nick. At 7.00 pm they all assembled in Mrs Waller's living room. Mrs Waller sat in the middle of a three-seater settee with Mrs Allen and Mrs Harris either side; DI James sat on one of the matching armchairs and Nick in the other. Moira grabbed a dining chair and sat next to Nick. The atmosphere was very tense.

Once settled, no-one said a word until DI James gave a little cough and said, 'when you are ready, Nick.'

Nick cleared his throat before starting, this was his moment. He imagined himself as Sherlock Holmes, ready to unmask a killer. If he'd had a pipe, he would have taken one last puff. 'As we know, five years ago young Peter was enticed into a car while I was playing football on the Green with Gordon and Paul and never seen again. A few weeks ago Moira suggested that we try to find out what happened to him. Our first task was to try and discover who actually took him and why. The only lead we had was the blue Hillman Huskey. DI James gave as the name of a suspect – Billy Watkins. We quickly established that he was the driver. Later discoveries confirmed our initial thoughts that he was not involved in any of the nasty business that followed. With the help of my mum it was established that the second man was Billy's best friend, a chap called Eddie. I'm not sure how much he was involved, but I'll come back to him later. The main culprit, you'll be surprised to hear was a catholic priest called Father John. He was recently arrested by the police for some other misdemeanour, but for some unknown reason....' Nick gave DI James a dirty look. '....has not been charged and has now disappeared.'

Nick noticed that Mrs Waller was struggling to hold back the tears.

'After an intense interrogation Billy Watkins finally told us what actually happened to Peter.'

At this stage DI James was shaking his head in disbelief. Nick ignored him.

'He told us that they had taken Peter to Father John's Chambers and had persuaded Peter to remove all his clothes. But before anything could happen, Eddie lost it and attacked Father John. According to Billy, as they grappled on the floor, Eddie shouted out "get him out of here". Peter quickly puts his clothes on, grabbed his shoes and his wooden rifle and ran towards the door. Billy followed and forced him into his car. His intention was to drop Peter off where they picked him up, but when they reached the junction of Folly Lane with Verulam Road, by the garage, Peter jumped out of the car and legged it. That was the last time anyone saw him. If you remember it was pouring with rain that day, so we can only assume what happened next. But I think we are right in thinking that Peter called at his friend Andrew's house for shelter. Finding out that he was not at home or remembering that he was on holiday he made his way to the Anderson Shelter to shelter from the rain; well we know the rest.'

Nobody spoke for a few seconds whilst they digested the information. Mrs Waller took a few deep breaths before saying, 'shall I make some tea?'

'That would be nice,' replied DI James.

Nick gave Moira a gentle nudge and she quickly understood and stood up and said, 'let me make it, I think Nick still has a few more things to say.'

DI James gave out a noticeable sigh; Nick ignored him. Moira disappeared into the kitchen.

Nick continued, 'the question I kept asking myself was - what made Eddie flip? But I think Mrs Waller knows the answer to that.'

Mrs Waller was staring at her feet.

'Shall I continue Mrs Waller?' said Nick, in a slightly sarcastic tone.

Mrs Waller sniffed and gave a gentle nod of the head.

'You may or may not have guessed that Eddie's surname was Reynolds and Eddie Reynolds was a very close friend of Mr and Mrs Waller. In fact, he was the Best Man at their wedding.'

Nick paused for a second allowing this information to sink in. He could see how the interest was rising.

'He was such a good friend that he used to keep Mrs Waller company when her husband was away overnight driving. I believe that this friendship overstepped the mark and that Peter is really Eddie's son,' said Nick, and he smiled to himself as he waited for the reaction.

Mrs Allen and Mrs Harris both gasped and Mrs Waller burst out crying. Nick stood there with a smug expression on his face. DI James just stared at him. Moira returned with a tray of teacups, and passed them around. After a while Mrs Waller composed herself and started to speak. 'Please don't think badly of me, it only happened the once. Cyril was on an overnight run to Scotland and Eddie said he would keep me company. Cyril was happy with this arrangement, he felt guilty leaving me alone at night. Well this particular evening Eddie brought a couple of bottles of Milk Stout with him. As Mary knows, it doesn't take much to get me tipsy and one thing led to another. In the morning I felt guilty and so furious that I told Eddie I never wanted to see him again and banned him from ever coming to the house. I think Eddie felt the same because I never saw him again.'

'Didn't Cyril think it was funny him not coming round anymore,' asked Mrs Harris.

'That was the strange bit, he never mentioned it.'

'Did he know that Peter wasn't his?'

'If he did he never mentioned it, he was the perfect father.'

The questions were forming exponentially in Mrs Harris's head. 'How did you know that Peter wasn't Cyril's?'

Nick stood up and asked 'can I answer that?'

'Quiet Nick,' said Mrs Allen. 'I think it's better if Alice told us.'

Disappointed at not being able to impress everyone with his detective skills, Nick sunk back into his chair. Moira smiled and stroked his hair.

'At first I wasn't sure,' Mrs Waller continued. 'I didn't think that after doing it just the once it could be Eddie's. After all it wasn't as if Cyril and I didn't do it, in fact Cyril was quite a randy little sod. At first I didn't even think about it, Cyril was a good father and he doted on Peter. But as Peter got bigger I noticed he had a strange birthmark on his side. It was exactly the same as Eddie's. Apparently it was a hereditary birthmark. His father and grandfather had the same mark. I'm not sure if Cyril was aware of this, but if he was he never mentioned it.'

'Okay, Nick' said DI James. 'I know you are dying to tell us, so go on – how did you know about the birthmark?'

Nick thought about not telling them but his vanity got the better of him. Excitedly, he continued. 'Well, it was when I was interviewing Eddie's fiancé; I asked her if she had any photos of Eddie. She had an old biscuit tin full of photos and I started to go through them and found this one of Eddie posing in his swimming trunks.' Nick handed the photo to DI James. As you can see the birthmark is quite prominent. It was then I remembered seeing the same mark on Peter when we used to play in his paddling pool.'

'It looks as if you have wrapped the case up, young Nick,' said DI James rising to his feet. 'You've done a great job and I'm sure Mrs Waller is very grateful and will stop throwing stones at you.'

Mrs Waller gave a small smile and mouthed thank you.

Mrs Allen looked up and said, 'You might as well go now Nick, Mary and I will stay and look after Alice for a while.'

Nick looked at Moira, nodded, said their goodbyes and left with DI James. Outside DI James shook Nick's hand, thanked him and drove off back to the station.

'Well,' said Nick, 'what shall we do now?'

'Let me think,' replied Moira. 'My house is empty, so let's go and check each other for birthmarks.'

'Excellent idea.'

As they walked hand in hand they noticed Nick's brother Richard, playing football on the Green with his friends Stephen Lester and Paul Bates. Richard, complete with his all green goalkeepers kit, was playing in goal and diving all over the place. They watched for a while, before continuing their walk. It was then that Nick noticed another boy, dressed in an Army uniform and holding a wooden rifle marching round the field. When the boy saw Nick, he stopped and saluted; Nick returned the acknowledgement.

'Who are you waving to?' asked Moira.

Nick smiled, 'just an old friend.'

Tuesday 15 September

'Nick, can you come down for a minute,' shouted Mrs Allen from the bottom of the stairs. Nick was just trying to make his hair respectable; he had arranged to meet Keith and Don for a trip to the Sandridge Youth Club. Running down the stairs he replied, 'What's up, Mum?'

'Mrs Harris is here, she's worried about Moira,'

Standing in the kitchen was Mrs Harris, with more than a worried look on her face.

'Is Moira alright?' asked Nick, as his mouth was getting dryer by the second.

'I'm probably worrying about nothing; but it's six-thirty and Moira hasn't come home from school yet. She always lets me know if she is going to be late. Did she say anything to you?'

'Never mentioned a thing,' replied Nick. 'Have you phoned Dympna, she always travels home with her? What did Elizabeth say; she must have been on the same bus?'

Moira, Elizabeth and Dympna all attended a Catholic High School for Girls in Welwyn Garden City.

'I knew Elizabeth would be late, she had a detention, so she didn't see her; unfortunately Dympna's not on the phone.'

Nick thought for a second, 'tell you what, I'll cycle to Dympna's and see if she's there. If not then we'll widen the search. Just let me make a phone call.'

Dympna Wilde lived in a nice 3-bedroomed house in Francis Avenue, on the New Greens Estate; Nick arranged to meet Keith and Don there. They all arrived about the same time. Nick had explained that Moira was missing and they had agreed to help him locate her. Nick knocked on the front door and was pleased that Dympna answered. She looked surprised to see the three boys standing there. Dympna was of average height with dark brown shoulder length hair. She had a pretty face with a pale Irish complexion.

'Sorry to bother you,' said Nick. 'But we were wondering if Moira was here.'

'No, afraid not,' replied Dympna. 'Why do you ask?'

'Her mum's a bit worried she hasn't come home from school yet. When was the last time you saw her?'

'I left her on the bus. We catch the 330 from Welwyn, its takes Moira virtually home. I get off at St. Peters Street and catch the 325.'

'How was she, did she seem worried at all?'

'Not at all, in fact I've never seen her so happy, you must be doing something right.'

Nick blushed.

'Did you notice anything strange, any weird people on the bus taking more than a normal interest in two very attractive girls?' Nick failed to notice Don and Keith shaking their heads.'

Dympna thought for a while then suddenly said, 'funny you should say that; there was a man on the bus, he looked familiar, but I couldn't see his face. He had a hat on and was wearing a scarf, which I thought was weird as it was quite hot.'

'Was he still on the bus when you got off?' asked Nick.

'Now you mention it, I think he was.'

'I think that's all,' said Nick, turning to Keith and Don. 'Anything I've missed.'

The boys shook their heads.

'Okay then, we'll be off. Thanks Dymp, you've been most helpful.'

'What now?' asked Keith, as they mounted their bikes.

'Let's go back to my place to see if there have been any developments.'

Mrs Harris was still waiting in the kitchen when the boys arrived back at Nick's home. Her look, when they entered the kitchen told them Moira had not been found.

Mrs Allen was the first to speak, 'there was a strange phone call for you Nick, while you were out.'

'Who from?' asked Nick.

'He didn't say. He just said that he had something of yours and if you want it back, come to the place where we first met and come alone.'

Nick felt remarkably calm as he stood outside the changing room at the Cunningham Hill playing fields. The sun was setting and there was a chill in the air. He gave a small shudder before opening the door to the changing room. The scene was as he expected and hoped. Standing there was Father John, not looking his best. He must have aged at least ten years in the ten days since he last set eyes on him. Next to him, sitting on the bench was Moira, her hands and feet bound and her mouth gagged. She looked at him in desperation; he did not return the look.

'Have you found my football shorts?' asked Nick, in a simpleton voice.

'What?' asked a confused Father John.

'My football shorts, you said you had them. They're new and my mum will be really angry if I've lost them. And I've got football practice at school tomorrow; I don't know what to wear if I can't find them.'

'I haven't got them,' screamed Father John.

Nick was looking around the changing room, mumbling to himself. 'I think you are really cruel making me come here. You shouldn't say things like that, it's not nice.' After looking around and satisfied that he shorts were not there, he made for the exit.

Father John was panicking, 'What about Moira?' shouted Father John.

Nick stopped, turned round and asked, 'have you seen my football shorts, Moira?'

Moira just shook her head.

'They must be somewhere,' sighed Nick, as the turned back and walked out of the hut.

Father John rushed after him; big mistake. As he left the hut Keith jumped on his back, Don ran towards him, head first, and butted him in the stomach. Winded, he fell to his knees; Don swung a punch and caught him on square on the chin. He fell to the ground. Before he could move Keith kicked him in his side. This was followed by Don kicking him square in the face. It didn't stop there, all the anger that Don had bottled up inside him was suddenly released as he repeatedly kicked Father John. Nick left him to it as he returned to the changing room and casually walked over to Moira and untied her bonds.

Once the gag was removed, Moira took a deep breath and said, 'what kept you?'

'I had to finish my tea first,' said Nick, before Moira embraced him with a big hug.

Back outside they observed the now unrecognisable Father John lying motionless and unconscious on the ground with Don, hands on knees, panting like the winner of the Grand National. Keith was standing next to him looking a little worried.

'Is he dead? asked Moira.

'I hope not,' replied Keith.

'Should we call for an ambulance?'

'Not a good idea, but the police should be here soon, so I think it would be best if we made ourselves scarce.' said Nick.

'How do you know that?' asked Keith.

'I asked my mum to phone the police anonymously at 7.30pm and leave a message for DI James to say that Father John is hiding in the changing rooms at Cunningham Hill playing fields.'

'He's bound to know it was us,' replied Keith.

'But he can't prove it,' said Nick, as he heard voices in the distance. 'I think they're coming, let's cut across the field. We can get out at Cunningham Hill Road.'

The boys picked up their bikes and disappeared as the sun finally set in the west.

Wednesday 16 September

Nick and Keith were already seated when Don joined them in *Sally's Inn* café. The mood was very solemn as they sipped their milkshakes. Even Anna, the waitress noticed and had decided not to continue with her usual teasing.

'How are you today, Don?' asked Nick.

'Confused,' he replied. 'On one hand I feel better, you know, like a huge burden has been lifted from my shoulders, on the other hand, I'm shit scared that I'm going to get into big trouble.'

'I shouldn't worry, like I said, they can't prove a thing.'

'Do you think the police will come after us?' asked Keith with a worried look on his face

'Let's put it this way, I bet you a pound to a penny that our favourite detective walks into this café in the next half hour.'

'So what do we do now?

'I'll put a few songs on the juke-box, and then we wait.'

They didn't have to wait long; five minutes later, to the sounds of The Honeycombs singing *Have I the Right*, DI James entered the café. After ordering his usual double espresso, he sat down next to Keith.

Trying to look surprised, Nick said, 'what do we owe the pleasure of your visit?'

'You know why I'm here, so let's not play games,' replied DI James.

Nick noticed that Anna was looking over, with a very worried look on her face.

There was a short silence before Don said, 'how is he?'

'Not to good, he suffered a severe beating to the head plus multiple injuries to his the rest of his body.'

'He deserved it,' mumbled Don.

DI James could sense the boys were worried. 'Don't worry; I'm not going to report you. I would just like to know what happened.'

For the next ten minutes the boys explained how Father John had kidnapped Moira and their plan to rescue her. DI James listened intensely and at the end of the narrative Nick asked, 'were you aware he was back in the country?'

'We had a call yesterday from Ireland, to inform us that he had gone missing, but I didn't expect him to come back here.'

'What will happen to him now?' asked Keith.

'That's up to you,' replied DI James. 'Do you want to report the kidnapping?'

The boys looked at each other before Don said, 'what do you think?'

DI James looked at the boys before answering; despite all the unbelievable things they have achieved, they were still children. He didn't think they needed all the hassle a court case would bring. 'I think we should leave it now; the church will take him back to Ireland and take care of him there. The doctors think that he may have suffered some brain damage, he took a hell of a beating.'

All three boys nodded in agreement. DI James stood up to leave, 'you three are remarkable lads, but I want you to promise me that you'll concentrate on you school work and leave me to catch the bad guys.'

'Of course we will,' replied a smiling Nick.

'Good, let's hope we do not have to meet for a long time.' What he had failed spot was that all three boys had their fingers crossed.

Visibly relieved Nick ordered three more milkshakes and was surprised when Anna said that she would bring them over. He was even more surprised when Anna said, as she placed each glass delicately in front of each boy, that they were on the house. They all looked up at her and said 'thank you.'

'My pleasure,' said Anna, with a nice caring smile on her face.

'Told you she would crack,' whispered Nick, as the Juke-box played his favourite song *She's Not There* by the Zombies

Aftermath

The funeral service for Peter Waller was held two weeks later at St. Michael's church, followed by an interment at the Cemetery in Hatfield Road. Mrs Waller had turned her back on the Catholic Church and was now a faithful protestant. The church was full; Nick thought that the whole of the estate must have turned up. Mrs Waller had insisted that Nick, Keith, Don and Andrew Chambers carry the coffin into the church. She had also requested that Nick read a poem; Peter's favourite –

Do not stand at my grave and weep,
I am not there; I do not sleep.
I am a thousand winds that blow,
I am the diamond glints on snow,
I am the sunlight on ripened grain,
I am the gentle autumn rain.
When you awaken in the morning's hush
I am the swift uplifting rush
Of quiet birds in circled flight.
I am the soft stars that shine at night.
Do not stand at my grave and cry,
I am not there; I did not die.

There was not a dry eye in the church, when Nick returned to his pew. Accompanying Mrs Waller was her estranged husband Cyril. Although stricken with grief, Nick noticed how much better Mrs Waller looked, even though she was dressed all in black. From what he could see her hair showed no sign of grey and she was wearing make-up that took years off her. The reception was held at the British Legion Hall in Verulam Road and everyone thanked the boys for finding Paul. Cyril Waller was extremely grateful and he slipped a five pound note into Nick's hand.

As the weeks went past Nick noticed that Cyril Waller was visiting his wife more often and it came as no surprise when he heard that they were going to give their marriage another go. But what pleased Nick even more was when they told him, before anyone else, that Mrs Waller was expecting.

With Nick studying hard at school, he was seeing less and less of Moira and when he was available she made some excuse, such as washing her hair or doing homework. He also noticed that when they were together, she wasn't as friendly as normal. It was clear that she was cooling off, so one evening he wrote her a letter, explaining how much he loved her and if she felt the same way to let him know. He dropped the letter off on his way to the paper-shop the next morning. She never replied. A few weeks later he heard that she was going out with a boy from the estate, locally known as Eddie Arsehole. For the years to come Nick never found out why she left him and always thought that they should have met in later years and then he would have definitely married her or at least – asked her.

REFERENCES

1. **The Billy Cotton Band** Show was a Sunday lunchtime radio show on the BBC Light programme from 1949 to 1968.

2. **Dovercourt Bay Holiday Camp** (1937 to 1980) a Warner Brothers Holiday Camp in Harwich, Essex. It was the location for BBC's Hi-Di-Hi.

3. **Saturday Club** was an influential BBC radio programme in Britain, on the Light programme and later Radio 1 between 1957 and 1968.

4. **Sue Bridehead** is the heroine in Thomas Hardy's Jude the Obscure.

5. **Keith Fordyce** (15 October 1928 – 15 March 2011) was an English disc jockey and former presenter on British radio and television. He is most famous for being the first presenter of ITV's Ready Steady Go! in 1963 but was a stalwart of BBC radio and Radio Luxembourg for many years.

6. **Muriel Young** (19 June 1923 – 24 March 2001) was a British television continuity announcer, presenter and producer.

7. **Noggin the Nog** is a popular children's television character appearing in his own TV series (of the same name) and series of illustrated books, the brainchild of Oliver Postgate and Peter Firmin. The TV series is considered a "cult classic" from the golden age of British children's television. Noggin himself is a simple, kind, and unassuming King of the Northmen in a roughly Viking-age setting with various fantastic elements, such as dragons, flying machines and talking birds.

8. **Maxwell Hawke** – Ghost Hunter was launched in the Buster comic on October 29th 1960.

9. **Ballito** stocking factory was opened in the early 1920s in Hatfield Road, St. Albans, and was among the leading names in hosiery.

10. **St. Michael's Church** pre-dates the Norman conquest and in common with the churches of St. Stephen and St Peter was always said to be founded by Ulsinus, Abbot of St. Alban's Abbey in 948AD.

About the Author

Allen Nicklin was born in St Albans in 1949 and has lived there ever since. Allen attended the Marshalswick School for Boys before taking an apprenticeship with Eastern Gas Board. In 1978 he qualified as a teacher and taught various subjects at the Hertfordshire College of Building and the St Albans College of Further Education.

In 2004 he took up the position of Lecturer in Mathematics at Richmond upon Thames College before retiring in 2012.

In 2009 Allen started writing short stories for his friends and family following a dare. This is his second published novel.

Allen is married with two daughters.